PRAISE FOR *ON SKEIN OF DEATH*

"Allie Pleiter skillfully knits together endearing characters, a leap-off-the-page setting, and a delightfully perplexing mystery with this debut."

—*USA Today* bestselling author Laura Bradford

"Allie Pleiter's first Riverbank Knitting Mystery has all the elements needed for a successful series, particularly a great hook." —Criminal Element

"Pleiter excels at creating characters you care about, and *On Skein of Death* is no exception. . . . A well-plotted mystery, clever red herrings, and intriguing layers give the book its focus, and the lovely hint of romance potential will appeal to spark-loving readers like me without alienating mystery purists. I can't wait for the next book!" —Reading Is My Superpower

"Even those who have no particular interest in knitting or crafting will doubtlessly enjoy *On Skein of Death*." —Brianne's Book Reviews

Riverbank Knitting Mysteries

ON SKEIN OF DEATH
KNIT OR DYE TRYING

Knit or Dye Trying

A RIVERBANK KNITTING MYSTERY

ALLIE PLEITER

BERKLEY PRIME CRIME
New York

BERKLEY PRIME CRIME
Published by Berkley
An imprint of Penguin Random House LLC
penguinrandomhouse.com

Copyright © 2022 by Alyse Stanko Pleiter
Penguin Random House supports copyright. Copyright fuels creativity, encourages
diverse voices, promotes free speech, and creates a vibrant culture. Thank you for buying
an authorized edition of this book and for complying with copyright laws by not
reproducing, scanning, or distributing any part of it in any form without permission.
You are supporting writers and allowing Penguin Random House to continue to
publish books for every reader.

BERKLEY and the BERKLEY & B colophon are registered trademarks and
BERKLEY PRIME CRIME is a trademark of Penguin Random House LLC.

Knitting pattern by Amy Kaspar

ISBN: 9780593201800

First Edition: April 2022

Printed in the United States of America
1   3   5   7   9   10   8   6   4   2

Book design by George Towne

For Dede

CHAPTER ONE

My best friend, Margo Payne, was watching me closely.

That's not unusual. Margo always eyes my every bite when I taste a new goody from her shop. I'm used to my role as Unofficial Treat Taster for the Perfect Slice pie shop coming with a side of scrutiny. As friendships go, it's a pretty sweet trade-off.

Margo should know she has no reason to worry. I've loved every new creation she's ever made. In fact, I love the treats in her pie shop as much as she loves the yarn in my yarn shop. It's a marvelous little circle of admiration— perhaps it's a triangle if you add in my English bulldog, Hank, who is as fond of Margo's goodies as I am. Hank may be Y.A.R.N.'s official shop mascot, but the way he stares longingly across Collin Avenue toward Margo's windows, I could make an argument that he's also the official Perfect Slice Pup.

I was sitting in my knit shop, Y.A.R.N., on a Thursday afternoon in April. Surrounded by a kaleidoscope of colorful yarns, amazing textures, and gorgeous needlework, I happily tasted delicious pie made by a good friend. I'd say this was a wonderful day, but the lovely truth is that days like this are delightfully ordinary. The gathering table at the center of my shop is often filled with good food—brought by Margo, myself, my mom, or many of my customers. I'm often surrounded by knitters who are more like friends than patrons, by the historic beauty of my hometown of Collinstown, Maryland, and by the sheer bliss of doing exactly what I think I'm here on earth to do: make beautiful things with yarn and help others do the same.

But I digress—back to the pie. I took one more bite before putting Margo out of her misery. "Relax. It's delicious."

She exhaled as if my rave was ever in question. We've been friends—true-blue-tell-it-like-it-is friends—since high school. She knows I would tell her if it didn't meet my high expectations for Margo's pies (it has never happened). I love everything she bakes, and my dress size— which, no, I will not reveal—proves it.

"How did you manage it?" I asked with my mouth full. In this particular instance, the pie was more delicious than I'd imagined.

Margo gave a victorious smile. "Gluten-free pie— well, *good* gluten-free pie—is no easy feat, believe me." Her brown eyes fairly beamed. "But you know how I like a challenge. And so many people are asking for gluten-free goodies these days, I wanted to have something really tasty ready for the festival."

"This definitely is really tasty." I indulged in two

more bites. "You'll have gobs of customers once word gets out."

I was sure of it. While I have no such dietary restrictions, I have a handful of shop customers who complain that there are too many products out there where "gluten-free" equates to "taste-free." My recent tasting assured me Margo's pie would never be one of those.

"So are you going to go with the mini-tart free-sample thing?"

Margo and I trade clever ideas as much as we trade food and yarn. She's come up with some of the best promotions for Y.A.R.N. since it opened eight months ago. For weeks we'd been helping each other come up with ways for both our businesses to capitalize on Collinstown's upcoming big event. Thanks to the tourism acumen of town mayor Gavin Maddock, our town would be launching its first-ever See More Than Seafood Festival. The eleven days over two weekends would feature different foods to help visitors think of the region for more than crab and crab cakes.

Margo grinned. "You betcha. Bitty tarts to hand out to the first fifty customers this weekend. Then two more flavors next weekend."

"It'll work," I replied. "By the end of this—and for the rest of the season—they'll be lining up outside your door."

This festival was geared to be the early kickoff to Collinstown's tourist season. Not that we needed much in the way of manufactured publicity. Mother Nature does most of our work for us. This part of Maryland is gorgeous in the spring. Actually, it's stunning in the fall and charming at Christmas, too. Every season—not just the shellfish—gives people a reason to come to Collinstown. The beauty drew me back for a fresh start after my divorce, and it was the best decision I ever made—next to opening Y.A.R.N., of course.

I have to admit, I was skeptical of the big festival idea at first. I didn't think we needed themed weekends to tout our variety. If tourists came to Maryland for crab and such, that was fine. We'd wow them with all our other splendors once they arrived. But Gavin had slowly convinced me that the more we showed we had to offer at first, the easier it would be to entice new visitors to come for a variety of reasons. After all, I have dozens of different kinds of yarn in the shop. People come to explore and discover—why not the same for Collinstown?

So now I was pulling for Gavin to get a big win with his festival. Marketing concepts aside, we were done with a dreary March and our town felt ready to catch a fresh wave of excitement for the coming summer.

I finished off the small gluten-free coconut cream tart, not hiding my satisfied grin. "Your pies need to be part of every food festival. I mean, we can't let the restaurants have all the fun."

"You, too," Margo replied with a wink. "I'd never have thought of plant-based yarn. The cotton I figured, but all the other stuff? It's amazing. Vegan yarn—it's pure genius. How'd you ever get the idea?"

While the festival was mostly about food, I was rather proud of the way I'd devised to tie in with the event. "From a handbag, actually."

Margo raised an eyebrow. "I love a good handbag as much as the next woman, but do you want to explain that?"

"Well, you know the term 'vegan' is mostly associated with food. But it's broader than that. It applies to clothing and other industries." I held up the handbag in question, a very beautiful, very functional satchel bag in a spring-beckoning mint green.

"The day after Gavin announced his festival," I went on, "I was staring at this in a DC department store. I bought it just because I liked it, but the store clerk asked me if I was buying it because it was vegan. Some people don't like the idea of buying leather things, so things that aren't made from leather or another animal product can be considered vegan. In fact, the tag on the bag touted it as a vegan product."

Margo stared at the bag. She'd complimented me on it twice since I bought it. A superb handbag is one of life's great pleasures.

She nodded. "Makes sense. But I confess, I never thought about it that way."

"Neither had I, but it got me thinking. People don't realize yarn can be vegan, too. Sure, everyone's first thought is sheep wool or alpaca or Angora rabbits. And those are great fibers with all kinds of good qualities. But there is so much more out there. Loads of really interesting, beautiful fibers that aren't made from animal products."

"So they might come in for the wool but discover all the other stuff while they're in the shop."

"Exactly," I replied. "By the time I turned off the highway, I had the idea for a Wield More Than Wool weekend to go along with See More Than Seafood."

Always the kind of friend who is happy for anyone's success, Margo smiled and sat back in her chair. "Brilliant. I have a brilliant best friend."

I have often thought the same of Margo. "After that," I replied, "there was only one person to call. I had Julie Wilson on the phone within the hour."

Julie Wilson has been an outspoken advocate for animal-friendly, plant-based knitting fibers for the past two years. She designs patterns and imports plant-based fiber, but she is most known and loved for her gorgeous dyeing of yarn. Nobody, but nobody, creates the incredible colors she does. I'd been reading an article about her just the day before I bought that handbag. Granted, Julie treads the oh-so-thin line between aggressive and abrasive, but her work is extraordinary. Besides, I admire someone with that much passion for their message.

"And you booked her, smart you. But didn't you say she was . . . feisty?"

That was a gracious term for Julie's difficult personality. "She is."

Margo scowled. "Okay, but who needs difficult and feisty? Why would someone as nice as you bring in someone like her?"

I reached over to the counter behind me and picked up a shimmering, luxuriously drapey shawl in an indigo blue so rich, it would make most knitters weep.

"Oh." Margo fingered the luscious fiber in the same way I'd just fawned over her dessert. "That looks as good as my pie. I think I get it now."

I'd had that exact reaction when first seeing the yarn, and it only intensified once I started knitting it into the shawl Margo was now touching.

"It's a silk blend made by a Mumbai yarn company," I explained. "Their whole process is specially designed not to harm a single silkworm."

"That color. Wow."

"'Wow' is right. I already sold out the first shipment before Julie even got here."

Not that I make a habit of putting cash over courtesy, but I was hanging on to the notion that somewhere under that prickly exterior was a nice woman just waiting to come out. Really, how else could all the creative beauty flow out of that mind?

"Julie's stuff is amazing," I agreed with Margo. "And you're exactly right—not enough people know how much is out there. I've brought in all kinds of nonanimal fibers, and Julie will help me introduce people to them. So if I have my way, I'll have lines outside my shop that'll be as big as yours."

Margo packed up the little bakery box she'd brought from across the street. "And knitters have to eat. Everybody wins."

"Crocheters, too" came the call from Tina Hanson, nestled in one of the many comfy chairs scattered around my shop. "I don't suppose you've any more of those?"

Margo always brings extras for customers. Sometimes I wonder if patrons hang out in the shop for the treats as much as for the kinship of knitting or crocheting. Who cares? Either works for me.

"You can have the one that's left, but come by for more of those tiny tarts tomorrow," Margo replied. "And send all your friends."

Tina resumed her stitching. "Nobody has to ask me twice."

I share almost all of my customers with Margo. It's a nearly daily occurrence for someone to come in to Y.A.R.N. with a to-go slice of pie from across the street. And despite the full range of coffee supplies my shop assistant, Linda, keeps on hand, "coffee break" at Y.A.R.N.

almost always means a trip across the street for pie to go along with that coffee. I think it's the perfect arrangement of friendship and business.

"When does Julie get here?" Margo asked.

"She was supposed to come in this morning, but her connection got delayed in Denver. She should be here in about an hour, as a matter of fact. She told me she'd call me when her rideshare crossed the bay and I'll meet her at the Riverside Inn."

I'd booked Julie the nicest suite at our local historic inn and told Bev, the manager, to ditch all the down pillows, comforters, and anything else Julie might find objectionable. Julie might be a challenge, but I was ready.

What I wasn't ready for was George Barker, someone more prickly than Julie could ever hope to be. George barged through my door just then, red-faced and stomping right in my direction. "King George" had found near-daily reasons to be annoyed with me ever since last October when I'd announced that I, a mere yarn shop owner, dared to run against him for Chamber of Commerce president. George—who isn't called "King" for his exemplary leadership—considers himself a real estate mogul. To call him an unlikable, ever-selling walking ball of ego was an understatement. Peeved was the man's standard operating mode. But I admit, he did look particularly peeved today.

"What have you done now?" he shouted, pointing furiously behind him up the street toward his office.

Honestly, some days I think George is sure he owns every square inch of Collin Avenue. He doesn't.

"I don't know, George," I said with too weary a sigh. "But I'm sure you'll tell me."

George was just pulling in a breath to launch what I'm sure was another of his diatribes when Tina gasped. "Oh, my stars!"

Tina was a lovely lady and a dear customer, so her alarm meant more to me than George's ever-present panic. When Linda added a not-so-calm "Oh, no!" from her spot behind the register, it dropped a rock into the pit of my stomach.

"You're behind this!" George accused me, still not bothering to say what "this" was. "You did this!"

Margo, who was sitting closer to the window, stood up and began walking toward the door. George was on her heels like an impatient tailgater on the DC Beltway. As she looked out my shopwindow, her expression of "there goes George again" changed immediately to startled disbelief.

"Um . . . Libby?"

As I got up from my chair, I began to notice the other people on the street I could see through the shopwindow. They were all staring in the direction of George's pointing finger and Linda's wide eyes.

I heard it before I saw it. A sound I knew, but couldn't associate with Collin Avenue. It couldn't be.

It was. A bleat.

A whole lot of bleating, in fact. And quite a few car horns. And shouting. As if a herd of . . .

By the time I reached the door, my brain tried to wrap itself around the sight that met my eyes.

For some inexplicable reason, a sizable herd of sheep was making its way down Collin Avenue.

CHAPTER TWO

O kay," I said, mostly to myself. I tried to draw some connection between the absurd sight and George's irritation. It didn't take long for me to connect the dots. I turned to look at George, who bore a striking resemblance to a near-boiling teakettle. "I didn't organize a sheep parade."

He snorted.

"You think I did this?" In all our promotional brainstorming, this idea had never come up.

"Of course you did this," he shouted. "They're sheep! This is a yarn shop. Yarn comes from sheep."

For a split second, I thought about explaining that the whole point of my upcoming weekend was that yarn came from *far more* than sheep, but George's red face stopped me. Well, that and the particular sheep now paused in front of my store. My mouth fell open as I caught sight of the words "Wool Is Good" spray-painted on the large animal's thick fleece. *Spray-painted*. Like a walking woolly protest sign.

"See?" George sputtered. "Do you see that?"

Honestly, I didn't have an answer for George. He clearly thought I had organized this. In truth, I was as surprised as he was.

I heard Linda come up behind me. "Protest sheep?" Her voice held the same disbelief currently blanking my brain of a logical response. "That's a thing?"

"Evidently," I said, still stunned. Seriously? Spray-painted protest sheep?

"They're protesting *you*," George accused me as if he'd just been waiting for someone to hate me this much. Surely any shop owner evil enough to deserve such a protest had no business running for Chamber of Commerce president against a pillar of town progress like George Barker.

"Actually, no," I replied as calmly as anyone could be expected under such crazy circumstances.

In a flash, it came together for me. On our original schedule, Julie should have been in the hotel for a couple of hours by now. Due to a travel delay, it was likely she'd just be arriving. In the middle of all this. I sent up a small prayer of hope that she hadn't arrived yet and as such would miss this demonstration.

"Their beef is with Julie Wilson."

As if to prove my point, a second spray-painted sheep came to stand beside the first. The name Julie Wilson was painted inside a red circle with a slash through it— the universal "no" sign.

"Their *mutton*, actually," Linda offered under her breath, earning a growl from George and a please-don't look from me.

George's eyes were bulging now. "Our state has one of the largest sheep-and-wool festivals in the nation and you brought in someone sheep farmers hate. What were you thinking?"

It really bugs me when George is even the tiniest bit right. But some sliver of me was impressed that he'd done his homework.

"I knew there was some controversy with Julie, yes. But, George, nothing about my event is antiwool. Or any other fleecy, furry thing." I pointed to the sign up on the shop wall. "It says 'Wield More Than Wool'—as in *and*, not *or*. Gavin's festival isn't anticrab, is it?"

"Those aren't crabs and lobsters walking down my street."

It has always bothered me that George frequently referred to Collin Avenue as "his" street rather than "our" street. King George clearly felt his beloved Collin Avenue had been defiled.

"I need to go out there and—"

Oh, no. On the very short list of things that would make the present situation worse, George going out there was at the top. I fixed George with my darkest glare.

"You will not go out there and say anything. Let me go talk to these gentlemen."

Three bearded, very rustic-looking men were now clustered outside my door like malevolent magi. But no one was bearing gifts in this crowd. No shepherds abiding in the fields by night—not by a long shot.

When I opened Y.A.R.N., I envisioned a life of quiet creativity. Good coffee, gorgeous fibers, beauty coming into the world all around me. I did not plan on stepping outside my beautiful brick storefront to make peace with outraged shepherds.

"Well, you'd better do something," George practically hissed through his teeth.

"Linda," I called over my shoulder, "Julie hasn't called yet, so hopefully she hasn't arrived." I dearly hoped that was true. "But check with Bev just to be sure. And if Julie is here, ask Bev to do whatever she can to keep Julie in her room. I don't want this to turn into a confrontation."

Maybe I still stood a chance of defusing this before anything got out of hand. Because if Julie got within a hundred yards of this herd, there'd be no hope of anything but confrontation.

Taking a deep breath, I walked out the front door. Out of the corner of my eye, I saw Mayor Gavin coming up the sidewalk at a near run. Up and down the block, Collinstown residents and shop owners were coming out of stores and restaurants to view the wild sight, not to mention the traffic backed up by the sheep now meandering in both lanes. One ewe even cast a big unblinking eye at me as she nibbled on the spring flowers just planted in the pots in front of the shop.

I couldn't decide if it was a good or a bad thing that I recognized the oldest of the farmers. "Barney, isn't it?" I called in the cheeriest voice I could manage.

I have tried to foster good relationships with the sheep, goat, alpaca, and other fiber-animal livestock owners in the area. In January I'd hosted a whole local-fibers night with many of the local farms. Up until this minute, I had thought we were all in the same boat—um, pasture. Clearly I'd crossed some line in bringing Julie in.

"Where is she?" Barney demanded without any niceties. Anyone angry enough to spray-paint their own sheep evidently didn't have time for small talk.

I wasn't sure it was safe to answer. Could sheep stampede? They always struck me as slow and docile creatures. The occasional frolicking lamb, perhaps, but nothing bent on destruction. In fact, the flock looked rather annoyed, as if they'd been pressed into service as protest billboards when they'd really rather have been munching on a hillside somewhere.

I didn't rise to Barney's shouts, but kept my tone calm. "Why do this?"

The younger of the shepherds—who was actually much younger than I first realized, and one I hadn't met yet, reached into the pocket of his canvas work jacket and produced a smartphone. He held it up to show Julie Wilson's YouTube channel, clicking on a video just as Linda said, "I think I know why," behind me with the same video on her phone.

Another lead weight landed in my stomach. Julie was known for posting the occasional fiery outburst on her YouTube channel, but that was usually on Tuesdays. Her video two days ago had been rather peaceful, and I was foolish enough to think we'd escaped controversy in the windup to our weekend.

Wrong.

Only a few seconds into Julie's video, it became clear this particular episode was a scathing attack on inhumane sheep farming. The footage shown was rather ghastly, making the shearing look harsh and cruel. I've seen many shearings, and none of them looked like that. But even I knew Julie looked for stories and images that supported her belief that animals didn't need to be involved in our diets or clothing ever. Personally, I owned three sweaters made from wool that came from one of the farmers in front of me—perhaps even one of the very sheep in front of me. Wool is, after all, a renewable resource.

"It's *her* we want," Barney said with narrowed eyes. "She picks out one or two bad apples and makes us all look bad." His face softened. "I take good care of my girls."

He did. "I know you're not a bad apple," I replied. "But maybe a conversation is a better choice than this."

I motioned to the small crowd now gathered around the midstreet flock. One ewe *baaah*-ed as if to say, "Yeah, what she said."

Barney jutted his chin toward his companion's cell phone. "Jud, does that look like the kind of gal who has 'conversations' to you?"

Julie's angry face scowled over the phone screen. Barney had a point. Julie didn't look to be a fan of conversations any more than George did. Julie liked arguments. Arguments probably made for viral videos way better than pleasant conversation. Why did I ever think this yarn business would be peaceful?

At this point Mayor Gavin had reached the shop. He gave the scene a disgruntled growl as if this livestock outburst was the last thing he needed today.

Get in line, I thought.

"I'm not going to be able to keep Frank from coming out here much longer," Gavin said.

He was using what I referred to as his "mayor voice"—all deep and official and "don't mess with me." Frank Reynolds was Collinstown's chief of police. Frank didn't suffer fools well, but he also didn't have much crime to fight. The most Collinstown ever saw in terms of crime was the occasional overimbibing tourist, high school kids out for a joyride, or shoplifting.

Oh, and the little matter of the murder of a knitwear designer who came to my shop last year. I promise you, I have had dozens of successful events since then, but people do tend to remember the ones where the guest of honor turns up dead.

Barney's snarling face doubled my conviction to make sure he didn't get anywhere near Julie. "I'm not going to arrange for you to meet her like this," I declared in the closest to a mayor voice I could produce. "I don't think she's even here yet."

"Um, yes, she is" came Linda's worried voice from behind me. "Bev said she checked in twenty minutes ago."

So much for heading this off at the pass. "Well, then"—Barney started to move his flock down the street toward the Riverside Inn—"we'll just give her a little show to see out her window. My nephew works at the inn and he told me you booked her the corner suite. We know which window that is, don't we, girls?"

I kid you not, the sheep bleated in unison and followed their shepherd.

I ran on ahead, glad that even in my cutest shoes I was faster than the average ewe. I needed to reach Julie before things could get even more absurd.

B ev met me at the inn door. "It's been crazy in here."
"It's about to get crazier." I pointed behind me to the sheep, which were still a good fifty feet away.

Bev made a sound that was a cross between a gulp and a growl. "You've got to be kidding me!"

"A herd of *goats* would be kidding you," I managed to joke. "These are protest *sheep*. Against Julie."

My heart skipped a beat when I saw one sheep toddle up onto the sidewalk and look hungrily at the window box full of spring flowers outside the police station. Angie Goldman, who ran the desk at the station, might give Julie a run for her money in the cranky department if she caught sight of any sheep grazing on her beloved flower boxes.

"How bad is it?" I asked Bev.

Why hadn't Julie called me on arrival like she said she would? Still, Linda said it hadn't even been half an hour. Things couldn't have gotten that bad so soon, could they?

My question brought a dark look from Bev. "Do you have a sister, Libby?"

"No."

It only took me a second or two to make sense of that question. Julie's sister, Monica Wilson, was one of the chefs brought in for a series of festival classes and celebrity cooking demonstrations at some of our local restaurants. She had checked in yesterday.

"Julie and Monica?"

Bev put a hand to her forehead. That worried me—it took a lot to ruffle Bev's feathers. Then again, if Monica's temperament was anything like Julie's, it could spell double trouble.

"They've been bickering like kindergartners," Bev moaned. "'Your suite is nicer.' 'You have the better view.' 'I have more interviews than you.' I didn't know whether to send up biscotti or boxing gloves."

"Maybe both?"

Bev was a clever businesswoman who ran a top-notch inn. She didn't deserve to be playing referee between feuding guests like this. And I could tell Bev's considerable patience was running short. Looking past me at the approaching flock, she angled around me to stand at the curb in front of her inn.

Barney and his companions were lining the sheep on the street in front of the building, spray-painted messages facing the windows, which would include those belonging to Julie's suite.

"Don't you bring those sheep up on my sidewalk," she declared in tones to rival Mayor Gavin's command.

Police Chief Frank Reynolds came out from his station to stand beside Gavin with dual looks of bafflement and frustration. I was pretty sure there wasn't an ordinance on the books for this one.

Frank went straight up to Barney. "What's going on here?"

Barney's chin jutted out. "We're protesting that gal Libby brought in—that's what."

Frank adjusted his hat. I'd come to learn he did that when annoyed. "You're blocking the street."

"I'm exercisin' my First Amendment rights," Barney declared.

I wondered who had fed him that line. Barney was opinionated, maybe a bit stubborn, but not exactly the type to get political. Then again, it wasn't hard to see why he took Julie's comments personally.

Frank gave an irritated snort as a sheep bumped into his leg and bleated. "Your sheep have no Constitutional rights and they're blocking the street. Clear 'em out."

Gavin gave an irritated groan behind me, and I followed his gaze to a group of tourists on the other side of the street. Every one of them was filming the scene on their cell phone. The whole thing was just absurd enough to go viral . . . or end up on the evening news. Gavin had created the festival to gain the town publicity, but I don't think this was the kind he had in mind.

"You said she's here. I'm not leaving until I know she's seen us," the second farmer declared. He turned his glare in my direction. "You go bring her to the window of that fancy hotel room. Or better yet, tell her to come down here and face us. I'd like to see if she's got the nerve."

Nerve or not, I was going to do no such thing. A protest was bad enough. These farmers looked like they wanted to launch a rumble. Besides, I had no doubt Julie was already at the window, probably filming her own scathing commentary on the situation.

"You've got ten minutes." Frank made a show of looking at his watch. "If I don't see these sheep heading back up the street in ten minutes, I'm going to hit you with a flock of citations. Don't make me do it."

Bev pulled the front door of the inn open for me. She looked as if she didn't care how this ended as long as it was over fast. "Go on up there and see what you can do, will you?" she pleaded.

There's a chalkboard wall in my shop where people—myself, customers, friends, or anyone—can write what they think Y.A.R.N. stands for. Originally, it stood for "You're Absolutely Ready Now," as I reached for my lifelong dream of opening a yarn shop. Dozens of versions have gone up in the months since the store opened. Tina walked up and added, "Yumminess Abides Right Nearby," after she'd tasted Margo's tiny tart. It's a Y.A.R.N. tradition, one that I dearly love.

As for me and my current situation, "You Aren't Remotely Normal" felt more like it. I strove for a calm that edged out of my reach as I followed Bev into the lobby and headed for the stairs to Julie's room on the second floor.

I bet librarians never have problems like this. Why did I ever think a yarn shop would be a quiet career?

"At least my customers don't protest me" came a female voice as I rounded the landing.

"Oh, really?" came a voice I recognized as Julie's. "What would you call all those one-star reviews? 'Unimaginative' was the latest one, wasn't it?"

"Well, I don't see anyone spray-painting *my* name on walking mutton chops" came the shrill reply.

"That's a new low, Monica, even for you."

I heard a door slam as I reached the top stair.

The Dockhouse, arguably the nicest restaurant in town, was hosting Monica. It was one of six establishments that had brought in well-known regional chefs to create menus and host special weekend dinners featuring local fare that wasn't seafood. Monica Wilson's local cable cooking show, *Dish Up Comfort*, focused on comfort food, but there was nothing soothing in the tones of these two sisters. I didn't know if I should be proud or bothered that evidently I'd sprung for a nicer room for my guest than the Dockhouse had for theirs.

I found Julie in the doorway of her suite, staring at the door across the hall from her, presumably the one that had just been slammed in her face.

"Hello, Julie," I panted, a bit winded from taking the inn's stairs at a run. "I see you've arrived." I tried to sound cheerful, but I expect I fell rather short. "We've got a bit of commotion going on, hmm?"

"My sister needs to stay out of my business." Julie glared at the closed door, then realized I was mostly talking about the commotion outside. "Oh, yeah, that."

She looked rather pleased. She liked the chaos—that was clear.

I didn't share her fondness. "We'd like to clear this up as quickly as possible, if you don't mind. Would it be too much to ask for you to just show up at the window for a minute?" *And not yell anything confrontational?* my brain added silently. "The farmers have promised that they'll clear off the street once they know you've seen them."

That wasn't entirely true—Frank had commanded them but I'd not heard any sort of agreement from Barney and his buddies—but I wasn't going to split that hair . . . um, fleece . . . at the moment.

Julie shrugged and turned toward the bank of windows in her room, which looked out onto the street. I was surprised she seemed so willing to cooperate.

"They'll just be back," she said. "These types want to get the biggest bang for their spray-paint buck."

"This has happened before?" I probably shouldn't have been so shocked.

"You don't think these guys came up with this on their own, do you?"

"Pardon?"

"Some guy in Vermont was the first to try this stunt. It's happened at least half a dozen times. I'm pretty sure they all talk to one another." My jaw dropped as Julie went to the window, yanked it open, and called, "Hello there, heartless wool harvesters," to the crowd below. "Point made. You can go home and continue your reign of cruelty now."

I cringed, rather glad I couldn't quite make out what Barney yelled back. Whatever it was, it was sufficient to earn an irritated response from Chief Reynolds. I'm not quite sure how a wave can be sarcastic, but Julie managed it just before pulling the window closed.

"Doesn't that bother you?" I asked, although it seemed a pointless question, given the victorious look on Julie's face.

"Not at all. Controversy means awareness, and raised awareness is what I'm looking for."

Julie crossed her arms over her chest. She was a tall woman with unruly wavy dark hair, bold sharp features, and mesmerizing green eyes. Striking but not in a way most people would call beautiful. What was truly beautiful was the exquisite coral sweater she wore. The knitter in me noticed the color immediately. But the sweater also had a delectable texture, a cotton-blend yarn that wandered between lightweight and nubby. Any knitter would consider it the perfect spring sweater.

"Besides," Julie went on, "don't you think the spray-painted sheep pretty much make my point for me? Who would do that to an animal they cared about? Those sheep are just objects to them. Profit centers on four legs."

"They can't all be bad apples, can they?" I gestured to Barney and his flock below. "I've seen Barney's farm. He seems to take very good care of his flock."

Julie gave me a bless-your-heart look. "Did you know sheepshearing is a competitive sport in some parts of the world? I could show you photos of shorn Angora bunnies from Asia that would make you cry. My point isn't that there are some good apples like your Barney there. My point is, why do it at all when there are so many good alternatives?"

I thought of the dozens of cozy woolen knitted garments in my possession. *I like wool. I like all the fibers.* Then another part of my brain argued—in my mother's voice, no less—*You knew who she was when you booked her. Don't blame her for the opinion—that's why she's here.*

I opted for "You make a good argument."

It seemed a neutral enough response. I looked out the window, glad to see Barney and his compatriots herding the flock back up the street the way they'd come. I had no doubt I'd be hearing about this little escapade for weeks to come. I'd booked Julie Wilson to start a discussion, not a war. Now my goal of conversation had dissolved into chaos. And the festival hadn't even started. Speaking of which, I decided to get down to business with my guest.

"All the raw fibers you ordered have arrived, and the water you had shipped in, too. Pans, burners, a scale—it's all sitting in the warehouse ready for Saturday's workshop. How would you like to get ready?"

Julie herself had chosen the slightly startling name "Watch Julie Wilson Dye" for her hands-on fiber-dyeing workshop, which would take place on this first weekend of the festival. Every knitter I knew wanted to learn how Julie achieved her famously luscious colors, and tickets had been selling fast.

"We're almost sold out. People are very excited to come learn your techniques. And I've had dozens of orders for the custom color sight unseen."

Julie smiled at that. In fact, Julie Wilson creating a custom batch of an exclusive color for Y.A.R.N. was an enormous coup. No one knew anything other than it would be called Riverbank—and no one cared. If Julie made it, we all knew it would be beautiful.

"Then I've got everything I need right here."

She patted a large black wheeled crate I assumed contained the dye compounds for which she was famous. A lot of people clamored to know how Julie made her dyes, and that crate contained the answer. No wonder she brought it in person rather than shipping it ahead.

"Just let me into the space. I'll do the setup first and then bring these over when I'm ready to work." She pointed to the black case, confirming my guess that her dyeing compounds were inside.

"You'll make the first two batches tonight and tomorrow?" We'd talked earlier about the time frame for creating her stunning fibers.

"And then I'll do a smaller last batch in front of the workshop attendees on Saturday."

I confess I really wanted to watch her work to see how she did what no one else seemed able to do. "Do you need an extra set of hands to set things up?"

Julie shook her head. "No, thanks. I'm a one-woman operation. Just get me into the building and show me how to turn on the ventilation system. I'm good to go from there. Besides," she said with an unexpected wink, "the way I dye is hot, humid work, and I can get a bit cranky."

"A bit cranky" struck me as an understatement. I wasn't quite sure how to respond to that. Was Julie deliberately testy or just unwilling to water down her strong personality? Did it matter? After all, I'd watched enough cooking shows to know several chefs were known for their explosive personalities. What Julie did was just as much art as what her sister, Monica, did, maybe even more so. At least I knew enough not to voice that thought aloud.

I wrote down the address for the nearby warehouse we'd secured for Julie to work in and host the workshop.

Dyeing is far too smelly and messy a business to do in the shop, so I was glad an old manufacturing site with an excellent ventilation system a block away was available to host the crowd I'd hoped to draw.

"I'll meet you there in half an hour?"

Julie gave me the warmest look I'd seen from her yet. "Perfect."

Wouldn't it be a surprising outcome if I discovered a sweet, friendly person under all that bristle and artistic brilliance? It wouldn't be the first time. Yarn brings out the best in people, I always say.

CHAPTER THREE

Later that evening, I wandered among friends and guests at the festival's opening reception. I'd gotten Julie settled in with no further problems, and I was looking forward to this party. Not to single out any restaurant, Gavin had organized a cocktail hour for all the local businesses at the town hall. I watched Gavin stroll among the crowd, pleased that his launch was coming off nicely, until he met up with me at—where else?—the dessert table.

"Gotten many sheep jokes tonight?" he teased.

"Too many. I don't want to be known as Libby Beckett, Rabble-Rouser." I selected yet another of Margo's delicious shortbread cookies.

Gavin's eyes took on the warm gleam of memory. "There was a time . . ."

Right there was the lingering complication between

Gavin and me. There *had* been a time. Gavin and I had been a serious item in high school, dramatic and reckless in the way of all teenagers in love. A pair of ended marriages and the complications of our new lives had left us trying to figure out who we were to each other now. Or more precisely, who we ought to be to each other right now. Some days I classified the gentle pull between us as nothing more than nostalgia. Other days it felt like something worth exploring. I was pretty sure Gavin had the same emotional ping-pong going on in his head as well, even though we never talked about it.

Gavin's daughter, Jillian, and my mother, however, were perfectly happy to share their opinions on what we ought to be to each other. Gavin and I had spent the past few months putting the brakes on their nonstop attempts to match us up. We were trying hard to downplay our plans to steal a simple quiet dinner later this evening. It wasn't a date. We weren't looking for romance—mostly just peace and quiet between harried friends—but we knew you couldn't convince Jillian and my mother of that.

Gavin sipped his drink. "Maybe you and Esther can compare notes on how to handle the Wilson sisters." Esther owned the Dockhouse, where Monica would be serving as guest chef tonight. "From what she tells me, Monica's just as much of a challenge as Julie."

"Really?" I joked. "Has anyone rolled wheels of cheese down Collin Avenue to protest Monica's appearance there?"

"Not yet but the festival runs two whole weekends." Gavin's grin broadened as Jillian walked up. He pulled her into a hug. "Did I throw a good party, kiddo?"

Jillian rolled her eyes a bit like any fourteen-year-old,

but I could tell she was proud of her dad's accomplishments. "Not too bad. You could use better music," she suggested as she nodded to the elegant string quartet from the local college hired to play chamber music in the corner.

"You don't know what better music is. This isn't the crowd for the stuff you listen to."

Jillian turned to me. "Three of my friends sent me videos of the sheep thing. It's hysterical. Would you be okay with me putting it on my YouTube channel?"

I was sure it was probably all over the Internet already anyway, and I was rather impressed that she did me the courtesy of asking. "If you're nice about it," I replied, "and you include a link to Julie's workshop."

Jillian tucked a strand of hair behind her ear. "Actually, I was hoping you'd let me ask Julie for an interview."

After I taught her to knit last year, Jillian not only took to the craft, but decided to try to become a teenage influencer in the yarn world. She was "gaining traction," as she put it, and I have to admit I was proud of her. Mom and I were in a good-natured race to see who could send more followers to Jillian's channel, and even though I had a whole store full of customers to draw from, Mom was actually winning.

"If you remember the advice Caroline gave you," I answered.

Caroline was an entertainment journalist and a shop customer I gained about the same time as I introduced Jillian to knitting. Caroline was kind enough to be a mentor of sorts to Jillian in how to navigate the media world.

"I know, I know. Be polite, be specific, be ready to hear no," Jillian recited.

Given such wise advice, Jillian had actually conducted three very fine interviews with knitting designers and yarn manufacturers. I thought that was admirable for someone her age. Still, Julie Wilson's contentious personality could pose more of a challenge. I wasn't sure I was ready to expose a young girl—much less a young girl I liked very much—to the dark side of media attention.

Like any smart woman, I deflected. "Did your dad say it was okay?" After all, Gavin knew almost as much about Julie's snarky side as I did.

He looked cornered. "Not yet. I was hoping we could talk about it over dinner before I gave my permission."

"Oh, yeah, dinner." Jillian's eyes could be as playful as her father's. "Sure," she said, drawing the word out as if it hinted at a dozen things. "Talk about it over dinner. But she's right there, Dad. I could totally do it now. Then I could edit it while you guys are at dinner."

I'm not sure I'll ever get used to the idea of fourteen-year-olds being able to run circles around someone my age when it comes to technology. I'm happy when I can operate our store credit card machine without incident. Shooting, editing, and broadcasting video interviews before you can drive? It's a strange new world, to be sure.

"I still get to okay it before you hit the publish button," Gavin said, his eyes returning to parental seriousness.

"Unless you all stay out past my bedtime."

Again, she made the words sound as if she'd be waiting by the door the way my mother waited for me. And yes, Gavin and I had broken our share of curfews back in the day. Still, that's not the kind of thing I expect a father admits to his daughter until she's about twenty-five . . . if ever.

"Relax," I said, playing along. "I'll have your father home by nine thirty."

After the day I'd had and the days Gavin and I both had ahead, I'd have been thankful if we made it that long. I was exhausted, and we hadn't even started on Julie's events.

"Go ask her," Gavin said, "but don't take her away from other important conversations. She's here to sell tickets for Libby, not gain you followers."

Jillian smirked. "If I do it right, she can do both."

Smartphone at the ready, Jillian trotted off in Julie's direction.

Together Gavin and I watched her politely approach Julie Wilson and make her pitch, and then, in complete shock, we witnessed Julie turn into a warm, smiling mama bear, nodding enthusiastically to Jillian. Seconds later they walked over to a set of chairs where Jillian set up her phone to record them chatting.

"Well, I'll be," I said to Gavin. "The secret to unlocking nice Julie is your daughter. If only I'd known."

The two of them looked as if they'd been friends for months instead of minutes. Julie was even complimenting the bamboo-silk cowl Jillian was wearing. I knew Jillian had designed it herself, and could only imagine how impressed Julie would be when Jillian admitted it. Every knitter loves the idea of passing along their beloved craft to a new generation.

Gavin gave me a look. "I'm in trouble, aren't I?"

"Jillian? Well, yes. She's smart way beyond her years.

If we can keep Mom from corrupting her, she ought to go far."

"Too late. Rhonda's trying to talk her into running for freshman student council president when she gets to high school."

I cast my glance over to where Jillian was now having an animated conversation with Julie. "She should. But only because she wants to, not because Grandma Rhonda says she should."

Because I wasn't able to have kids of my own, it hadn't taken long for me to warm up to the idea of my mom adopting Jillian as her surrogate grandchild. Mom could be a handful, but she had a lot of love to give. When they weren't trying to fix Gavin and me up, the two actually made a pretty clever team. Jillian easily glossed over Mom's all-too-numerous senior moments, and Jillian's own mother hadn't been much of a parent, so I was happy for Jillian to have more positive women in her life.

The bright light of Jillian's smartphone was suddenly overshadowed by another set of lights coming from the far corner of the room. Conversation ground to a halt as Monica swept into the reception, tailed by a filming crew and a fast-moving in-charge-looking guy. I caught sight of the *Dish Up Comfort* logo on the cameraman's bag. This was Monica's husband and producer, Yale Wagner, with a crew in tow.

"I told him not to film at this," Gavin grumbled. "This is a social event, not a preview."

"She and Julie got into it back at the hotel," I warned. With a gulp of alarm I noticed Yale's bright green sweater. A *wool* sweater. "I hope no one's looking to stir up trouble here for the sake of entertainment."

Not thirty seconds later, the shouting started.

"Turn that thing off!"

Julie's voice towered above the murmurs of shock and curiosity in the crowd around the two sisters. They stood glaring at each other in the center of the room. Poor Jillian's interview had come to a screeching halt while Yale seemed intent on keeping his own camera rolling.

"I'm going to have to agree," Gavin said in a voice that sounded far calmer than I knew him to be. His tone was even, but everyone in the room knew he meant business.

Julie walked over and picked at the sleeve of Yale's sweater. "Seriously, Yale? Did you buy this one just for tonight?"

Now that I thought about it, two of the three sheep farmers had had wool sweaters on as they marched their flocks down Collin Avenue. I'd never wear wool in Julie's presence out of deference to her values. It never occurred to me until tonight that someone would wear wool to deliberately annoy her. From the frown of weary irritation on her face, it happened a lot.

"How come Esther gets to have press for her chef tonight and we don't?" Tony Vigali asked. Tony owned the Blue Moon and made some of the best Alfredo and tiramisu in the county.

"No one gets press tonight," Gavin announced. "Turn it off, please."

Only Chief Frank could make the word "please" sound more like a command, and out of the corner of my eye, I saw Frank moving toward the sisters, ready to back Gavin up.

"No one?" George Barker cut in. Why did this man

materialize wherever drama started in this town? "Wasn't your daughter just interviewing the yarn lady?"

I held my breath, waiting for Julie to take supreme offense at being called the yarn lady. I rather liked it when people called me that—given the shop name and my passion for the craft, it does happen frequently—but I doubted Julie would.

"My daughter's YouTube channel is not press," Gavin replied.

I could see him regret that statement almost as fast as I did. Jillian's eyebrows furrowed down into an insulted glower as she shoved her cell phone into her back pocket. Gavin was going to hear about that one when he got home tonight, surely.

Yale walked up to Gavin but didn't signal for the cameras to stop rolling. "I thought you'd want *Dish Up Comfort* to cover the festival. It's why you brought Monica here."

"It certainly couldn't be her cooking," Julie grumbled loud enough to be heard.

While I will admit to several downsides to being an only child—being the only person to deal with Mom being chief among them—this display of sibling rivalry made me grateful.

"We've invited several media outlets to cover the festival *starting tomorrow*," Gavin said, emphasizing the final words. "Tonight is a friendly celebration."

There was nothing friendly about the looks Julie and Monica were currently exchanging. In a diversionary tactic, I stepped between them to tap Julie's elbow. "Have you tried one of Margo's pies? She owns the shop across the street from mine and they are delicious. Let's go get ourselves a slice, shall we? Let Gavin handle them."

Julie cast a dark look over her shoulder before allowing me to nearly tug her in the direction of the pie slices set out on a banquet table in another corner of the room.

"You knew she'd be here," I offered in a can't-we-all-get-along? tone. "Have you two always fought like this?"

Julie picked up a slice of the most decadent of Margo's chocolate pies—*good choice*—as I was reaching for one myself. I find chocolate to be a time-honored coping strategy—one I heartily endorse. There aren't too many stresses in the world that a dose of chocolate and an hour of knitting can't soothe.

"No," she said with an angry—and perhaps a bit sad—glance back at Monica and Yale.

Despite the single word, Julie's eyes and tone told me there was a lot of complexity behind her answer. Since when have families ever been simple? It's been just Mom and me in the years since my father passed away, and we're as complex as they come. The social tangles of Sterling's family were part of the reason our marriage stopped working. While he seemed to thrive on the intrigue and complicated expectations, I found it exhausting. I also found his infidelity and deviousness intolerable, but that's another matter.

"You are both impressive artists. And we all know artists can be temperamental," I said as kindly as I could. "Perhaps while you're here together, you can find a way to appreciate each other again."

I was surprised to hear my mother in those words. People loved Mom because she managed to see the good in everyone. And she is a good person herself. She's just edging out of forgetful and into what looks all too much like early-onset memory loss. I pushed that thought aside with another bite of delicious chocolate pie while I watched Julie take a bite of her own.

"Not likely. Not with Yale here."

I had to agree. "He doesn't look like he's much in favor of you two getting along."

"He's got his reasons. Besides, conflict makes better ratings. It's one of his favorite sayings. And we all know Yale lives for great ratings."

I followed Julie's eyes to look at the couple. "He does seem very eager to promote her."

"Her cooking?" Julie asked sharply. "Or what her cooking can do for him?"

"But they were married before she got her cable show, right? He must care for her." It suddenly felt like a dangerous assumption. Perhaps I should have been guiding this conversation away from the topic of Monica and Yale.

Julie declined to reply, which was a reply in itself. I chose a new topic. "I think Jillian has great promise as a knitter and an influencer in the knitting world. Were you having a good interview?"

Her expression softened. "Good kid. Smart. She told me you taught her to knit."

"Jillian is one of my favorite students. I have no doubt she'll surpass me in her knitting skills one day. Probably very soon." I decided to try a compliment. "And I hope she has as much influence on our craft as you do."

"Our craft could use a few new voices," she agreed.

Again, I caught a hint of something behind the sharp edge in her words. Perhaps she really regretted how her relationship with Monica had gotten this bad. They were still sisters, after all.

Even though I knew it would tank my planned peace and quiet with Gavin, I opted to ask, "Are you sure you don't want to come out to dinner tonight after the reception?"

To be honest, despite the I-work-alone vibe, she looked just the tiniest bit lonely. And she was my VIP guest, after all.

"No," Monica replied. "After this I'm taking the dye compounds over to the warehouse and getting started on the first batch. Where are you going to eat?"

Now I was sorry I'd asked, because I had to admit, "The mayor and I have reservations at the Dockhouse."

Julie's eyes narrowed. "Where Monica's cooking."

"Well, yes, but I'd cancel that reservation so that we could go somewhere you'd be more comfortable."

I would. I was looking forward to the chance to spend time with Gavin, but that could wait until after the festival. Especially if Julie wanted company.

She gave a small unattractive snort. "I'd bring a fire extinguisher if I were you."

The warning tone of her words caught my attention. "What on earth do you mean by that?"

"I'd be willing to bet she sets something on fire. Monica makes mistakes when she's nervous. Things tend to burn. And Yale is making her nervous."

So is the way you're fighting, I bet, I thought.

"I'm sure it will be a lovely meal. But I'd still change my plans for you, really," I insisted. "Collinstown has lots of great places to eat, as you can see. We don't even have to go fancy. We could grab a burger or even takeout from Tom's Riverside Diner. They do a fabulous cheeseburger."

She just didn't look to me like someone who wanted

to spend the night alone in a warehouse mixing up chemicals and tints.

"I don't do dead cows."

Oops. How could I have forgotten, even momentarily, that Julie was a vegetarian?

She waved me away. "I'm fine. Go enjoy your dinner. Who knows? Maybe I'll be wrong and this time nothing will catch fire."

I gave a small gulp at Julie's supreme lack of optimism.

Noting my expression, Julie backpedaled. "Relax. You'll have a great meal. Monica is capable of one— under the right circumstances."

That sounded as much like a sisterly backhanded compliment as I've ever heard. Now I didn't know whether getting to keep my dinner date with Gavin would be a good thing . . . or a bad one.

CHAPTER FOUR

Fire?" Gavin raised an eyebrow as we sat down at our table at the Dockhouse an hour later. "She said 'bring a fire extinguisher'?"

"Lower your voice," I shushed him. "It was just Julie being mean."

"Those two seem to be good at that."

We ordered drinks. I'd kept off the wine during the town hall reception, but right now a good pinot would be very welcome. I changed the subject.

"Did you smooth everything over with Jillian?"

"I'll be regretting that for a few days." Gavin gave an eye roll his teenage daughter would admire. "I didn't mean to knock her project, but I wasn't wrong. Her interviewing Julie isn't the same thing as Yale sticking that camera in everyone's faces."

"I'm surprised—and grateful—he isn't here. Monica's in the kitchen tonight, after all."

Gavin looked around. "Monica told me he was out getting B-roll shots of the town, whatever that means. If it keeps his camera crew somewhere else, that's fine with me."

As if they'd heard that cue, Yale and one of the cameramen I'd seen at the reception walked in the restaurant door. Yale stopped at our table on the way to a booth near the kitchen.

"Mayor," Yale greeted Gavin with a rather curt nod.

"Mr. Wagner," Gavin returned with an equally cool formality. "Did you get your B-roll shots?"

"Not all of them. I want to get a few high-angle ones in the evening light. I'm just popping in to check on Monica. Make sure she's feeling well settled."

His voice had just the touch of controlling tone I knew too well from my days with Sterling.

"What is B-roll anyway?" I asked.

"I don't think you had the chance to meet Libby Beckett. She owns the yarn shop hosting Julie."

"B-roll is establishing shots. Landscapes, street scenes, visuals to put in between the action." He extended a hand. "So you're the shop owner. My grandmother was a knitter. Monica's mother is, too."

"Was she?"

I hear some form of that reply often. Everyone seems to have a mother or an aunt or a grandmother who either knit or crocheted. You can usually see it in their eyes if they find the memory heartwarming or old-fashioned. I'll be the first to tell you knitting is current and artistic and alive and well in today's generations, but I'll admit to a certain bias in my enthusiasm. Still, Jillian is a perfect example of what's happening in the yarn world, and why people like Julie raise such an interest.

"My grandmother taught my mother, and she taught me," I continued. "Teaching new knitters is one of my favorite things."

"She taught my daughter, Jillian," Gavin added.

I decided on a brave tactic. "Does Monica knit by any chance?"

It had never occurred to me to ask until just now. It might offer a bridge between them—I'd seen crafts do that before. Several people at opposite ends of the political spectrum came to forge a friendship while in my store. Knitting connects us a lot more than other things divide us, I've always thought. Why not Monica and Julie?

"Not much since Julie made it her soapbox."

Clearly, that couldn't serve as a way to reconcile the sisters. There was a lot of turbulent water under that sisterly bridge. And besides, it wasn't really my place. Mom did enough butting in for the both of us.

I chose to shift topics yet again, pointing at the small card listing the specials Monica was making tonight. "You must eat a lot of Monica's cooking. Do you have a favorite to recommend?"

Yale scanned the card. "Oh, the four-cheese truffle mac and cheese definitely. The meat loaf is good, but the mac and cheese is exquisite."

He made that nearly cartoonish gesture of kissing his fingertips before waving them in the air like some French gourmand.

Gavin hid his groan, but I knew him well enough to still see it in his eyes. He had little patience for people who put on airs. His direct practicality made him an excellent mayor in my opinion, even if he did need to occasionally remember to soften his edges.

"That's what I was planning," I replied. A boatload of gooey, cheesy carbs sounded delightful. "And your recommendation for dessert?" Even though I'd had a slice of pie at the reception, I was still planning on another round to finish off my dinner.

"Oh, the apple cobbler. It's my very favorite thing she does."

Pride sparkled in his eyes. I got the sense maybe he really did admire his wife's talents. Julie's cut about him being opportunistic wasn't all wrong, but it didn't strike me as the full story. Perhaps Yale Wagner was actually a nice guy who was just over-the-top proud of his wife.

"Good to know. I look forward to enjoying your wife's cooking," I said with a smile.

Yale patted his stomach. "I always do," he replied, then checked his watch. "Wish I had time to tonight."

He headed off toward the kitchen, out of which Monica came, had a rushed conversation with him, then retreated back behind the swinging doors. She looked harried and stressed. Then again, I expect a restaurant kitchen during the dinner rush is a stressful place.

"I don't like him," Gavin offered as he scanned the card of specials. "Esther tells me Monica was much nicer to deal with than he was. 'Exquisite,'" he muttered. "Who says that?"

I narrowed one eye at my dinner companion. "In fact, I used that very word yesterday to describe Julie's work. Did you see what she was wearing tonight?"

Julie had changed into a top of the most *exquisite* flax yarn knit up into an ethereal floating tunic. And the color—a rich, undulating green—was gorgeous.

"I like yours better." Gavin's eyes gave a hint of the

gleam that used to undo me in high school. "That's new—did you knit it for tonight?"

One of my very favorite things about Gavin is how he notices my knitting. It's always nice to receive a compliment on something I wear, but Gavin finds a way to let me know he is impressed by the fact that I have knit it. I touched the sleeve of the smart cotton pullover I was wearing. It was in a deep red with a scalloped boat neck. I'd just finished it two weeks ago in preparation for tonight's reception.

I felt my cheeks heat up. "It's one of Julie's designs. She's so talented."

"Well, you are, too."

The conversation warmed up from there, and the dinner became what it was originally planned to be—a quiet chance for us to catch up. Margo would have insisted it was a date, and my mother and Jillian would have been right behind her, chiming in with their agreement. I wouldn't use that word. Not yet, at least. Gavin and I were close friends who cared about each other, but neither of us had mustered the courage to cross *that line* despite the continual meddling of others. We'd been so serious in high school, I think we both feared that if we did get involved again, things would get very deep very fast. Both of us had been sufficiently burned in our marriages to be gun-shy on that front.

Just as the conversation veered toward the fancy dinner we'd had before our prom night, we were saved by Gavin suddenly catching sight of something over my shoulder. I turned to follow his gaze and saw George Barker coming to our table after scanning the room.

"Have you seen Yale Wagner?" he asked with urgency.

"He was here a while ago," Gavin replied, "but just for a brief chat with Monica. He said he and the crew were heading out to get evening shots of the town."

George gave a smug smile. "Excellent. I told him to do that." Then he found someone else evidently more important to talk to, and buzzed off toward another table without much of a farewell.

I could easily picture George providing Yale with a list of suggested marketing concepts. The man's selling game was always on.

"You don't think he's trying to talk Yale into a real estate reality show?" I asked.

Gavin polished off the last of his meat loaf. "I wouldn't put it past him. I guess wherever Monica goes, Yale goes with cameras rolling. I was hoping to dodge ending up as an episode. We just wanted her to draw customers."

I looked around the packed restaurant. "Well, she certainly has done that. And Bev tells me the inn is sold out for both weekends of the festival." I cleaned my plate of the delectable macaroni and cheese I'd had for dinner. "We may have gotten off to a rocky start, but I think you have a success on your hands. This was delicious."

"I take it we are ordering dessert?"

"Of course."

It was always a point in Gavin's favor that he welcomed my love of desserts. My ex-husband, Sterling, never stopped me from ordering, but he had a subtle way of making me feel bad about it. He never ordered himself, just looked at me with a not-quite-hidden air of disapproval as he sipped his coffee.

"I'm taking Yale's advice and ordering the cobbler. If he likes it better than the mac and cheese, it's got to be *exquisite*." I fought the urge to use Yale's gesture just to tease Gavin. "What are you having?"

"I'm going for the carrot—"

His words were interrupted by a loud alarm. The kitchen door burst open and smoke billowed into the room while a busboy yelled, "Fire!"

CHAPTER FIVE

Thankfully, the small fire seemed to produce more drama than damage. Gavin and I stood among the pack of restaurant patrons waiting outside for the smoke to clear. Most of us doubted we'd be welcomed back into the restaurant to finish our meals, but Esther seemed reluctant to call the night to a close. She bustled between customers and fire department officials, trying her best to keep everyone in good festival spirits—rather a lost cause in my opinion, but I admired her efforts.

To say Gavin stood with me on the sidewalk wasn't quite correct. It was more like worried pacing. Not that I could blame him. It had to look like his carefully planned festival was spinning out of his control. Gavin and drama are not good friends. It's why I so admired the great job he was doing with Jillian. Being the single dad of a teenage girl is a drama-soaked undertaking for someone like him.

As Gavin made his twelfth lap of the sidewalk, Chief Reynolds walked up to me. "Minor electrical fire," he said, staring back at the wide-open doors and windows of the restaurant. "Wire on one of those massive industrial mixers."

I knew the size and strength of the machine because Margo had one. I used to joke we could bathe Hank in that thing when he was a puppy.

"Will everything be okay?"

Gavin seemed to need to hear the answer.

"For the most part. Smoke's nearly all gone already, and she's got another mixer. The fire chief says he expects the Dockhouse can serve again tomorrow."

I've known Frank Reynolds long enough to know when he hasn't said everything he's thinking. "But . . . ?" I cued him.

Frank gestured that we walk farther down the sidewalk away from the other displaced diners.

"But what?" Gavin added, looking even more concerned.

Frank glanced over his shoulder before turning back to us. He leaned in. "The firefighters are telling me it doesn't look accidental. The mixer wires were stripped in three places. Too neatly to be just regular wear and tear."

Gavin's jaw tightened and he gave me what Jillian might call side-eye. "Are you saying someone set that fire?" he asked Frank.

"Looks that way."

Gavin now glared at me. "You have to tell him."

That caught Frank's attention. "Tell me what?"

"Well," I began, "you've already seen how Julie and Monica may be sisters, but they're not exactly friendly."

"I've got four sisters," Frank replied. "They're not exactly friendly most times, either. But no one's set anything on fire . . . yet." Given that Frank was nearly ready to retire, that was a pretty good track record. I had always wondered where Frank's peacekeeping skills came from. "But those two . . ." He'd been at the hotel and the reception, so he knew all about the sparks flying between the Wilson sisters of late.

"Earlier today Julie joked to me to bring a fire extinguisher when I came to dinner at the bistro tonight. I had invited her, just to be nice to my guest, and I'd even offered to go somewhere else if she felt uncomfortable."

"I take it she turned you down," Frank replied.

"She did, but the jab is, well, eerily"—I hesitated to use the word—"suspicious, given what's happened. Julie sort of warned me there'd be a fire tonight with Monica cooking."

Frank's lips pressed together. "And even more suspicious given the fact that Julie was in the kitchen this afternoon. She told Esther she was leaving Monica an apology note. I have the feeling she left a little more than that."

I really, really didn't want to go down the road of criminal investigations with Frank again. "Crime-solving yarn shop owner" has never been on my bucket list, and I had no plans to add it now.

He took out the little notepad he always carries and slipped a pen from his shirt pocket. Clicking the pen, he scribbled down a few words.

"Where is Julie now? When's the last time you spoke to her?"

Great. My VIP speaker was now an arson suspect. That was not on my marketing plan for this event.

"I saw her last at the reception," I answered. "She said she'd rather spend the evening at the warehouse getting things ready for the workshop. There's a lot she needs to prepare and she said she'd rather do it alone."

"Rather convenient. So the thing's not at your shop?"

Frank's not a knitter. I have several male knitting customers and one really talented male crocheter, but I don't count Frank among either of those.

"No. Dyeing takes a lot of harsh chemicals. There are fumes and powders, so you have to be careful about ventilation. That made the warehouse on Willow Street the perfect place. We rented it out for the weekend." I checked my watch. "She's probably there now."

"I think we need to have a little chat with Ms. Wilson. Can you call her to come over here?"

I reached into my handbag for my cell phone. "I can try. But she may not come or even answer her phone if she's in the middle of a batch."

I had tried dyeing my own yarn once, and it required a bunch of rubber gloves, hot water, smelly chemicals, and careful timing. I don't even like to pick up the phone if I'm in the middle of a tricky row of stitches.

Sure enough, my call went straight to voice mail. I kept my message to a general "call me when you get this," not wanting to raise undue alarm.

"So you have no personal knowledge of Ms. Wilson's whereabouts at the time of the fire?"

Frank's words sounded way too serious for my taste. I'd hoped never to get tangled in a criminal investigation again—this was supposed to be a quiet, profitable year. The flashing fire truck lights all around me were currently shouting otherwise.

"No, I don't." I didn't care for the hard way my answer settled in my stomach.

"And she made a prediction to you about a fire happening here tonight. And she was in this kitchen earlier today. Unsupervised." He slipped the notepad back into his pocket.

"Unsupervised?" Gavin asked.

"Most of the staff hadn't arrived yet, and those that were there were out front, busy with preparations. In other words, Julie had plenty of opportunity. Let's go down to the warehouse, Libby. It's time to talk to your dye lady."

I had no choice but to walk down to the warehouse and have an unpleasant conversation with Julie Wilson.

It could all be circumstantial, I told myself as we turned toward the direction of the warehouse. Then again, Julie had been in the kitchen, she was mad at Monica, and "I was in a big warehouse where nobody saw me" isn't much of an alibi.

"Would you mind if we stopped by the shop and I picked up Hank?" I asked.

On the one hand, walking to the warehouse would put me halfway home and I didn't want to double back after the long day I'd had. On the other hand, I found myself wanting Hank's excellent sense of judgment about people. I could always tell a lot from the way Hank responded to anyone and the way people responded to Hank. Since Julie hadn't met Hank yet, it seemed to me their meeting might confirm—or disprove—my intuition that while Julie and Monica bickered, they'd never go so far as to actually harm each other.

"Fine by me," Frank agreed. "Go pick the fellow up

while I tie up a few details here with the fire department and I'll meet you at the warehouse." Frank looked at his watch. "Fifteen minutes, if not less."

Gavin checked his watch as well. "I'll walk you over to the shop and the warehouse, but then I've probably got to get back." He grimaced. "I'm sure Jillian has a few more choice words for me."

"She'll have cooled off by now," I said as we began walking, even though I wasn't actually sure of that. "You were just trying to defuse the situation."

Gavin gave a *harrumph* of doubt as he stuffed his hands into his jacket pockets. "She gets upset at the tiniest little things lately. And she's become a champion grudge holder. I feel like I can't do anything right where she's concerned."

"Mom will tell you I was even worse at her age. I can't believe I'm saying this, but maybe we *should* get the two of them together more often. I'm sure I could dream up some project for them to do this weekend at the shop."

We turned onto the block that held my shop, and even from this distance, I could see Hank curled up on his window bed, awaiting my return. I love the front of my shop with the wonderful carved wooden Y.A.R.N. sign above the door, the red brick, and the big display windows bursting with yarn and knitted garments. And often the world's sweetest English bulldog.

"I'm willing to try anything," Gavin remarked. "Even Rhonda."

As he caught sight of us approaching the shop, Hank dashed off his window spot and bounded to the front door. The door was barely open before my legs were covered in happy bulldog jumps and nudges. Even on my worst days, Hank's greetings are a steady source of joy.

"Hello, boy," Gavin said, bending down to receive a slobbery greeting.

I take it as no small endorsement that Hank loves Gavin. And Jillian. Mom insists Hank is trying to tell me something. I make a point of reminding her that even Hank can be wrong, because he liked Sterling. No intelligent woman is going to run her social life solely based on her dog's recommendations.

"We're gonna make a stop on the way home. Okay, boy?" I called as I gathered my bag of shop paperwork and Hank's leash from the office.

H ank, Gavin, and I actually beat Frank to the warehouse, turning the corner just as Frank's squad car pulled up on the curb. It was a midsized industrial-looking structure, clearly more functional than most of Collinstown's other buildings. A throwback—if you will—to the days when the river provided power instead of the electric company. The warehouse was painted a very industrial and uncolonial rusty yellow; most people considered it a bit of an eyesore for our quaint and picturesque town. Still, none of the several proposals for a new use for the space had yet met with success.

"Think they'll actually turn this into loft apartments?" Frank asked as we headed up the sidewalk to the entrance.

Not everyone considered historic Collinstown to be the place for loft apartments, and there had been a bit of a dustup at the last zoning board meeting.

"That's the request in front of the zoning board, yes." Gavin stared at the artless square space. "Not everyone's thrilled."

There's tradition, and then there's stagnation. I wasn't one of the people who thought loft apartments spelled Collinstown's cultural doom. Young artistic people liked loft apartments, and I was very much in favor of young artistic people.

"It's a much better use than sitting empty most of the time," I offered. "Even if it's the perfect space for Julie's event at the moment and—"

Frank's shout cut me off. "Someone's barred the door!"

I rushed up to see a long stick pushed through the double handles of the warehouse door. "Open it!" I yelled.

Frank threw his weight into the stick, knocking it from its position. He and Gavin joined forces to pull on each of the handles.

"It's locked," Frank said.

"Oh, wait. I've got the other set of keys." Fear tangled my fingers as I dug in my handbag for the keys. Out of the corner of my eye, I saw Hank backing away from the door. "Keep Hank away. The odor's got to be pretty strong in there."

I tried the first key on the ring as fast as I could, but it wasn't one that opened this door.

"So the fans should be running?" Frank asked as I tried the second with no success.

The hair on the back of my neck stood up. You could just see the pair of circular holes that held the huge set of fans. Rather like big round eyes in the yellow walls peering out over a section of the building's black tar roof.

"Because they aren't."

I tried the third key as my throat started to close up in

panic. "Those fans *need* to be on." I jabbed the final key anxiously into the lock, relieved to hear the tumblers turn. "Julie?" I yelled. "Julie, we're coming in!"

Frank and Gavin pulled on the doors and they swung open. All of us—even Hank—fell back at the wave of powerful fumes that billowed out from the warehouse. We stumbled in the wedge of light cast onto the sidewalk through the doorway, eyes watering and coughing. No dyeing process I had ever seen produced fumes like this.

And Julie was in there. I didn't think a human could breathe inside. I held the light shawl I was wearing over my nose and went to push my way into the doorway when I felt Gavin's arm shoot out in front of me.

"Don't go in there!"

"I have to! Gavin, she's in there." Some part of me knew Gavin was right but the irrational do-something urge was winning over any wise caution. "Julie!" I called between breaths that burned in my lungs. "Julie, are you in there?" My words were swallowed by a coughing fit.

Wiping my stinging eyes, I turned to Frank. He was already on the phone to the paramedics, calling in a medical emergency. I'm not sure if it was the fumes or my own dread that sent me tilting off-balance as Gavin pushed the door shut. He reached his other arm around me, pulling me and Hank farther back.

"What if she's in there?" I shouted, pushing against his restraint. "We can't leave her."

"*If* she's in there," Frank said, "she's going to need someone with an oxygen tank to go in and get her. Nobody should be breathing whatever that is. It could be toxic."

Toxic. The word sank into me like a knife. Strong chemicals, yes, but toxic meant bodily harm. Julie knew what she was doing. She was careful. It was why she wanted to be doing this part of the dyeing herself, not in front of an audience where someone could get overcome. Besides, most traditional methods of dyeing plant fibers didn't need the strong chemicals wool dyeing required.

Then again, what about Julie was traditional? I had no idea how she achieved the colors that had made her famous. I'd never asked her if the chemicals she used were dangerous. She was so secretive about her formulas, I doubted she'd have told me even if I did ask.

Gavin pulled out his own phone. "I'll call the fire department. Maybe they can get a ladder up there to free up the ventilation fans."

"Do something—do anything!" I shouted, pacing in horror. Not only had someone blocked her exit, but now the ventilation that should have protected her had failed. My brain conjured up pictures of Julie coughing, groping through the fumes to find the doorway, stumbling the way I had just done.

As the red flashing lights of the ambulance began to shine up against the building, I tamped down the surge of fear that my VIP guest had come to harm.

While I was sure it was only minutes, it seemed like hours before the emergency workers could get inside to open the windows. Desperate for something to do, I called Bev on the slim hope that Julie had returned to the hotel.

"No. And, Libby," Bev said with doom in her voice, "I just discovered the second key to Julie's room is missing." Bev's historic inn used big beautiful brass keys instead of mundane plastic key cards. "I used my master to check in her room to make sure nothing looked disturbed. Everything looks okay, but she's definitely not in there."

During the unbearable amount of time that passed before the fire department raised a hook and ladder up to unjam the ventilation fans, Frank pulled Gavin and me aside. He'd picked up the large branch that had been blocking the doors, and had it sitting on the hood of his squad car.

I gasped at what I saw. It wasn't an ordinary stick. It was a staff. We were looking at a shepherd's crook.

"Is that what I think that is?" Gavin asked.

He had good reason to sound astonished. I think the last time I'd seen a shepherd's crook was in the church Christmas pageant. Not exactly the tool of choice for your twenty-first-century sheep farmer.

"Someone jammed the warehouse door with a *shepherd's crook*?" I couldn't believe the words leaving my mouth. Today had gone from contentious to absurd to downright unbelievable. "Who'd do that?"

Frank and Gavin looked at each other and said in ridiculous unison, "Shepherds."

"My nephew works at the inn and he told me you booked her the corner suite"—wasn't that what Barney had said? My whole body flinched at the thought of Barney behind this. *No. Why go this far?*

A shout cut off our consideration of the gruesome fact as the okay came from the crew for us to enter the building.

I handed Hank to one of Frank's lieutenants and Gavin and I dashed inside. We began a frantic search for Julie amid the giant steaming pans, electric burners, racks, and other equipment. Despite the missing key, I kept up the desperate hope that Julie had just gone out somewhere to clear her head. That she'd walk up, laughing off someone's attempt to trap her, pleased and smug at how they'd failed. I prayed with every struggling breath that I wouldn't find Julie collapsed somewhere within the building.

In fact, I didn't find her. The paramedics found her first.

I heard Gavin yell something and dashed toward the sound of his voice with my shawl held over my nose and mouth. I found him and two paramedics behind a set of tables, crouched down over Julie's body. Her limbs were motionless and covered in the splatters of her dyes. It was a horrid, garish sight. Blotches of colored powder covered her face and hands, her hair and arms. Smears of the colors were over her shirt and apron and even over the protective dust mask lying a few feet away from her on the floor.

She was backed into the far corner of the large room, a long way from the door we'd been pounding on to rouse her. With a wave of nausea, I noticed she was under a bank of grimy windows long rusted shut. Desperate color smears on the windows told me she'd tried to get them open.

It wasn't dye that tinged the tips of her fingers and her lips and the pallor of her skin. It was death. Julie had been asphyxiated.

CHAPTER SIX

I fell against the wall myself, overcome with the thought of Julie's life ending in such a horrible way. She was an expert dyer. She'd know the proper precautions to take. She'd been very particular about the building, its ventilation system, and who would be allowed to be present when she worked with the strong chemicals. "Beauty ain't cheap. In fact, it can be downright dangerous," she had said of the secret process that created her exquisite colors. My head spun with the thought that Julie had paid too high a price for her colors this time. Who had barred her exit from the building like that? Had the sheep farmers taken things a step further, and had they really meant to kill her?

I stared at her body, at the splashes of colors that stained her clothes and the lifeless gaze of her deep green eyes, mortified but unable to look away.

"Libby." I heard Frank's voice behind me and yet distant. "Step back."

I felt Gavin pull me away from the body. Somehow I registered the resignation in their voices, the odd and sad shift Frank talked about when a situation turned from rescue to recovery. That was usually more about accidents on the river, when the coast guard was called once boats were found without their passengers from a mishap on the water.

"Mishap" was too weak a term for what had happened here. "Accident" didn't apply, either. "Tragedy" came close—a mean-spirited act turned deadly.

"I shouldn't have let her do this alone," I said to Frank as we watched the ambulance doors shut.

No one was working frantically inside to save a life. Now their job was to transport Julie's body to the coroner's office for an investigation. A *death* investigation. The word "death" echoed in my thoughts as if bouncing off the walls of the large empty space.

"Don't do that, Libby. You told me she wanted to do this on her own. You offered to help her—didn't you say that? And if you had, then you would have been trapped in there with her."

Gavin's alarm at that failed to keep me from slipping down a steep slope of guilt. I was losing the battle to the ridiculous notion that my shop was cursed. Last fall Perle Lonager had been killed during one of my events. Now Julie Wilson had died. Who would want to do an event for my shop ever again? Would even the customers start to fear coming into the store? I couldn't seem to stop my brain from swirling in a million catastrophic directions.

We made it out of the space, and I sank down on the

curb. My legs simply gave out underneath me. The officer who had been holding Hank released him and he dashed to my side. He recognized my distress—as dogs so often do. He did the only thing he could—coming over to sit close to me, his chubby jowls pointed up at me with eyes that seemed to say, "I'm right here."

Commotions draw crowds easily in small communities like Collinstown, and I noticed a knot of curious onlookers standing across the street. I felt on display, marked for all the world to see as the woman who had invited Julie Wilson to her death. With nauseating anguish, I remembered the tongue-in-cheek title Julie and I had come up with for her workshop.

"Watch Julie Wilson Dye" now struck me as the furthest thing from clever. It was ghastly. The urge to run around town and pull down every poster, every flyer, and somehow yank back every email surged over me. My hands started to shake even as I clutched Hank like a canine life buoy in a storm.

"Why did I let this happen?" I moaned to no one in particular.

"You didn't let this happen," Gavin tried to reassure me as he sat down on my other side. "Someone blocked the door."

With Gavin on one side and Hank on the other, I ought to have felt a little bit better, a little more bolstered to face the grim situation. I didn't.

"But it was locked. It should have been okay closed. That's horrible, but it shouldn't have—"

"But then the ventilation system somehow failed." Gavin's words barely reached through my panicked fog. "That's really what killed her, I suppose."

I was staring at the ground, fascinated in my shock at

how the flashing emergency vehicle lights reflected off the pavement and off the faded yellow walls of the warehouse. Frank's black shoes walked into my vision.

"Libby," he began, "you need to come over and look at this."

His words might have been pleasant, but there was no mistaking the dark edge in his voice. So dark, in fact, that Gavin immediately rose and all of us—even Hank—started walking. Frank led us to the far corner of the lot where he'd moved his black-and-white Collinstown police chief sedan. The trunk was open.

Frank stood in front of the car and met my eyes with a combination of sympathy and concern. "None of this was an accident. The ventilation fans were in complete working order. Well, they *were*. Until someone stopped them."

The sidewalk seemed to lurch under my feet, and I felt Gavin's hand reach out to steady my shoulder.

"It couldn't have been Julie." I gulped as the night air seemed to thin around me. "She'd have had no reason to turn them off," I went on. "She told me herself ventilation is the most important thing when she dyes."

My brain was spelling the word "d-y-e-s," but my ears heard "she dies," and I felt my whole body recoil in horror.

Frank nodded toward the car trunk. "These were jammed into the blades to stop them from rotating."

More shepherd's crooks.

"They wouldn't!" I shouted, even though I had no reason to believe that. Well, no reason except I couldn't imagine any sane person doing such a thing. "They're angry and insulted and a bit stubborn, but Barney and the others . . . they wouldn't . . ." My voice trailed off in a baffled, wounded whimper. "Would they?"

Frank looked back at the two curved staffs sitting in his trunk. "If they didn't, someone wants us to think they did. Put the combination of where those staffs were placed together, and—"

"Julie Wilson was murdered." Gavin's voice held the resignation of someone whose pet project had just become his biggest nightmare.

"There's a slim chance Julie's death wasn't intentional." Frank ran a weary hand across the back of his neck.

"How do you figure that?" I nearly moaned.

Nothing about this seemed like a fluke. It all seemed horribly deliberate.

"It could be that whoever did this only wanted to scare her or just make her too sick to hold her workshop. But either way, they meant her harm, which means it's murder whether or not they meant it to be. This was no mistake. This was premeditated and designed to send a very clear message."

"She's had death threats before." The fact popped out of my memory, buried deep in a conversation Julie and I had had two months earlier.

Frank's eyes widened. "She told you that?"

"She was proud of it, actually." I glanced at the pair of staffs and thought I would never see another Christmas pageant shepherd or Little Bo Peep illustration without being slightly ill. Peaceful shepherds abiding in the fields, watching their flocks by night, did not carry murder weapons.

But maybe the angry sheep farmers sending their

flocks down Collin Avenue in protest did. Would they have gone this far? Did anyone's view on alternative knitting fibers go this far? It seemed impossible.

A new thought turned my stomach to ice. "Does this mean Julie didn't cause the fire in Esther's restaurant?"

"No, she still could have." Frank pinched the bridge of his nose. "Julie left the note for Monica in Esther's kitchen well before dinner, so that gave her plenty of time to have messed with the wires earlier and still have gotten back here in time to . . . fall victim to this."

He was trying not to say "die." Most likely because I seemed to physically flinch anytime anyone used the word.

"We'll have to let the coroner's office establish a time of death to know for sure. And whatever the toxicology reports can tell us."

"Julie Wilson is dead." My brain struggled to hold the thought. "Julie Wilson was murdered."

"Seems to be the case," Frank said.

"What do we do about the festival?" Gavin sounded outright despondent. "We can't keep it on if someone has been murdered, can we?"

Frank shut his trunk with a declarative *thunk*. "Are you asking my opinion, Mr. Mayor?"

Gavin shrugged. "I guess I am."

"Keep going. Whoever did this wanted to cause trouble. Either just for Julie or for everyone. The less trouble we let him have, the angrier he gets. And angry criminals tend to make mistakes. So I'm advising that publicly, we treat it like an accident. For now."

"Well, I can't just keep going. My VIP guest is dead." I leaned up against the car, feeling wobbly. "Even if I could do the event without Julie, I'm not sure I'd want to."

"No," Frank replied, "I don't think *you* can keep on. But we can try with the rest of the festival. And announce this as an accident, like I said."

I looked at Frank. "Isn't that lying?"

"If someone intentionally murdered Julie out of spite, having it treated like an accident will just make him or her mad. And like I said, an angry killer usually makes mistakes."

Killer. Murder. The words hit me like a hard rain, stinging and chilling my bones. A new thought stole my next breath.

"We'll have to tell Monica." My heart sank. "The last conversation they had was an argument. An awful one. Who could live with that?"

"Telling Monica is my job." Frank's words were meant to calm me, I know, but they fell far short. "You just get yourself home. I don't want you back inside that warehouse until our techs have had at it."

"I'll see she gets home," Gavin said.

Normally I'm not much for Gavin's protective side, but tonight I welcomed it.

I suppose I shouldn't have been surprised to see my mother waiting on my doorstep. News—especially dramatic bad news—travels at the speed of light in small towns like this. Anytime more than two emergency vehicles converge on one place, I have no doubt phones all over Collinstown light up like a telethon pledge drive.

"I forgot my key," Mom said, giving Hank a head scratch as if it was perfectly fine to show up unannounced on my doorstep at nine fifteen on a Thursday night.

"You don't have a key," I corrected her.

It was this trick she played on herself—and me—a sort of maternal gaslighting. If she kept insisting I had given her a key, I would eventually cave and give her one rather than have to refute her declaration time and time again.

Not happening. I love my mother, and I'm grateful I have a key to her house, but I am wise enough to know that reciprocating would end badly. "Call before you come over" is not in my mother's worldview. Mom comes from the era when you didn't need to lock your doors and true friends just let themselves in. Now she locks her door, thankfully, but still believes in unannounced social calls. If you love someone—and are reasonably sure they love you—dropping in is totally okay. Not to me, and therein lies the problem.

"How was your nice dinner?" Mom asked as I opened the door.

Gavin and I exchanged looks. Could she really not know?

"It got cut rather short," I explained, "by the accident."

I heard Frank's advice ringing in the back of my mind.

Mom's eyes widened. "I heard all those sirens. What happened?"

Gavin sighed. "I've got to get home to Jillian."

His words had an apologetic good-luck-with-that tone. Explaining all this to Mom would be about as much fun as the dressing-down he'd get from Jillian for belittling her YouTube channel. The evening was going to end badly for both of us.

"What happened?" Mom asked again.

"There was a fire at the restaurant." It seemed too simple an explanation for everything that had happened tonight.

"At the Dockhouse? That's awful. Was anyone hurt?"

Not at the restaurant, but my special guest was asphyxiated just a few blocks away, my brain silently shouted. There was so much chaos, it was hard to choose where to begin.

Mom walked over to my stove and picked up the teakettle. She is one of those people who believe all difficult times should be weathered with a hot beverage in hand. It's not a bad strategy, although I have to admit I considered taking a mug over to the bar and filling it with a good stiff Scotch.

I pulled in a deep breath. Tea aside, this meant Mom was settling in for a good long visit. Half of me wanted peace and quiet; the other half didn't really want to be alone after what I'd just seen.

"The kitchen caught fire during Monica Wilson's dinner," I began, leaving out any mention of sabotage. "Well, actually just a mixer. But there was lots of shouting and smoke. No one was hurt, thankfully." *Not there, at least.*

Mom filled the kettle. "Glad to hear it. I was down by the river at the diner with Arlene and we saw all the fire trucks and police cars. I suppose restaurant kitchens are bigger. There certainly weren't that many for my fire."

My weary brain jumped awake at the last two words, and I nearly dropped the pair of mugs I was getting out of the cabinet. "Your *what*?"

Mom gave me her best it's-nothing smile as she put the kettle on the burner.

"Mom, you just said 'my fire.' What fire?"

I couldn't believe the question was leaving my mouth. Fire? Mom had had a fire? How did I, her only daughter not twenty minutes away, not know my mother had a fire? Where was the small-town gossip mill when you needed it?

"Oh, I just had a little mishap last week, that's all. The firefighters—very nice boys, all of them—told me it happens all the time."

I doubted that. A whole lot. I applied a calm I surely didn't feel to my voice and asked, "What caught fire, Mom?"

"The kitchen. Same as your friend there."

I thought of the billows of smoke coming from behind that poor busboy and nearly choked. "Your kitchen caught fire? When?"

"Last Tuesday."

Her tone was infuriatingly ordinary. Which made me worry this might not be the first time Mom had had "a little mishap."

"And it wasn't the whole kitchen. Just the pot. Eggs make the most dreadful mess when they boil down dry." She began rooting through my cabinets for cookies, settling on a tin of shortbread ones from Margo's shop. "Ooo, Margo's. These are my favorites. I had to throw the whole pot away, you know. And that smoke smell. It's much harder to get rid of than you'd think. How's Esther holding up?"

Granted, I was feeling bad for Esther's wonderful restaurant, but I was having a bit of trouble getting off the fact that my mom had *set her kitchen on fire*.

"Why didn't you tell me?" I was trying not to shout and not doing a very good job at it.

Mom gave a glare. "Because you'd get like this."

"I think I'm entitled to get like this," I countered, grabbing the tin from her. "You should have told me. Now I have to top off the night that my VIP guest choked to death with news that my mom set her kitchen on fire?"

Mom grabbed the tin back. "I did not set it on . . . Wait. What did you just say?"

The stress of the night flooded up over me and I found myself fighting back tears. "Julie Wilson. We found her in the warehouse. Fumes. From the yarn dye. Mom, she's dead."

I hadn't meant to say anything. Now I couldn't seem to keep it in.

Mom's face transformed from stubborn irritation to motherly concern. "Dead? Julie is dead?" The tin rattled onto the counter as she pulled me into a hug. "No. Oh, no. It can't be."

"It is," I moaned into her shoulder.

Despite my many years as a successful adult, I felt young and fragile. Cursed, even. I couldn't bear the thought of another life being lost in connection to my shop.

"What happened? I thought that was the whole reason you chose that place."

I told myself not to spill the whole story, to keep to the accident tactic Frank advised without any mention of suspicions and deadly shepherd's crooks.

I went and found a tissue and dried my eyes to give myself a bit of time to think. I settled on "There was an accident with the ventilation."

"Those giant fans on top?" Mom pulled a tissue from her own pocket and dabbed a spot I'd missed.

"Yes. They were jammed." *On purpose by someone*, my brain corrected, but I didn't dare speak that aloud.

"The place was thick with terrible fumes when we got there."

"Elizabeth, that's just awful. Did they check you out? Did you breathe any of whatever was in there? Or did Gavin? Or Hank?"

"No. I admit, I was ready to rush in there but Frank and Gavin stopped me."

Mom's hand flew to her chest. "Well, thank God for Frank and Gavin." The teakettle whistled and she fetched the teapot down from my cupboard. "What a dreadful thing. She didn't seem like a very pleasant person. Barney was going on and on about her at the diner. Still, no one deserves that."

The diner. Leave it to my mom to be at Tom's Riverside Diner getting a cheeseburger while a fancy food festival was launching in Collinstown. I blinked, realizing what she'd just said.

"Barney was at the diner tonight?"

Barney lived pretty far out of town. And it wasn't as if he could just park his sheep in the parking lot while he ducked in for a burger. He had to have come back into town on a second trip if he was eating at Tom's. What would bring Barney into town twice in one day? I didn't like the answer that blared like an alarm bell in my mind.

"He was there. A whole bunch of them were there. Very proud of his little shenanigans today, he was. And you know how Barney gets when he has too many. Some men get happy when they drink. Barney just gets meaner."

"Did he say anything?"

I handed Mom a pair of tea bags and she added them to the water she'd poured. I didn't bother with a plate, but set the full tin of shortbread down on the kitchen table, taking three for immediate consumption while my brain collected facts.

Mom clicked her tongue as she set the cozy—beautifully knit and felted from thick forest green worsted wool—over the teapot. "He said all kinds of things. Boasted. Sheep down the middle of the street. And spray-painted, to boot. It's all just silly. A letter to the newspaper would have been just as effective if he wanted to get his point across. Did you know Angie said she had to clean up two piles of sheep dip in front of the police station?"

I shook my head. I hadn't thought of the outcome of that protest other than Julie's irritation. I wouldn't have been surprised if Gavin ordered the town street cleaning truck up and down Collin Avenue first thing tomorrow morning. Most avenue shop and business owners had decorated and taken pains to be spotless for the festival's first weekend. I hoped most of those extra touches had survived the flock's visit. Still, it was Barney's return visit to town that I found more intriguing, given what we'd found at the warehouse.

"So Barney was at the diner celebrating with a bunch of the other farmers?"

"Oh, I suppose you could call it celebrating." Mom brought the teapot and the pair of mugs over to the table. "One minute they were very proud of themselves. The other they were fighting like bulls. Or rams, I suppose. And the drinking. Barney had so much beer, I thought Tom ought to call him a cab, but you can't tell a pig-headed old coot like Barney that he can't hold his booze."

"When? Around dinnertime?" The twisting in my stomach told me that was no coincidence.

Mom stared at me. "Well, that is when most people eat dinner. Why?"

I pushed out a breath. Somehow I was going to have to gather my wits enough to explain to Mom why I was asking all of these questions about Barney without revealing that he might have killed Julie.

CHAPTER SEVEN

All that sugar, all that tea, and all that death did not make for an easy night. I found myself walking into the shop with dragging steps Friday morning. I couldn't bring myself to phone Linda the night before, so I merely sent her a text asking her to meet me at the shop an hour before it opened.

Linda is one of those people who is the coolest head in the room in a tight spot. She often joked that her former job as the loan officer at a big-city bank meant "disappointing people for a living," so I was glad her stalwart, encouraging heart found a home at Y.A.R.N. She's the kind of petite but feisty woman to whom the phrase "small but mighty" absolutely applies. I expect even her college-age children know you can't pull anything over on her. Still, even she sank down into one of the shop's big upholstered chairs at my grim news.

"I thought you were going to tell me we had extra

tickets to sell as a result of all the excitement," she gasped. "I can't believe we're doing this again. Hard to hold a dyeing workshop when the dying's already happened, isn't it?"

I knew Linda's off-color joke was an attempt to face down the absurdity of all this, but she was giving voice to the panic I'd been trying all morning to ignore.

"I can't believe it, either."

We'd had a celebrity guest meet a grisly end— strangulation by yarn—at a previous event. Somehow the multiple successful events we'd had since then no longer mattered. I was fighting the sense that I was drowning in my own misfortune. Cursed.

Linda held out her hand. "Have you got a list?"

She knew me well. I was up long after Mom went home and again well before the sun. I'd spent those hours filling a yellow legal notepad with a list of things that now needed to be done.

"At least this is a smaller crowd. And the ticket prices weren't as high as last time." I sank farther into my own chair. "It feels selfish to be worrying about ticket refunds when someone just died."

"And the way she died," Linda commiserated. "What an awful accident. The warehouse owners must be going crazy right now."

Indeed, I was proud of myself for managing to keep the situation couched as an accident. Still, I couldn't help but think gasping for breath and choking on toxic fumes seemed like a horrible way to die.

"No way to defend yourself from a killer you can't see."

It felt cruel to let the landlords think their building

had somehow been at fault, but I trusted Frank knew what he was doing.

Linda's eyes went wide. I'd given just too much away. "Killer?" she asked.

"The fumes," I amended quickly. "Killer fumes."

Linda leaned forward in her seat. "Libby Beckett, you're the worst liar I know. What aren't you telling me?"

Gavin and Frank would probably have slapped my wrist for that slipup, but suddenly I needed to talk about the whole thing to someone. I needed a discreet and trustworthy ally, and Linda was one. Cautiously, I told her about the door, the fans, and the shepherd's crooks. I left out the bit about Barney's diner bragging session, although I fully intended to fill Frank in on that as soon as possible.

Linda's eyebrows furrowed as she came to the conclusion anyone would. "Barney and his buddies? Doing something like that? He's a bit of a curmudgeon—I get it—but *murder*?" She tucked her strawberry blond bob behind one ear, eyes squinted in thought. "Although it seems a bit dumb, don't you think? Pointing the finger straight at yourself like that? I mean, do sheep farmers even use shepherd's crooks anymore?"

I'd had the same thought earlier this morning. "Unless it's someone wanting us to think the sheep farmers did it. They are her most likely enemies, after all."

I scanned the printout I'd made of the ticket holders, glad to see we had emails and cell phone numbers for every one. At least this wouldn't become a long slog of painful phone calls to let people know the event was canceled.

"I don't know," Linda said, rising to put on the coffeemaker. "Didn't you tell me Julie got into it pretty badly with her sister yesterday? And if Julie was mad enough to mess with the mixer like that . . ."

While Margo considers calories to be the best tool for problem-solving, Linda believes caffeine is the way to go. Me, I let whoever of them is nearest choose my coping mechanism. Today was feeling as if I would require both.

"Well, there's that, too. We can place Julie in the Dockhouse kitchen in the hours before the fire. And Julie predicted to me that Monica would have a kitchen fire."

Linda turned and gawked at me. "Could it be those two were trying to kill each other? Literally?"

I felt a shiver as I continued sinking into my chair. "I can't figure any of this out. I can't believe there's another murder connected to my shop." I caught the Watch Julie Wilson Dye poster out of the corner of my eye and pointed to it. "Can we take that down, please?"

"Absolutely."

Linda's efficient nature kicked in. She filled the coffeemaker with grounds and water, then deftly yanked the poster from the clips that held it up on the wall. She tucked it, and the stack of event flyers on the sales counter, into a nearby cupboard and then turned to me, hands on her hips.

"And don't you go thinking you have another murder to solve. That's Frank's job."

"I solved the last one." It was an odd thing to be proud of, but I had taken great satisfaction in seeing justice for the brilliant young designer Perle Lonager. "Evidently I'm pretty good at it."

"I make a mean French toast," Linda countered.

"That does not make me a chef." She pulled mugs off a tray and a carton of creamer from the small fridge. "Speaking of chefs, what are they going to do about the food festival?"

"Frank wants Gavin to keep it going. They're going to list Julie's death as an accident to deny whoever it was publicity for the point they were trying to make. The entrance Julie used was on a dark side of the building, so we don't think anyone saw the crook in the door before we did. Step one is Frank going to talk to Barney. Which means he needs to know something Mom told me last night. Can you make that coffee to go and get those emails started?"

"On it. And hey, Libby."

"Yoo?"

"I'm sorry. All this. You don't deserve it, and neither does the shop."

I swallowed hard. "Neither did Julie."

When I called Frank's office, he told me to meet him at the Riverside Inn instead of the police station. He and some officers were getting ready to go over Julie's room and he thought I might be of help.

"I don't know that I can be of any help here," I admitted as we stood outside Julie's suite, waiting for Bev to use her master key to unlock the door.

"I don't, either," Frank replied. "But since I don't know what I'm looking for, you might catch something related to that yarn stuff that I might miss."

I started to say, "No one kills anyone over 'yarn stuff,'" but I realized my own experience had proven that theory wrong. It's never just yarn stuff anyway—it's all the human emotion tied to it. Still, I could follow Frank's thinking. And if he had enough faith in me to ask my help with the case, then I was eager to offer whatever assistance I could.

Alarm made me suck in my breath as Bev opened the door to utter chaos. "I thought you told me no one ransacked Julie's room," I exclaimed at the sight.

"No one has" came a voice from behind me.

I turned to find Monica looking nothing like her usually elegant self. I hadn't heard her come out of her room across the hall. Her hair was a mess, her eyes looked tired and teary, and the set of her shoulders broadcast stress and grief. She looked every bit like a woman who'd just lost her sister, no matter how much I'd seen them bicker.

"Like I said to Bev yesterday, Julie is—*was*"—she swallowed hard at the correction—"as messy as they come."

I was reminded again that their last conversation had been a bitter, petty squabble, and my heart went out to the woman.

"Monica," I said, walking over to give her a hug, "I'm so sorry."

She waved me off, walking into the room. Not everyone's a hugger, and we had only just met.

"That's my sister, leaving chaos wherever she goes."

Frank, Bev, and I followed Monica into the space.

"Please don't touch anything," Frank advised all of us as he passed out latex gloves. "If you want to pick something up, ask me first." He looked at Bev. "Find that second key yet?"

Alarm drew Monica's features taut. "Someone has a key to Julie's room? What kind of security is that?"

"We're treating it as a serious breach of security, I assure you," Bev replied.

"Because that's what it is," Monica said sharply. "Something in here could be related to Julie's accident."

"Which is precisely why I'm here," Frank assured her.

I hoped I hid my flinch at the use of the word "accident."

"This investigation has my full attention, Ms. Wilson." Frank walked over to her. "I'm sorry for your loss, ma'am. There's no need for you to stay if you find this difficult."

Monica gave a sort of whimper as she turned in a slow circle about the room. Clothes billowed out of an open suitcase on the floor beside the bed, with items tossed over chair backs, lying on tables, and hanging from doorknobs. The boxes of dyeing supplies I'd seen earlier were gone, having been moved to the warehouse, I assumed. A few unused measuring cups and plastic containers stood in a box in the corner. An impressive collection of super-healthy snacks—nuts, granola, dried fruit, protein bars—cluttered other surfaces. I found it hard to believe Julie had been in here only for hours; it looked like a herd of health-conscious frat boys had been in here for a week.

I watched Frank turn an evidence bag inside out and use it like a glove to pick up a drinking glass. I noticed a smear of Julie's deep burgundy lipstick on the rim.

"Mind if I borrow this for DNA, Bev?"

"Whatever you need," Bev replied. "I'll keep housekeeping out of here until you give me the okay." With that, she left the room.

I watched Monica's eyes take another sweep of the space. A touch of something—grief, panic, an under standable sense of being overwhelmed—flashed in her eyes. She seemed to have trouble catching her breath.

"If it's all the same to you, I'd rather not be in here."

Were I in her shoes, I didn't know how I'd feel. I might want to linger and try to get a sense of my lost sister's presence. I also might find the whole thing suffocating. Grief doesn't pay much attention to logic.

"Of course," Frank said.

I have always admired Frank's ability to be both compassionate and in command at the same time. It's a good quality in a small-town police chief—and in a friend.

"But I will need a statement from you eventually. That can happen later today, and I can save any questions for then."

Frank's kind tone seemed to heighten the threat of tears in Monica's eyes.

"I really am sorry for your loss," I said. "Your sister did the most beautiful work."

"She was a giant brilliant pain in the ass," Monica said with a sniff. "So talented and so annoying at the same time, you know?"

I tried to send her an understanding smile. "Most great artists are." I remembered Frank and Gavin's agreement. "What about today? Are you going ahead with your events? I have to think most people would understand if you don't."

She shrugged. "Sitting around will only make it worse. I've done the hard part, calling Mom and Dad. They're so upset to be in Europe on a cruise right now. They're at sea, so it might be as much as a week before they get here. But they've called their travel agent. Yale is pulling strings, and everyone's doing their best to get them here as soon as they can."

I couldn't imagine being a parent and having to wait to come help your daughter deal with something like this. Or even dealing with it yourself. Every detail seemed to pile up to more heartache.

"I'm so sorry." I tried to think of anything else to say. "Is there anything we can do to help until they get here?"

"Right now the best place for me to be today is in the kitchen. I'll go mad if I just sit around here."

"I can understand that."

Whenever any problems or troubles hit, the shop is where I want to be. I do my best thinking and problem-solving with yarn and needles in my hand. And my customers are the best friends I have in this town.

"But I do mean it. Call me if you need anything."

"Gavin and Esther said the same thing," Monica answered. "I'm sure Yale and I will be okay."

Her voice quavered just enough on that last word that I knew she didn't quite believe it. Who would have with such a fresh tragedy? Seemed to me, even the sister who drove you nuts was still your sister.

With a curt nod to both Frank and me, Monica went across the hall to her room and shut the door. The sound struck me as much more of a sad, quiet click than the angry slam I'd heard just yesterday. The finality of it sank under my skin.

I turned to Frank. "When are you going to tell her it wasn't an accident?" It seemed cruel to add a lie to everything else Monica was facing.

"When I'm sure they weren't involved." Frank pushed his hands into the latex gloves with a practiced motion.

I balked at him. "Surely you don't think Monica did it? She was at the restaurant. And she has nothing to do with Julie's antiwool stance."

Frank merely grunted and started sorting through papers and clothing, carefully peering at things and turning them over.

"What are we looking for?" I asked.

"Anything that looks like a reason to kill her."

Frank's matter-of-fact tone chilled my spine. I wasn't a police officer, and I didn't much care for the rounds of playing detective I'd done to date.

"What does a reason to kill look like? A wad of hundred-dollar bills stashed under the pillow? Diamonds? State documents?"

Frank didn't appreciate my nervous joke. "From your standpoint, what did Julie have that someone might want?"

I didn't have a ready answer for that. I hadn't seen expensive jewelry on Julie to make me think she had lots of money. She had a certain notoriety, true, but it wasn't as if you could steal that.

"I don't know." I pulled on the pair of gloves he'd given me and started delicately poking around the room the way Frank was doing.

He picked up a plastic bag with half a dozen skeins of brilliant purple yarn. "Other than her loud mouth, is this what she's famous for? Why you brought her in?"

"Yes," I answered in awe of the deep hue. "Nobody gets the kinds of colors Julie does. Dyeing plant fibers is a trickier business than protein fibers."

"Protein?" Frank raised a gray eyebrow at the term.

"Protein fibers are the ones that come from animals. Wool from sheep, cashmere from goats, angora from rabbits, that sort of thing." I began peering at the books and notes on the bureau, hoping something would catch my eye as significant. "Those take to dye much easier than plant or synthetic fibers. But Julie can somehow . . ."

My words fell off as I found something I would definitely classify as significant: a flat, hand-stitched silk pouch roughly the size of a manila envelope. The word "Recipes" was embroidered in brilliant green on the flap.

"Can somehow what?" Frank asked, walking over.

I undid the little silk cord that wound around a button to hold the pouch closed. The pouch was empty. "Frank, I think I might have found what you're looking for."

CHAPTER EIGHT

Recipes?" Frank looked skeptical. "Like for chocolate chip cookies? I thought the other sister was the cook."

"Think of it more like formulas. And in Julie's case, more like secret formulas. Julie won't reveal how she gets the colors she does."

He scowled. "I don't get it."

I reached over to pick up a hank of the yarn, one that traveled in waves from a gorgeous emerald green to a deep indigo and back again.

"Julie is famous for her colors. She's one of the few people who are able to get these kinds of hues in plant fibers. Everyone wants to know how she does it. But of course, she won't say how."

"So the how is in her formulas," Frank finished my thought. "Her recipes."

"Which aren't here." I pointed to the silk "envelope."

"I think this could be the place where she stored them. And it's empty."

Frank carefully took the item from my hands. "Wouldn't she need the recipes with her when she was doing the dyeing? And why not have them someplace more secure—a laptop or something?"

There was that. She'd have needed to refer to those formulas when dyeing the yarn, so it didn't make sense that she had left them back here.

"Maybe she just left the pouch? Maybe she mixed the dry compounds here and took them over to the warehouse to add the liquids? I don't know. But maybe she felt storing them anywhere on a computer meant they could be hacked. Or stolen. I don't keep my passwords anywhere on my computer. They're in a little book hidden in my house. Maybe it's the same thing."

Frank peered inside the silk pouch. "You can just as easily steal this. *If you knew what you were looking for.*"

I walked over to the wastebasket and peered inside like I'd seen detectives do on television. "Frank, look."

It was an empty jar of dye powder. That didn't seem right for someone as secretive of their formulas as Julie. Why wasn't this at the warehouse with the other supplies? It took me a moment to work out what felt off.

"Wait. This can't be one of the ingredients Julie uses."

"Huh? Why?"

I held the plastic bottle up to him. "These are acid dyes."

"Acid?"

I pointed to the smaller print on the label that read: *for silk, wool, and protein fibers.* "These dyes are for the kinds of fibers Julie never uses. She'd never get the colors she creates from these—they'd fade on things like cotton and bamboo and flax." A thought struck me. "Unless she figured out how. What if she figured out some secret ingredient to add to make the dye react and stick?"

Frank squinted at the tiny print. "Her secret formula."

If Julie had figured out a way to make acid dyes work on plant fibers, it would explain how she managed the brilliant colors. And why she took such pains to hide her tactics. But if someone else knew . . .

"Frank," I went on, "lots of the chemicals you have to add to acid dyes can be toxic. So if someone knew she was using them—"

"They'd know blocking the ventilation system could harm her," Frank finished.

"But how would the sheep farmers know that?" I asked. I barely knew how the process worked and I was immersed in the fiber world.

"Maybe they don't know the difference. Maybe they just know dye fumes can be toxic and assumed Julie used them." Frank scratched his chin. "Their wrong guess just happened to be right in this instance."

"I suppose so."

I still had trouble picturing Barney and his buddies committing murder. Being a stubborn old coot who cared about his sheep enough to name every last one of them didn't make Barney seem like the type of person to send Julie to her death. Even if he did hate what she stood for.

Frank peered into the empty jar. "So these dyes need a second chemical to work?"

"On the fibers Julie uses, yes. At least I think so."

"Can you get me a list of what those chemicals are? I could give them to toxicology."

"I can make a few calls. But if Julie's using something else—her secret ingredient, if you will—I don't know how we'll know what to look for."

Frank held my gaze. "We didn't know what to look for here, but we found it, didn't we? You've got a nose for this, Libby."

"I wish I didn't." Yes, knitters know to look for patterns and we often have to unravel what's in front of us to find the one stitch that threw everything off, but I didn't like using my skills this way. "What now?"

Frank put the jar into a plastic bag. "I'll take this back to the station and let the boys do a little research while you make your calls." He checked his watch. "I promised Angie we'd go to the pasta thing at two."

Ah, the festival was still going on. Angie was the police receptionist, and Frank's budding romance with her was the worst-kept secret in town. I'm sure he thought no one had realized how adorably sweet he was on Angie, and she on him. As much as I wanted to jump all over our new theories, I didn't have it in me to insist that Frank break his festival date with Angie. Especially since I would probably have to spend the next hour shuttling between the store and the warehouse, making sure every ticket holder knew today's event was canceled.

Canceled. The word seemed too ordinary for the terrible thing that had happened. An event was canceled, but a life was lost. Not lost, *taken. Stolen.* No amount of controversial-opinion yelling seemed worth that price. And I hated to think that someone I knew, someone whose sheep produced yarn I purchased and carried in the store, might have done it.

"You go have a good time with Angie." I offered a hopeful smile. "Who doesn't want to learn how to make pasta?"

"Me," he replied with a reluctant smirk. "But she really wants to go."

His expression was so sweetly lovestruck, I had no doubt that if Angie wanted to drag him to one of my knitting classes, he'd show up. It warmed my stressed-out heart to know life was still going on in happy ways around Collinstown.

"I'm really more of a cheeseburger and chicken-wings kind of guy."

Maybe, Chief, I thought to myself, *but you're as romantic as they come.* My ex, Sterling, would have bought me four top-notch pasta-making machines before he'd have devoted the time to take a class like that with me. Sterling always seemed to find Collinstown a bit backward to his high-powered DC taste, but I never saw it that way. Folks in Collinstown weren't old-fashioned; they just never forgot what was really important.

"I bet you'll have a great time," I assured him. "Angie will probably cook something delicious with whatever pasta you make."

I don't know why Frank felt he had to hide his relationship with Angie. Half the town already knew, and I had never found anyone who wasn't one hundred percent in favor of the match. Some days I wanted to grab Frank's shoulders and shout, "We all know, for Pete's sake. Just date her publicly. We love the both of you."

But I never did. For one, that level of nosy was Mom's arena. And for two, Frank just might put me in cuffs if I did.

By Saturday morning I got the okay to clear the workshop supplies and Julie's yarns out of the warehouse. The cavernous space chilled my skin—and not just because the huge ventilation fans had been running full speed for over a day. The fresh air rushing in from the open windows felt biting rather than bracing. The blast of heat and humidity that hit me when we had pulled that door open Thursday night was long gone. For a place that was supposed to have housed the magic of color creation, the space struck me as a cold and gloomy gray.

Frank and I walked in to see several folding tables set up along one wall. Half a dozen hot plates, now unplugged, sat next to a collection of metal kettles like the kind you'd use to make tea. Plastic pitchers sat in rows on another table, the remnants of dark dyeing liquid in several of them. Tongs, measuring spoons, and other utensils were scattered across tables and counters. Packages of "blank" yarn Julie had shipped in—white or cream fibers ready to be dyed—were piled up on one table. Rows of huge square tubs, like the kind you see at catered buffets, were laid out on other tables, but only two of them were filled with dyed yarn. Farther off to one side, two rows of wooden laundry racks Julie had asked us to supply stood empty, still waiting for the yarn to hang to dry. Our celebrity guest hadn't gotten very far in her dyeing before she'd been overcome.

I stood still, struck by this scene of art in the making. It was as if someone had hit a giant pause button in the middle of Julie's creative efforts. Some of these seemed to be the exclusive Y.A.R.N. color, rich in ripples of deep blue and green like the river that ran through town.

"This must be Riverbank," I said to Frank.

"What?"

"She was dyeing an exclusive color for us. Riverbank. It's what she was making when she . . . died."

I knew the color wasn't the means of her death—at least not directly—but it still felt as if our particular color had killed her. Beautiful as it was, I couldn't bring myself to touch any of it.

"We took samples of the yarn and the liquid in each of these vats," Frank said. "If she was dyeing with this stuff, why is the liquid clear?"

This really wasn't my expertise. "I think because all the dye went into the yarn. You know, absorbed."

Frank's brows furrowed. "So why doesn't the yarn smell? Those fumes were strong. Wouldn't it still be in these things?" He gave the strands a dubious look, as if they still might slither out of the pan like octopus tentacles and do him harm.

I had wondered the same thing, since the yarn we were looking at didn't seem to have been rinsed. "I don't know much about any of this. I always thought the harm was in inhaling the powder, but no one really knows what process or what ingredients Julie used."

Where were those formulas? If she had a file of them, they should have been here.

"Do you want all this?" Frank asked. "The lab says it's safe."

In truth, I wasn't sure. Even if it was to be our exclusive color, I wasn't in a rush to be the owner of Julie Wilson's last batch of yarn ever. Still, wouldn't it have been a worse thing to let even these few skeins go to waste? It looked like they would still turn out nicely. They didn't seem to be ruined. Shouldn't I do whatever I could to salvage them?

While Julie had never shown me any swatches of the color she had planned for Riverbank, I didn't need to see it. I knew it would be wonderful. The yarn in front of me managed to live up to its name. It looked like our river. Somehow she had also managed to capture the silver-white of moonlight reflected in those waves, and I could see the water traveling as I stared at the thick loops of tied yarn. They were dark, almost mysterious, but they were also beautiful. Even without the benefit of whatever full process Julie had intended to use, she had managed to create beauty. At least I hoped so.

"I guess we can just pull it out, rinse it, dry it, and see what we get."

At least that would have been the next step with any standard dyeing process. I had no idea what Julie would have done.

"So they're not ruined? Overcooked?"

He'd told me his pasta hadn't turned out so good. I had to admit, the whole scene did look like a colorful pasta dish in the making.

"Hopefully not."

I wanted to believe in how beautiful the skeins were now, how beautiful they might be when they dried. But I also feared they would somehow look dark and deadly to me no matter how they turned out.

Frank nudged the vat, sending little ripples through the liquid that just barely covered the long hanks of fiber. "These look heavy. You want some help?"

I didn't want to pull Frank away from his job of catching Julie's killer. "I'll be fine."

After I gave them their rinsing "baths," it wouldn't take much muscle to hang the wet yarn on the wooden laundry racks in the center of the room to dry. Once I decided to do it, I discovered I was actually looking forward to the process. It would be the closest thing to a goodbye, a memorial, that I would get to give Julie. I was grateful the raw yarn she was using was all fiber I'd purchased for the event—it gave me no guilt to use the yarn, and I didn't feel as if I was stealing anything from her.

After all, someone else had stolen her very life. The least I could do was try to save her last work of art.

"Maybe just help me with this first tub."

I grabbed one of the two rubberized canvas aprons I'd brought with me and handed it to Frank, along with a set of long rubber gloves. Normally, you wore such protective gear for stains and heat, but given the lethal circumstances, I wanted to take extra precautions in case there was anything sinister lurking in the clear dye water, lab results or no.

Frank lugged the pan over to the industrial sink and tipped it to drain the water out. "Really does look like blue spaghetti and . . . whoa." He stopped midpour.

"What?"

Frank used one of the nearby sets of tongs lying on the counter and fished something that looked sort of like a pair of pliers out of the water.

"Wire strippers," he said grimly. He pulled a plastic evidence bag from his pants pocket and slipped the tool inside. "You're not going to tell me there's a yarn-related need for wire strippers, are you?"

I swallowed hard. "No."

Julie had declined my dinner invitation so she could set Monica's kitchen on fire.

"Well, now we have evidence to go along with the fact that we can place Julie at the scene of the fire. If she were alive, I'd have enough to charge her. But seeing as—"

"It's safe to come in here, right?" a voice interrupted him.

Frank and I turned to find Yale Wagner and his cameraman. With the camera running.

"Shut that thing off," Frank barked as he deftly slid the bagged wire strippers into his pocket. I wondered how many times a week Yale heard that phrase. The man seemed to have no scruples against filming anything. It made me wonder if Monica appreciated the inside look into her life Yale continually gave her fans. I'm not so sure I'd want so much of my life played out on the screen.

"Are you kidding? This will be fascinating stuff."

Not half as fascinating as what we'd just found, I'd have said.

Frank walked toward Yale with his palm flat out, facing the cameraman's lens. "Active crime scene investigations are *not* fodder for your television show."

Yale's eyes narrowed. "Barker said you'd give me trouble." He grunted and finally waved a stop-taping hand to his cameraman when Frank glared extra hard. "Had a lot to say about you, actually."

"Been talking with Barker, have you?"

I secretly wondered if it was more like George talking to—probably selling to—Yale. I decided to change the subject. "How is Monica holding up?"

"She's upset. She and Julie never got along, but . . ." His voice trailed off.

Attempting to set fire to your sister's kitchen is a few notches above not getting along in my book. Had Julie meant to rattle Monica or truly to harm her? We'd probably never know now that Julie was gone.

Fire smoke? Toxic fumes? The thought of choking on either gave me goose bumps.

"It's a terrible thing to have happened," Yale continued. "She's not doing especially well. But she'll hold up. She always does."

Sure, I lost an event, but this woman had lost her sister. And even if their relationship had deteriorated to the point where Julie would have actually sabotaged her sister's mixer, now all hope for any kind of reconciliation was gone. That seemed a lot to bear in the middle of a cooking festival. I almost always knit when I was upset or sad—did cooks do the same thing? I'd heard Margo use the term "stress baker," so maybe so.

The cameraman seemed a bit bored by all the sad personal talk. "I'll be outside, Yale. Call me when you're ready to shoot in here."

That won't be anytime soon, I answered in my head.

Yale waved him off. "Yeah. Sure." He looked around the room. "I didn't think it'd end like this." He tucked his hands in his pockets and shrugged. "They ought to love each other, you know."

No one had ever said what was in the note Julie had left Monica. Could it have been an apology? The wire strippers seemed to shout otherwise, and it wasn't my place to ask. Then again, I suppose even those could have been planted by someone.

"I've never had a sister," I offered, mostly to Frank on account of his several sisters. "Do they all fight like that and still love one another?" I've had some doozies of fights with Mom, and I still love her to death, so I suppose it's true.

"They do—did, I think," Yale answered before Frank. "Just didn't know how to show it without stomping on each other's nerves. Sort of a you-always-hurt-the-ones-you-love thing. Monica's really wrecked about it. Her folks are in pieces, especially since they're having such trouble getting back."

"It must be terribly hard on the family, to lose your daughter and your only sister like that." I looked around, once again reminded I was not only surrounded by the colors Julie loved, but that I was in the place where she died. "Like this."

Yale's eyes followed my gesture to the lines of pans and bottles. "They did a version of the same thing, when you think about it. Following recipes, cooking up creations. They are—were—both talented. Just each had a bit of trouble seeing it in the other. Being here just seemed to make it worse."

I hadn't thought about it in that way, but Yale was right. Sometimes it takes someone outside the family to see the family bonds. My father used to say, "It's hard to see the label from inside the bottle." I could always see how Sterling's family went to great lengths to cut one another down, and he always laughed it off as friendly sarcasm. It wasn't.

Frank pulled out his notepad. "Did you see Julie at the Dockhouse on Thursday night? Or in the afternoon before the reception?"

"No, but she must have done something to tick Monica off." Yale said.

I thought it was interesting that Yale didn't mention the note Julie had left. Had Monica not told him?

"Monica gets careless when she lets her temper get the better of her. I wasn't that surprised to hear she burned out the mixer motor, to be honest."

So Yale didn't know the mixer's wires had been stripped. "Julie said Monica's had more than her share of kitchen accidents," I offered. "Is that true?"

Yale gave a resigned grunt. "Regretfully. And I was hoping to get through this weekend without a mishap.

It's one of the reasons I stopped in at the restaurant—I usually like to give Monica a wide berth when she's cooking, but she was really on edge. And I was worried Julie would try something, frankly. I almost turned the appearance down when I found out Julie would be here."

Fights? Fires? Not being able to be in the same town? These sisters were starting to sound like they were capable of doing anything to each other.

CHAPTER NINE

All kinds of brunches were happening around Collinstown Sunday morning, but I stayed home until the shop opened at noon. I knit, said a few prayers for Monica, Yale, and the safe return of Mr. and Mrs. Wilson, walked Hank, and generally tried to regain my bearings.

Jillian came into the shop a little after one. I liked that she was a frequent visitor to Y.A.R.N. Gavin's daughter was a talented knitter and a budding designer, and I had no doubt that I'd be hosting an event for her own career one day. She was as natural a talent on the stage as she was at the needles, so even if she didn't become a knitting celebrity, I thought she stood a pretty good chance of being a celebrity who knits. I've met three Broadway stars and two B-list movie stars who are devoted knitters, and I always take notice when a celebrity showcases their love for yarn and needles.

"Hi, Ms. B." She slid a backpack off her shoulders and onto one of the table chairs, as at home in the shop as I'd want any customer to be. "Dad's busy with the festival, so he gave me some money to come by and pick out some yarn for a new project."

I smiled, both at her enthusiasm and Gavin's indirect support of my shop. I often wondered how much of Gavin's mayoral salary went right back into Collinstown businesses. He was always careful to buy local whenever possible.

"Who doesn't like picking out yarn for a new project?" I left sorting my new shipment of circular needles and walked over to her. "What did you have in mind?"

"I was doing more research on Julie Wilson last night, and I came across a tank pattern in flax. It looked cool. Got any of that?"

I knew exactly the pattern Jillian meant. "I do. In some of her best colors." I led Jillian to a basket of flax yarn in gorgeous jewel tones. "Look at these."

Her hands went straight to a celery green and a sky blue. The girl had an eye for color—I'll give her that.

"You'd look great in either of these."

"I thought I might use them both. Stripes, I mean." Jillian had one of the marks of a great knitter—she always did something with a pattern to make it all her own. "You think she'd be okay with that?" She looked unsure, as if altering the pattern of a dead woman constituted some sort of artistic insult.

"I didn't know Julie well, but I do think she liked that people had their own take on things. I'm sure she wouldn't have minded." Using the past tense where Julie was concerned still left a sour taste in my mouth.

She fingered the yarn. "Why's it so scratchy?"

"Well, it is now, yes. But it won't stay that way. Flax softens up when you wash it. So it'll feel scratchy and stiff while you knit it, but it'll come out like this when you're done."

I handed Jillian the shawl I'd knit a month ago in preparation for Julie's visit. The thing draped like silk and shimmered in the sunlight.

"Oh, wow. Yeah, I'll do it in this yarn. Can I wind it here?"

We often wind yarn for customers. We have a nifty little contraption that does the job fast. Only I've discovered sometimes a customer wants friendship as much as they want fiber, and then I usually opt to sit at the table and chat while we do it the old-fashioned way—one person holding the yarn while the other winds a ball. Jillian was a fan of the second way, which usually meant she had something on her mind that she wanted to talk about.

"Sure," I said. "I've got some of that cream soda left in the fridge. Want some?"

Gavin will never know that I keep a stock of cream soda hidden in the back room so I always just "happen" to have some on hand when Jillian stops by. I do the same with dog biscuits, too, so don't go reading into that gesture.

Conversation aside, I would have suggested Jillian wind the yarn here, because flax is notoriously hard to keep wound. All that slick stiffness means it seems to delight in springing out of control, which is infuriating when you're trying to knit. I grabbed a strip of nylon netting—the kind you find in the produce section at the supermarket—and snipped off two wide strips.

"Put the balls in these once we've wound them," I advised. "They like to go haywire."

Even as I spoke, part of the ball undid itself as if to show off its rebellious tendencies. No wonder flax had been one of Julie's favorite fibers.

"I see what you mean," Jillian said with a laugh.

"How's school going?" I ventured after we finished the first of four balls. She had requested a soda and hand winding, after all.

"Okay," she said with a marked lack of enthusiasm.

"So not great." From what I remember about middle school, nothing about eighth grade was even close to great.

"Well, no."

"School stuff or kids stuff?" I knew from Gavin that Jillian was a straight-A student, so I doubted it was the former.

Jillian's eyes narrowed as we started the second ball. "Hailey Connors."

Jim Connors was our local state representative and an attorney in town. Nice but intense. "What's up with Hailey?"

"So she's super popular, okay? She and her five friends practically run the school. They all have boyfriends and *all* the clothes. She never talks to me."

Evidently some things about middle school never changed. "I know the type, yes."

I was holding the yarn this time, and Jillian's hands sped up as she wound the ball. "So two weeks ago, she starts asking me all these questions about my YouTube channel. She wants me to show her my knitting, what editing software I use, all kinds of stuff. I spent two whole weeks showing her what I know." Jillian looked up at me. "Me, sitting at the Corner Stone, having coffee with Hailey Connors."

The Corner Stone was the trendy coffeehouse and smoothie bar two blocks down. They made excellent coffee, but for the kids it was the place to see and be seen. Nothing made me feel older than stopping by the Corner Stone just after school let out. I didn't have to be fourteen to know what it would feel like to be having smoothies there with the most popular girl in school.

"She even subscribed to my channel and got that whole group to subscribe." There was a giant unspoken "But . . ." hanging off the end of her sentence.

I asked, "Then what happened?" although it wasn't hard to guess.

"This week Hailey launched her own makeup channel. And she hasn't said a word to me since. She stopped commenting and liking my videos. Stupid me to think maybe we were friends."

My heart hurt for the girl. "She was just using you to show her how to do what she wanted?"

Jillian merely nodded. "Then poof, she was outta here."

"Doesn't sound to me like Hailey is a friend worth having. The popular girls rarely are, if you ask me."

"Grandma Rhonda said you'd understand 'cuz you weren't popular in school, either."

As much as I am touched that Mom "adopted" Jillian as the grandchild I wouldn't ever give her, I could go without being branded "unpopular" by my own flesh and blood. Sometimes I think backhanded compliments and well-intentioned digs are Mom's native language.

"Well, Sharon Peterson never said a single word to me all through school, so you're one up on me."

I left out that Sharon Peterson was on her third husband and owned a sad little travel agency just outside of Baltimore last I'd heard. I'm not one to gloat.

The yarn uncoiled itself from the ball Jillian was winding, springing off to wind up a pile of sky blue spaghetti in her lap. "Yikes—I see what you mean."

I pointed to the three or so inches of netting on the table in front of her. "I wasn't kidding about those little nets. Just keep the balls in there and pull gently, and you'll be fine."

We were halfway through the last ball when Jillian looked up at me and said, "So I'm trying to figure out what to do about my episode."

I had been wondering the same thing. "The one with Julie?"

"Yeah. We were actually having a pretty good time talking. I liked her. But . . . we didn't get to finish it on account of her sister showing up."

"That did sort of throw a bucket of cold water on things, didn't it? Can you use the parts you did finish?"

Jillian put down the ball—but not before tucking it safely into the small stretch of netting. I like a young woman who listens to advice—according to Gavin, those are rare. Then again, I have a mother who almost never listens to advice, so I'm not so sure it's an age thing.

"Should I? Post the interview, I mean." She gave a little swallow. "Dad told me he thinks it was the last interview she ever gave."

That seemed a heavy load for someone so young. "I see your point." I thought about her question for a few moments before I asked, "Do you like the interview? The parts you've got?"

"Yeah. She had a lot to say and she wasn't afraid to say it. I like that."

I smiled. "Me, too. Julie stood for something. She

didn't let people who disagreed with her stop her from doing what she thought was right." That seemed a good lesson for someone Jillian's age, especially in a world full of girls like Hailey Connors. I was in no hurry to see a put-down from a mean girl crush the creative spirit of someone like Jillian. "What do you think Julie would want you to do?"

"She talked about wanting to reach knitters like me. You know, my age. She even offered to put a link to my interview on her web page. I didn't expect her to be that nice."

I carefully set down the hank of yarn, ensuring it didn't tangle. "So are you thinking of posting it?"

"When I'm ready." She chewed her lip. "Which I'm totally not . . . yet. But later I think I will be."

"You can ask Caroline," I suggested. "She might help."

I didn't know much about media coverage of recently deceased fiber activists, but I was sure Caroline would help Jillian think through what to do.

"It's a bit creepy since she's dead and all, but she also had some really cool stuff to say. I feel like I ought to use it. And not just 'cuz she's the most famous person I've ever interviewed."

I admired Jillian's sensible nature—her father had done well by this young woman. "I think Julie would like that you didn't let her interview go to waste. And while I don't have nearly her following, I'll post a link to your interview on the Y.A.R.N. web page."

"You would?"

I felt a bittersweet twinge that she was surprised. "Of course I would. I think you're pretty cool yourself, you know."

Jillian shrugged and picked up the ball to continue

winding it, but I tucked her small proud smile away in a corner of my heart.

Weekends need to be busy in a tourist town like Collinstown. So I was glad to see the town bustling from the festival despite what had happened to my portion of it. Still, after Jillian left, the shop felt too quiet for a Sunday afternoon. Looking out at the line of people queued up for Margo's tarts, I told myself to be happy someone was having a great weekend.

It just wasn't going to be me.

I paused for a moment of self-pity as I packed up the little dyeing kits we'd made for the workshop attendees—ones we might now never sell. I made myself say another little prayer—this one for the festival. I couldn't do much for See More Than Seafood, but I could ask the Almighty to make sure the kitchen fire and Julie's death would be the festival's only catastrophes. And then I laughed out loud at the absurd nature of such a prayer and kept working.

My packing pity party was interrupted half an hour later as Arlene, one of Mom's troupe of friends she calls the Gals and a regular customer of the shop, came in. "Oh, good, you're here." She carried something large and flat in a paper bag.

"Where else would I be?"

My words had an unfortunate hopeless tone. I certainly wasn't going to be at the warehouse packing up after Julie's sold-out workshop, was I?

Arlene set the package down on the big round table in the center of the shop and came over to hug me. "I can't believe what happened. I wasn't ever that interested in dyeing my own yarn, and I think now I won't ever be. Talk about a don't-try-this-at-home kind of thing."

"But you had a ticket to the workshop," I reminded her, pushing the button to open the register drawer. I figured I might as well issue her refund now, since Arlene had paid cash.

Arlene reached over and pushed the drawer back shut. "I'll take it in yarn, hon. And *of course* I bought a ticket. It's you. I'll buy a ticket to everything you do, even if it's a class on raising cashmere goats. And I'll never do that, either."

Arlene's no-holds-barred loyalty put a huge lump in my throat. I muttered a damp-sounding "Thanks" and hugged her right back.

"Now," said Arlene, pushing me back to hold both my shoulders like a favorite aunt, "I was gonna save this for next week, but it seems to me you need it now." She nodded toward the flat package lying on the table.

"What's that?"

"Open it up and see."

I walked over to the table and peered inside the paper. "You didn't!" I gasped once I saw what was inside. I turned to balk at Arlene. "You didn't!"

She grinned ear to ear. "I most certainly did."

Half laughing, half sniffling, I slid the poster out of its paper covering and stared at it. *Give Me LIBBertY!* shouted the poster, with the L, I, B, B, and Y colored red in the intentionally misspelled word so that my name stood out. Below it was a drawing of a knitted scarf, whose stitches spelled out, *Libby Beckett for Chamber President.*

I gawked at Arlene, then back at the poster, then back at Arlene's delighted smile. "That's not a real scarf," she said, but then added a mischievous "Yet."

"You made me a campaign poster?"

Given the rebellion against King George that my candidacy represented, it was brilliant. After all, Patrick Henry had enjoyed some success with it back in 1775. I felt a little bad about how steamed this clever poster would make George—but only a little.

"I made twenty-five of them, actually. I knew there was a reason I took that screen-printing class over at the arts center last fall."

Arlene was always taking some kind of art class. I loved how much of a lifelong learner she was—most especially right now.

"We can't really put these up, can we?"

It wasn't like I was running for mayor. The public didn't vote. Just the shop and business owners who were members of the Chamber of Commerce.

Arlene narrowed her eyes in mock scorn. "Don't you be telling us Gals what to do. If we want to support our favorite business by decorating a few store windows of our other favorite businesses, that's what democracy is all about." She leaned in. "But this one's just for you. I figured you could use a bit of a boost today."

I held up the poster, fighting the urge to hug it to my chest. It felt like a giant bold valentine—exactly what I needed in my somber state.

"It's perfect. I should tell you it's inappropriate . . . but I can't quite bring myself to do it."

"I hear you, honey." Arlene's conspiratorial giggle was just what the doctor ordered.

CHAPTER TEN

Lots of churches have prayer shawl ministries. My church—Collinstown Community Church—is one of them. I don't often have the time to volunteer to knit the soft, fluffy wraps that are prayed over and given to people in need of healing or comfort, but I always donate yarn. I've sent more than a few volunteers their way, too. Prayer shawls are one of the most powerful uses of yarn and needles I know.

I wouldn't consider myself an intensely spiritual person, but I do recognize the importance of certain nudges. When I get an insistent nudge to give someone a prayer shawl, I try never to ignore it. Even if I don't know the person well.

Which is how I found myself knocking on Monica's door at the inn Monday morning, in possession of a prayer shawl and a nervous stomach. For courage, I recalled the words of Jeanette, one of Mom's Gals who had lost her husband last year. "Even if you end up saying something stupid," Jeanette said, "it's so much better than saying nothing at all." Even if Monica found my gift intrusive, I decided it was the least I could do.

Monica's drawn and weary face met me as she opened her inn room door. "Hello." It was more in resignation than greeting.

"I'm so sorry to intrude, but I wanted to give you this."

Her face softened as I handed her the little bag drawn tight with a piece of yarn that matched the shawl and a small card explaining what it was. She surprised me by saying, "Come in."

Despite the upheaval of the current situation, Monica's room was tidy. She appeared to be the exact opposite of her sister in so many ways. I found it hard to focus, given all that had happened, and my office was a total mess. Monica, it seemed, fought disorder with order, right down to the exacting lineup of pens on the room's desk beside files stacked in pristine order. Despite what I knew to be Bev's excellent housekeeping, the bed was already crisply made, right down to the military corners that looked out of place on a historic four-poster bed.

"This must be so hard for you," I offered, trying to sound as compassionate as possible. "I'm still amazed that you chose not to cancel your events. No one would blame you."

"No," came Monica's near-immediate answer. "I won't do that. I need to . . . keep busy."

As if she'd suddenly run out of all that necessary busyness, Monica slumped down on the upholstered couch in the room. With a weary wave she motioned for me to take a seat in one of the chairs. It was like watching a person deflate, leaking out all the vibrancy that had been there earlier.

I do enjoy presenting people with prayer shawls and love to watch anyone receive a knitted gift, but I still felt rather out of place, given Monica's deep and fresh grief. I felt as if I knew too much. I had no idea if Frank had told her about the wire strippers we'd found. I certainly didn't think it was my place to share that news, but the weight of knowing it pressed on my shoulders. I hoped for a chance to ask Monica what was on the note Julie had left for her—if she'd left any note at all. For all I knew, it could have just been an excuse to get into the kitchen and strip the mixer wires.

Monica seemed so lonely. She ought to have been surrounded with friends and family now, not her late sister's event host.

"It's awful your mother and father can't get here quickly."

"It wouldn't change anything, would it? Mom and Dad will be here soon enough. I know they're trying." Her tone sounded as if she was too spent to care. I thought again that it might not be the best choice to carry on with her events, despite her intentions.

Monica fingered the short length of yarn holding the bag shut. "Mom was the one who taught Julie and me to knit, you know."

"So you do still knit?" Yale had made it sound like she'd given it up.

"Not anymore, and not like Julie. I hardly ever have time to do it. Besides, it's *her* thing." She gave the word a sharp edge but still swallowed hard. "Was." Monica looked like someone who needed to talk.

"You two seemed to have a difficult relationship."

Rather an understatement, given the circumstances.

Possibly attempted arson seemed to qualify as a level above difficult.

She gave a dark laugh. "That's putting it kindly. We fought. All the time. I swear Julie's favorite thing to do was to start an argument."

That seemed to open the door for my question. "Was that what was on the note? More arguments? Not an apology?"

Monica looked at me. "Note? What note? There wasn't any note."

"Esther said Julie asked to get into the kitchen at the Dockhouse to leave you a note. I think we all assumed it was to make amends."

Monica's laugh held a bitter edge. "Amends? Julie? Never. No, there was no note. She'd have been more likely to set my kitchen on fire—that I'd believe."

Hadn't she? We were all but certain Julie had, weren't we? Maybe Frank wasn't sharing that theory with Monica until he knew more.

"I'm sorry the last words you had with her were an argument."

I'd always been grateful to have the chance to say a long and loving goodbye to my father before he died. It's so true that you never know when getting the last word really will be your last word with someone. It was a goal of mine to someday get to the point where I could have a civil and even kind conversation with Sterling, but I wasn't there yet.

"I loved her," Monica said, tears filling her eyes. "She always made it so hard, but I tried. I know it doesn't look like it, but I did."

I could understand how she seemed to need the world to know that. "Families are complicated." To help move her off the wave of tears that seemed to threaten, I pointed to the bag. "Would you like to open it? Are you familiar with prayer shawls?"

She welcomed the task. "No."

I gave her a quick explanation of the ministry as she undid the tie and pulled the lovely burgundy wrap from its bag. "They didn't have one not made from an animal fiber, so this one's a wool blend. I hope you don't mind."

I actually had looked. There was one shawl knit from a synthetic yarn, but it was a cheery lime green, and that didn't seem to fit the occasion.

Monica chuckled and sniffed. "Wouldn't that gall my sister?" She ran her hand across the fringe that decorated each end of the large wrap. "Then again, it didn't take much to offend Julie." She looked up at me. "It's lovely. Thank you."

She pulled the wrap over her shoulders, and I marveled at how the color suited her. Mom would tell me that was no accident. Mom's belief in serendipity matched her belief in God. It wasn't a bad way to go through life, believing everything happened just the way it was supposed to.

. . . Except dead yarn dyers. I was nowhere near ready to put that down to "supposed to happen."

Monica pulled the wrap tight and hugged herself. "Mom always said Julie or I would have one too many accidents someday."

Much as I tried to respect Frank's strategy, I hated the idea of letting Monica keep thinking Julie had died by accident. Why withhold things like that from people? This woman was grieving. She'd been victimized by what had happened that night in more ways than one. She deserved the truth, didn't she?

I settled for "It's an awful thing," which at least felt like truth.

"She was always so careless." Monica got up and walked around the room. "She told me she threw together chemicals like it was a game. That's not always a good idea, even in cooking." She turned to look at me. "If it made her sick or she passed out but created some gorgeous color, it was worth it."

"Julie told you she passed out from some of her dye mixes?"

Even I knew some protective equipment was required. And we'd found a particulate mask near Julie's body. If she hadn't used it, that seemed foolhardy, even for a rebel like Julie.

Monica waved a hand in the air at my shock. "You knew Julie. So sure all the rules didn't apply to her. Had a million demands for other people, but wouldn't listen to a soul."

I decided to take a chance. "Julie's dye recipes seem to be missing."

"This isn't the first time. She lost them for a whole day last time we tried to spend time together. She went nuts, thinking someone had stolen her precious secret formulas. Of course she found them the next day in one of her messy piles. You saw her room."

"We think we know where she kept the formulas, but they aren't there. Do you have any ideas where they might be?"

"Oh, I could guess." Monica walked to the bureau, opened a drawer, and proceeded to pull out a silk envelope just like the one we'd found in Julie's hotel room. "I don't suppose you found something like this?" It had the same "Recipes" label embroidered on the front.

"We did, exactly. It was on the floor in her hotel room. But there was nothing in it. It doesn't seem like a very safe place to keep something as important as Julie's dye formulas."

Monica ran a finger across the intricate shiny fabric. "Well, maybe not safe, but special. Mom made them. We each have one."

Now it made sense. I'd been wondering why Julie had chosen such a place. She struck me as the kind of person to guard her "secret weapons" more closely. The silk envelope was a surprisingly sentimental choice. I guessed there was more to Julie than the abrasive artist most people saw. Only now no one would get to know.

Monica sighed. "I was mostly joking—I didn't even know she kept hers."

I met Monica's eyes. "I think she cherished hers, actually. Julie's dye recipes were probably her most treasured possession. Sort of a place of honor, I guess." It warmed me to be able to offer that tiny bit of comfort to a grieving sister. And fight as they had, she was still a sister in grief.

"I really am sorry for your loss," I said, meaning it. "It's a terrible thing."

Monica teetered on the edge of tears. I hoped Frank would solve this one quickly so that we wouldn't have to keep up this pretense of an accident for long. Noble motives or not, it felt way too much like lying.

"Will you be all right?" I asked, touching her arm. "Is there anything you need?"

She stiffened. "No. Yale's here. He'll take care of everything." She pulled in a deep breath. "That's what he does, isn't it?"

There was something about the edges to her words. I

got the impression things weren't especially wonderful between Monica and Yale at the moment. But that really wasn't my business, and I had no intention of nurturing Mom's skills for meddling.

"Can I have it?" she asked.

"What?"

"The recipe holder. Can I have the one that belonged to her?"

Monica seemed to be touched to have rediscovered this connection to her sister. I'd probably have clung to it in her situation.

"It's with the police right now," I hated to inform her. "But I'm sure Frank will let you have it the minute he can release it."

"Why?" Monica asked, and I realized I'd slipped up. That was the trouble with lies. They took so much attention and energy.

"He's got all kinds of things related to Julie's death," I backpedaled. *Like the wire strippers used to set your kitchen fire.* "He's very thorough about those things. I have no doubt you'll be hearing from him soon enough about when you can take everything back. You said your parents were on their way from Europe, but is there anyone else we should call? A boyfriend, roommate, or something?"

Monica gave a dark laugh at that. "Julie? My sister didn't do relationships. Not well and not for long."

She hugged the shawl closer to her shoulders as if her sister's ghost had just passed through the room and chilled her. I couldn't say it hadn't.

"People cycled in and out of her life quickly. Mom would always say, 'Julie's just too strong a dose for most people.'" She choked up a little on that last line.

I had to say it. "I'd say you're amazingly strong to keep your event schedule. In light of what's happened."

It made me wonder if that would be true once Frank felt it safe to voice his suspicions—which now seemed much closer to facts—that Julie's death and Monica's kitchen fire had been no accidents.

"It's who I am. If I don't cook, I'll just die." She caught the potency of those words and slapped one hand over her own mouth. "I can't believe I just said that."

I tried to smile. "It's just a saying. And I get it. Knitting is the first place I turn when I'm upset, because like you said, it's who I am."

A tear stole down Monica's face. "Do you know Julie used to always joke, 'I'll just die if I can't dye'? She wiped her cheek. "Not so clever sounding now, is it?"

"She died doing something she loved" sounded too trite to use as a reply. Not with the image of those blue and grimy window smudges of struggle burned into the back of my mind. I settled for "You've been through a terrible shock. Give yourself a break."

The exhausted look returned to Monica's face. "Thank you again. It's a very kind gesture."

I picked up my handbag. "Come by the store anytime you like. It's a nice place to just sit and collect yourself. And lots of Julie's beautiful things are there. Do you own any of her yarn?"

Her weariness turned to regret. "I don't. Rather telling, isn't it?"

"Come by the store and pick something out. On me. I'd consider it an honor."

Monica managed a small smile. "You know, Julie always said knitters were the kindest people in the world.

Much nicer than restaurant customers or food critics. Thanks. Maybe I will."

I hoped she would. I'm not much for pop craft psychology, but it seemed to me it would go a long way toward healing for Monica to knit something beautiful with the fibers her sister made.

I was just coming back from the inn when George came stomping out of his office door. He clutched one of the Give Me LIBBertY signs in his hand, and his scowling face would have put Barney's to shame.

"So this is how it's going to be, is it?" he barked. "We've sunk to mudslinging?"

I pulled in a steadying breath, dearly hoping no one had been bold enough to try to put one of those signs up on the tree outside George's office. Provoking George, while frightfully easy, was never a good idea. He'd nearly had a stroke last year when Mom and her Gals decorated that tree with yarn for Collinstown Yarn Day because he felt it gave me unfair advertising. This went much further than that.

I held up a hand. "Arlene made those. I didn't—"

"I know Arlene made these," he cut in. "I'm sure you thought you were very clever putting her up to it."

I did think the posters were clever. But they were also none too subtle in their dig at King George. I should have taken the higher road and stopped Arlene before it came to this. To be honest, I was just so pleased to have someone make such a show of support.

"I didn't put her up to it, George. This was all her idea. I'm sorry if—"

"Do you know the history of that? To whom it was spoken?"

George gave "whom" such an edge, it sounded like an expletive. So George *did* know people called him King George. Half of me was sad that he knew. The other half wished he would wake up to how he ordered people around. His wife, Vera, was actually a nice woman. Did he order her around the way he tried to command everyone else?

"I know, yes. But, George, it's just a play on my name. I don't think she meant it the way you're taking it." My gut pinched at the white lie, but I couldn't think of another way to de-escalate the situation.

George shook the sign. "The hell she didn't."

I had never heard George swear. A small surge of pity rose up. I had always thought George was oblivious to how people disliked him. His words and the sharp, hurt look in his eye told me he did know on some level. Just not enough to change.

"What do you want me to do, George?"

"Tell them to take them down."

On the one hand, that seemed like an easy solution. On the other hand, there were now an equal if not greater amount of Barker for Chamber President signs scattered around town. I'd seen them on public places—telephone poles, et cetera. That told me George and Vera had likely slammed them up in retaliation, whereas I knew Arlene had gone around to shops and politely asked permission to post my signs. I wasn't ready to concede the whole thing to his tantrum. No one can take an inch and run a mile like George Barker.

I needed a fast compromise. "How about we declare

this a sign-free race? I mean, we've never had signs be-fore, have we?"

While this was mostly because George had run unop-posed for the last four terms, it seemed a good tack to me.

"They *all* go down?" George looked horrified.

"Not your real estate ones. Just the ones about the campaign." It was then that I got a very dangerous idea. "Why don't we just have a town hall meeting instead? A candidates' forum." A shocked, rational voice in the back of my head started yelling, *What on earth are you thinking?* Handing George a microphone would be like parking a candle next to a box of fireworks.

"Like a debate?" A competitive gleam lit his beady little eyes.

"I'd hope more like a discussion," I backpedaled. There was no way out of this now. Margo would slap my hand but grin like a fool as she did it. "We can each share our vision for the town."

George was very fond of his vision. I was either giv-ing George his dream or handing him enough rope to hang himself.

"Why don't I ask Mayor Gavin if he'll set it up?"

George nodded. He loosened his vise grip on the poster and his shoulders lowered a few inches. "I think that's a great idea. A chance to lay out our visions for the future of Collinstown."

There was just enough derision in his words to make me think he didn't believe I had any vision for Collins-town. He wasn't entirely wrong. My initial motivations for running were just to put an end to George's reign of snarky power. I was more running *against* George than *for* anything. And now? Now I was going to have to be *for* something. So while I had accomplished defusing to-day's George bomb, I'd set up a new challenge for myself.

It also struck me like a fast-pitch softball that I'd just committed myself to a whopping dose of public speaking—not exactly my favorite pastime. I'd better sign up for a bunch of coaching from Mayor Gavin. I could just see the look on Gavin's face when I went to him with this idea. He'd probably make some joke asking me if I'd lost my marbles. I was wondering the same thing myself.

"Great," I said with more confidence than I felt. "We'll pick a date for after the festival if Gavin agrees."

"Right after the festival. And of course he'll agree," George declared.

I wasn't so sure. I held out my hand for the sign. "Let's start with that sign. I'll call Arlene and ask her to fetch them all back. You do the same with yours."

"I'll put Vera on it within the hour."

Evidently he did order poor Vera around. I watched him pivot on his heels and head back up the block, fighting the urge to shake my head.

I should have gone straight into the shop—I'd been gone several hours as it was—but I gave in to the urge to stop in the Perfect Slice instead. I waved to Margo while she was on the phone with a customer, then walked over to her window and plucked the Give Me LIBBertY sign from its prominent position.

She balked at me as she hung up the phone. "What are you doing?"

"I'm gonna need this back."

"Why?"

"Bring me a big slice of coconut cream and come sit down. I've just gotten myself into a load of trouble."

CHAPTER ELEVEN

I can't really say what made me drive out to Barney's farm Tuesday morning. Frank had already questioned him—none too kindly, I expect—but nothing concrete had come from it. At least not that the chief had shared with me.

I suppose I wanted to see for myself if Barney really was capable of something so sinister. He'd obviously denied any part in the incident or Frank would have locked him up. Tossed him in what he often called "our special accommodations"—which had to be wording Angie thought up.

As I drove past the roadside fence of Barnyard Farms, I caught sight of the protest flock. Their red protest symbols had half washed off in last night's rain, leaving them looking a weary, blotchy pink. It was better than bloody, I suppose, but I still felt a ridiculous urge to apologize to them as they looked up at my passing car.

"I'm sorry you all got dragged into this," I said to

absolutely no one. "I'm sorry we all got dragged into this, actually."

While I half expected at least one of them to look up at me with knowing sheepy eyes and bleat, "Tell me about it, sister," of course none of them did. They barely even registered my passing as I pulled into the long lane that ran up to Barney's house and barn.

Even before I turned off the ignition, Barney came loping out of the barn with an annoyed look in his eye. "Guess this is my week for company."

"Really?" I replied, not quite sure whether or not to reveal what I knew.

"Frank was up here yesterday asking all kinds of questions."

I got out of the car and pasted a friendly look on my face. That took a bit of effort with the vision of shepherd's crooks in doors and ventilation fans dancing in my brain. "Well, that is his job."

He walked right up to square his shoulders at me, direct as ever. "Much as I'd have liked to, I didn't do harm to your nasty lady."

So Frank *had* confronted him. I chose not to reply.

"Oh, I know Frank thinks I did on account of those crooks, but come on, Libby. You and I both know how silly that is."

As silly as spray-painting your sheep and parading them down Collin Avenue? "What did Frank tell you?"

Barney tucked his hands in his pockets and rocked back on his heels. "That he wasn't one hundred percent sure that lady's death was an accident."

I found it interesting that Barney seemed to be going out of his way not to mention her name. "What do you think?"

"I didn't like her. Not her, not what she stood for. It's hard enough to eke out a living as a sheep farmer these days without nutcases like her giving people ideas. You don't like wool? Fine. Don't buy wool. But don't go telling folks they're some kind of awful for liking it." He walked over to the fence and gave a small whistle, and I watched in amazement as the sheep trotted over to him like loyal puppies. "Did you know it's healthy to shear a sheep? It's good for 'em."

"I had heard that, yes."

I had. Even though I'm not in the sheep business, I watched a story on the news a year or so back about a merino sheep found lost in the wild that hadn't been shorn in six years. The poor fellow could barely walk and had all sorts of skin problems from carrying around more than sixty pounds of excess fleece. He was nearly blinded by the fleece covering his eyes. If Julie contended that shearing was cruel to animals, I didn't see how that poor sheep's unattended state was any less cruel.

"'Course they put up a bit of a fuss when they're young, but all my girls enjoy it after they figure out it don't hurt and feels good."

One of the ewes, still sporting the splotches of her protest message, pushed her black face into Barney's open hand in a gesture that looked very much like affection.

"There are things about their health we can't usually tell until we shear 'em. And even you know there's no better fiber in the world for keeping warm and such." He stroked the ewe's ears with obvious love. "No, sir, I don't like her kind."

"Enough to kill her?" I almost asked. "Well, you certainly made that clear."

Barney chuckled. "Most fun I've had in months. When that Wagner fellow sent me that video of what the other farmers had done, I went straight to the hardware store and bought me a case of red paint."

"*Yale Wagner* sent you that video?" I could barely believe my ears.

"Yup. A couple of weeks before she got here. Funny name for a guy, don't you think?"

"Why did Julie's brother-in-law show you a video of other sheep farmers protesting her?" It sounded suspiciously like inciting a riot. Or the sheep version of a riot.

"I got the feeling he wasn't much of a fan of hers neither. He said he thought it'd be newsworthy. Beating that Julie woman at her own game. I liked the sound of that."

I bet Yale had liked the sound of that, too. Great television in the making. Did it matter at all that it deepened the divide between his wife and her sister? I gave Barney a you-should-know-better scowl.

"Oh, come now. I didn't mean any harm by it. Me and the boys just wanted to get our point across as clear as she got hers."

"You protested my event, Barney. And Gavin's festival." I felt as if I was scolding a schoolboy for a prank that had gotten out of hand. That wasn't too far off the truth, was it?

"Not you, her. We woulda left the festival alone."

I decided to get to the heart of the matter. "And the crooks in the fans? Mom said you were knocking back quite a few at Tom's diner that night, all proud of yourselves. Was it about more than just your parade?"

Something flashed across his eyes. Regret? Fear? It was only for a second before he jutted his chin out. "I just got done telling you I didn't do that. Come off it, Libby. I was proud of the girls. We made our point. And we made the local TV station, too."

"Her death also made the local news."

I wanted to make sure he understood that the stunt hadn't been harmless at all. He could deny all he wanted, but I wasn't convinced that he was innocent. Besides, even if Barney hadn't been the one to shut down the ventilation system, I could have argued that he had egged on whoever had.

"Aren't you listening? I didn't have nothin' to do with how she died. I told Frank that, too."

"And you have no idea who might have done such a thing?" I felt brave enough to press my point. "It might have been what killed her, you know. She suffocated in the dye fumes."

We didn't actually know that for sure yet, but it was pretty obvious from where I stood.

Barney turned on me. "Are you saying you think I *killed* her?"

My own desire to see Julie vindicated shouted down Frank's warnings about classifying her death as murder. "I think it's possible someone did."

"That's exactly what Frank said," Barney muttered.

I felt better about stepping over that line now that I knew Frank had already crossed it.

"I didn't put those crooks in that door or on those fans," he declared so loudly, some of the sheep scattered at the noise. He did that gesture rural men so frequently used to show annoyance—swiping off a ball cap, running a hand over their crew cuts, and shoving the cap back on their heads with frustrated force. "What kind of fool person would leave something like that behind if

they did?" He seemed genuinely ticked at being associated with the act—much more than Mom's suspicious
description had led me to believe. "Might as well have
signed my name on her forehead. Shepherd's crooks. For
crying out loud."

The same thought had occurred to me. Barney could
be a bit of a blunt instrument at times. I'd heard him
spout off more than once at a town council meeting—or,
as Mom had witnessed, when he'd had a few too many in
the local bar. But he didn't strike me as the kind to make
such an obvious blunder as to sign a murder with a clue
that pointed so blatantly back to him.

Which led me to the next logical conclusion: "What
if someone wants us to think you did it? You did announce your dislike of her pretty loudly."

My father's constant childhood advice to never use
the word "hate" when talking about another human being still stuck with me. "You can hate an act, you can
hate an idea, you can hate brussels sprouts, but you can't
hate a person."

Barney narrowed his eyes. "You sayin' I've been
framed?"

His question worried me. I was sure Frank had come
to the same conclusion—probably faster than I had. Why
hadn't he raised it? This was why it was dangerous to
play junior detective; I was likely to mess things up for
the people who knew what they were doing.

"It's possible, don't you think?" I posed.

His lined face scrunched up into an irritated frown.
"Well, who'd want to do that?"

Barney, like most prickly people, was oblivious to
how much he rubbed people the wrong way. Perhaps he
thought the whole world loved him and followed him

like his sheep. Trust me, they didn't. In fact, I'd say that if someone really had framed Barney, they'd picked a likely target. I saw Barney's gentle way with his animals, but most people didn't. They just saw the crotchety old coot who griped about a long list of things every time you bumped into him at the hardware store. They, like Mom, would all too easily embrace the idea that old Barney had finally had enough and gone homicidal.

"I don't know, Barney." I tried to take a helpful tone. "Can you account for where you were before you were at the diner that night?"

He scowled. "What, are you taking lessons from Frank on this?"

So Frank had already asked him for an alibi. "I'm just upset about my event."

That was true. I was upset. I did want to find out what had really happened to Julie. I felt as if I was suffocating under the weight of another murder associated with Y.A.R.N. In the middle of the night last night, I had shot up, wide-awake from a terrible nightmare that someone had barred me inside my house with a shepherd's crook and set the house on fire. After all, if someone had hated—yes, I decided it was okay to use that word in this context—Julie enough to end her life, they could have been considering real harm to Y.A.R.N. for hosting her. Or to me.

Barney grunted. "I didn't do it. I wasn't anywhere Frank could write down in his little book when it happened. I don't own any stupid crooks and me and the girls have said our piece on it." He adjusted his hat again in a way that let me know our conversation was over.

As I was turning toward my car, Barney said, "Sorry 'bout it all."

I turned back. "Sorry" was the last thing I would have expected from him.

"Thank you. It's a terrible thing. It was going to be a really interesting event. And she did beautiful work."

The moment of grace I'd seen in Barney's eyes faded, replaced by the sour look that usually filled his features. "Shoulda stuck to that."

As I drove back down the drive, the raised heads of sheep seeing me off, I found I couldn't say if I thought Barney was innocent or guilty. Both seemed entirely possible. And now I knew that Yale Wagner was more agitator than spectator in this drama. What did that mean?

I was still busy pondering the whole tangle when something on the side of the road caught the corner of my eye. I slammed on the brakes, pulled off to the shoulder, and got out of the car to look.

There, up against the far corner of the fence lining Barney's farm, was a shepherd's crook. Almost exactly like the ones Frank found at the warehouse.

I'm not sure what I did was legal or even ethical, but I invoked the junior detective's margin of error and did it anyway. I ran back to my car and grabbed one of the plastic grocery bags I always keep in my glove box. Using it, I picked up the staff and tucked it in my trunk.

I didn't know if Frank could get prints off weathered old wood, but I was sure going to give him the chance to try.

CHAPTER TWELVE

I set the basket of pineapple fiber yarn down on the counter at the Corner Stone coffeehouse and smoothie bar Wednesday morning. "So, what do you think?" I asked Paul Everly, the friendly and energetic former tax auditor who ran the place.

Paul stared at the cheerfully decorated basket. I'd run my idea by him over the phone earlier, but I figured he needed to see what I meant to truly understand the clever scheme Linda and I had come up with yesterday afternoon. Without Julie's inspiring speeches and demonstrations, I needed an alternate plan to draw people into the shop and sell the load of plant fiber yarns I now had on hand.

Paul picked up one of the brightly dyed mini skeins that filled the basket. "Pineapple smoothie yarn? This stuff is made from pineapples? Really?"

He sniffed the yarn as if it came in scratch-and-sniff varieties. I had just come from the florist with a basket of rose fiber yarn and she'd done the same thing.

"The fiber from the plants, actually," I explained. "Not the fruit itself. But still, I figure people who like smoothies might like the idea of pineapple fiber yarn. You keep the dollar for every skein you sell. But if they bring the tag to the shop, I give them a discount on anything they buy."

"Really?" A woman buying a smoothie next to me at the counter leaned in and peered into the basket. "From pineapples? Can I see that?"

I would qualify my smile as only half smug as I handed one of the mini skeins over to the curious woman. "Feel how soft it is. And don't you just love the colors?"

"You're the yarn shop lady, aren't you?" the woman asked. "I've been meaning to come in. Can I crochet with this?"

"Absolutely," I replied. "I'm Libby."

"The Give Me LIBBertY gal, right? Very clever." She slid her mini skein across the counter to the young woman ringing up her smoothie. "I'll take one. No, actually, give me one in each color. For each of my friends over there."

She pointed to a trio of women sitting over by the window. They reminded me of a younger version of Mom's Gals. "I'm Sylvia." She held out her hand.

I shook her hand and pulled out three more mini skeins and added them to the one on the counter. "When you bring these into the shop, Sylvia, I'll give you a discount on whatever you buy. We have groups of friends come in and knit or crochet together all the time."

Paul perked up with the energy of a new idea gleaming in his bright blue eyes. "Tell you what. If you buy one of our travel mugs and use that yarn to make a cozy for it, I'll give you your first three refills at half price."

"I like the sound of that," Sylvia said.

She added a Corner Stone travel mug to her purchases. I'd sold my first four mini skeins and hopefully met some new customers.

"Pretty clever deal you two have worked out here. That's the kind of person who ought to be running our Chamber of Commerce, if you ask me."

Paul grinned. Arlene had told me he'd been one of the first people to post a Give Me LIBBertY poster. "I couldn't agree more." He shifted the basket to a prominent place beside the cash register. "How many more of these you got?"

Suddenly the pile of event-related yarn gnawing at me from my stockroom didn't seem so daunting. "Loads."

"I'm thinking we're gonna need it."

The sense of a partnership went a long way in calming the anxiety I'd been fighting. Every business was bound to have its ups and downs, but the more we collaborated, the stronger we became.

Just as my coffee was ready, Gavin came up behind me. I'd asked him to meet me here for my second agenda item of the morning.

"Early Easter baskets?" he asked as he nodded toward the little display. Given the bright spring colors and the rattan basket, it did look like an early Easter decoration.

"Not exactly. This is my festival comeback plan. It's sort of my version of Margo's tiny tart tastings."

Gavin furrowed his eyebrows as he read the Pineapple Smoothie Yarn tag. "Why do I always find myself asking you to explain things you're doing with yarn?" Gavin asked. "You didn't ask me here to do something with this, did you?"

I bought our coffees and settled us in at a booth. "You're not involved with this part." I tried not to emphasize the "this part." "I need your help with something else."

I was just about to launch into my request for Gavin to coach me on the finer points of public speech and debate when Frank walked in. He pointed a commanding finger at me and said, "Don't leave until I talk to you. I've got a question."

Within a minute or so he set his to-go cup of basic coffee—Frank didn't do what he called "those ridiculous fancy coffees"—down on the table and took a seat next to Gavin. "Is there a yarn-related reason why toxicology found sodium hydroxide in Julie Wilson's system?"

"Sodium hydroxide?" I asked. "What is that?"

"It's closely related to sodium carbonate. More commonly called soda ash." Something about the way he used the word "commonly" told me there was something uncommon in why he was asking me.

"Well, there is a yarn-related reason to use soda ash," I explained. "It's used in many dyeing processes. Especially the ones with plant-based fibers like Julie used. So I suppose I wouldn't be surprised. But no one really knows what she used, so I can't be sure."

Frank leaned in and lowered his voice. "Would she have a reason to use pure chemical-grade sodium hydroxide?"

"Is there a garden variety?" Gavin asked.

"As a matter of fact, you could buy lye—which is essentially what sodium hydroxide is—at any hardware store," Frank replied. "But not this stuff. The grade they found in her system was the industrial-chemical kind. Highly caustic. Not the kind of thing just any old person should be messing with. Burns the skin. Burns the eyes. Burns lots of things, actually."

"I didn't see any burns on Julie's skin. Where'd they find it?"

Frank grimaced. "There were some burns on her face and hands. The color in the dye powder hid it until they cleaned her up. But it was the dose she breathed in that did the real damage. Basically, it disintegrated her respiratory system. The guys tell me if you combined that sodium hydroxide with a few other easily available substances, you could cook up a pretty lethal gas."

"But she had a fancy respirator near her. I remember seeing it." It would be a long time before the vision of her body left my memory.

"Which would mean she knew she was dealing with dangerous substances," Frank offered.

"Well, yes," I replied. "But honestly, I can't see why she'd have to do that. The way most people dye never needs more than a dust mask, some good rubber gloves, and maybe an apron. And ventilation. Julie was really insistent about the good ventilation."

Frank scratched his chin in thought. "So you don't know what she used. You weren't asked to supply any chemicals?"

"No," I replied. "And I wouldn't expect her to ask me. After all, her formulas were her big secret."

"And no one knows where those formulas are now?"

I thought of the decorated cloth envelope. "No. I'd guess they were in that empty cloth recipe folder, but not anymore. I would have thought they would be in the warehouse with her, but they weren't there, either. So she either hid them somewhere else, or someone took them. After all, Bev still hasn't found that missing key to her room at the inn." I had a hard time believing Julie's formulas were valuable enough to kill for, but who knew?

"Can you think of a reason she would have knowingly used a dangerous chemical like that in her dyeing process?"

"Common soda ash, yes. But that chemical?" I pushed out a breath, stumped. "Still, no one knows how she got the colors she did. Monica told me she threw substances together all the time and even got sick a couple of times from whatever she'd combined. Seems easy to believe she developed some kind of risky process involving something more dangerous than the common stuff."

Gavin was starting to look worried. "Julie should have been more forthright with you about any dangerous elements in her secret formulas."

I was suddenly following Frank's thinking. "Unless she didn't know it was in there. The jar we did find in her room was common stuff, nothing that should have harmed her. Could someone have sabotaged Julie's ingredients?"

Frank checked a page on his notepad. "This industrial stuff is a granular white powder. She might not have noticed it if it looks the same as whatever she normally used."

Gavin glanced at the container of sugar sitting at our table. "A million things are made up of granular white powders."

Frank looked back up at me. "And then there's the hot water."

"I wondered about that. Most people don't use hot

water for plant fibers, but I just figured it was part of Julie's method since she requested burners. She said it was hot and steamy work. And the water in those pans was still warm when we got in there. But why does the hot water matter?"

"Because according to my guys, this stuff will"—he read from his notes—"'boil explosively when added to hot water.'"

All kinds of nasty possibilities were storming my imagination. "Wait," I said, leaning in and lowering my voice. We were discussing a murder, after all. Not exactly standard coffeeshop conversation. "So someone could have swapped this dangerous stuff with whatever is the regular powder in Julie's supplies, and they wouldn't have had to be there to kill her because she would have started the reaction herself by mixing them." It was ingenious in a blood-chilling sort of way.

"That's one possibility. But they'd have to have seen Julie's formula to know that was possible."

And as far as I knew, no one knew Julie's formulas but Julie herself. "There's also the respirator. If she had that rather than a simple dust mask, Julie knew what she was doing was dangerous."

"And the lack of ventilation is what killed her," Gavin surmised.

This kept getting more complex by the minute. "We have no way of knowing without seeing her formula."

The three of us sat for a minute, contemplating what a tangled mess this had become.

"Then there's the crooks in the door and the fans. And the other one. How do those fit in to all this?" I asked.

Gavin's attention snapped to me. "There is a fourth crook?"

I told him about finding the shepherd's crook at the edge of Barney's farm.

"You didn't double back and confront him or anything, did you?" Mayor Maddock has a protective streak a mile wide, frequently aimed in my direction.

"Of course I did no such thing," I replied. It had actually never occurred to me, but I wasn't going to admit that to Gavin. "I brought it straight to Frank to see if he could lift prints."

Frank raised an eyebrow at my proper use of police nomenclature. I still hadn't decided whether to be proud or annoyed at my growing detective skills. This wasn't really a body of knowledge I was pleased to obtain.

The chief's response was a frustrated grunt. "It's nearly impossible to lift prints off any of those staffs. We checked them for fibers or plant residue, but we didn't come up with anything helpful."

"Well, it still points in Barney's direction, doesn't it?" Gavin scowled.

"Or it's just made to look like that," I revised. "After all, Barney literally paraded his dislike for Julie and what she stood for down the middle of town. And Julie said other sheep farmers have done something similar—that's how Yale knew to send him the video. You wouldn't even have to have known him to pick him out as a likely suspect."

Suddenly I wondered if Yale was behind this. Why? Nothing made sense.

Frank put his notebook away. "With no prints or fibers on the crooks, anyone is now a suspect."

Gavin sank his head into one hand. I knew he felt his marvelous festival had gained a huge dark cloud, and he wasn't wrong about that.

Frank tried to cheer him up. "The good news—if you can call it that—is that this seems to be about Julie. It's not an effort to damage the festival or the town. Or even you, Libby. We just happened to be the circumstances."

Gavin wasn't convinced. "I had one of the chefs pull out and go home yesterday. Jillian told me CollinstownProtest-Sheep has become a hashtag. That's not my definition of great press."

"Anyone can make a dumb hashtag," I tried to console Gavin. "Most of them last only days, if not minutes."

"This one can't die fast enough if you ask me."

Gavin's lips thinned at the verb. Suddenly "die" or "dye" had a connotation none of us welcomed.

"Julie told me she got protests like that all the time. We weren't her first herd of spray-painted sheep," I continued, finding the classification absurd. "If they wanted to bother her, they didn't. In fact, she actually seemed pleased Barney and his buddies did what they did. I think she enjoyed stirring up the controversy. Wanted it."

"Well, they may not have bothered her, but they certainly succeeded in killing her." Frank's jaw tightened. "What they won't succeed in is taking us down with her. We're going to nail this guy, whoever he is. Not Collinstown or your shop," he said, looking at me, "or your festival," he added with a steady gaze at Gavin, "is going down on account of this. You have my word. This idiot doesn't get the final say. Hear me?"

"Thank you, Frank."

But even as I thanked him, I thought of the bitter words I'd heard slung between Monica and Julie. They clashed so harshly with the regret that seemed to fill Monica's eyes and radiate off her. What if Monica was more than just the surviving sister?

"Unless 'this guy' is a she?"

"Monica." Gavin sank farther down into his seat.

Frank nodded. "Wouldn't surprise me. Sibling jealousy is one of the oldest motives in the book. Although she was visible at the restaurant at the time."

"You just said the killer didn't need to be in the warehouse with Julie." I took another sip of my coffee, then thought out loud. "She could have felt the protest gave Julie all the attention. I mean, they argued about who had the better hotel room. They were certainly competitive."

"Monica was the highest-profile special guest before Barney shifted the focus to Julie," Gavin added. "I did have two reporters ask if they could swap out their interviews with Monica to talk to Julie instead after the whole sheep thing."

"Really?" Maybe Julie's high-friction personality wasn't just her nature. Maybe it was extremely clever marketing.

"That'd tick me off if it was my sister. Or the star of my own TV show." The chief grunted. "So everyone's got a motive, and anyone could have used the crooks as a weapon."

"But who has the access to the sodium hydroxide and the knowledge to use it," I asked, "without hurting themselves?"

"Now, that," replied Frank, "is a question that needs answering." He produced a grim smirk. "Maybe we can add it to your debate with George?"

Gavin nearly did a spit take with his coffee. "You're debating George?"

So much for my gentle introduction of the idea to Gavin. "More like a town hall. To replace the highly objectionable campaign signs."

Gavin's scowl filled his face. "That's a terrible idea. Who are you going to find to moderate that circus?"

Both Frank and I smiled and nodded our heads in Gavin's direction.

CHAPTER THIRTEEN

As we walked out of the Corner Stone, Frank turned to me with a serious look in his eyes. "Keep your distance for a while, Libby. I've told Yale and Monica we have reason to believe Julie's death wasn't an accident now. Things are volatile. Don't go poking your nose around in things this time."

So like any upstanding but wildly curious citizen, I waited until Frank was in his office a full twenty minutes before I headed over to the inn to see Monica and Yale. It was just a sympathy call, a common courtesy. With a few carefully and sensitively asked questions.

Monica had not taken the department's current theory well. "They said it was an accident."

She looked at me as if I had lied to her as well. By omitting what I'd known, I suppose on some level I had.

"Frank thought whoever did this was looking to make

a public point. I think he hoped to frustrate his or her efforts by keeping his theories of murder quiet."

"You don't keep a murder quiet," Monica said with wounded eyes. "Who keeps a murder quiet?"

Yale looked aggravated, as if maybe he agreed with Frank. I could believe that Yale probably thought Julie's murder had somehow upstaged his fine marketing plans.

Monica sank down on the couch with a whimper. "Julie," she whispered with such regret I felt it tighten my own throat. "Murdered." Her shoulders seemed to fold in on themselves and she drew her arms around her chest.

"Monica," I said with the softest tone I could manage, "is there anyone who might want to see your sister dead?"

Yale laughed out loud at that. I agreed Julie had a talent for ticking people off, but I didn't see how it was worth a laugh. Even difficult people deserved to keep breathing.

"He's right," Monica conceded. "It'd be a long list. She gets threatened all the time. I kept telling her that the publicity wasn't worth it, that she should take it down a notch. Mom and Dad were after her to tone it down for months. She just kept right on. Not that she ever listens— *listened* to any of us." Her voice caught on the correction to past tense.

"Did she ever mention anyone in specific who had her worried, who made threats that seemed like histrionics at the time?"

Monica's head sank into her hands and I wondered if defying Frank's steer-clear order had been a good idea. To lose a sister to an early death was one kind of tragedy, but to have that sister murdered seemed another level of grief altogether.

"Julie did tell me she'd been threatened. Many times,"

I continued, hoping to get Monica to talk. "I have to admit, I was kind of amazed how easily she brushed it off."

"Brushed it off?" Yale laughed again.

I kept waiting for him to go over and console his wife. The fact that he didn't seemed cold. I hadn't seen them be very affectionate with each other their entire visit, but stress could do that to people.

"She enjoyed it," Yale went on. "My sister-in-law wasn't happy if she wasn't goading someone into an argument."

Again, being difficult wasn't justification for someone to die. Yale was getting on my nerves.

I met his irritated gaze. "Well, I don't know that I'd call emailing videos with protest ideas to Barney and his sheep farmer buddies anything less."

Monica's head shot up from her hands. "What?"

So she hadn't known. That spoke volumes, didn't it?

"Julie told me this wasn't the first time people met her with the kind of protest Barney staged. There are videos of people doing it online. Barney told me Yale sent him links to those videos before the two of you arrived."

Yale's irritated look dissolved into a guilty grimace. If they weren't a happy couple now, I'd just thrust a whopping wedge between them.

"Did you?" Monica demanded.

"It's not like you think," Yale backpedaled. "I was talking to some local farmers, trying to set up a farm-to-table thing for your lamb chops."

That struck me as ridiculous. Watching how some local farmer grew luscious strawberries or tended to happy hens that gave you beautiful eggs was one thing. Watching lambs frolic on the grass knowing you were going to butcher one and eat it for dinner? That seemed less like something informative and more like something guaranteed to ruin your appetite.

My attitude must have shown on my face, because Yale glared at me. "Every show needs B-roll. It can't all be shots of Monica, pots, and pans."

"I thought we agreed we weren't going to do the lamb chops," Monica declared, eyebrows furrowed. She'd shifted from sorrow to anger remarkably fast—the classic volatile chef personality, I suppose. "To keep things calmer with Julie."

I could just imagine how Julie would have responded to the promotion for a lamb chop dinner by her own sister.

"The farms are right here. We didn't have to use the B-roll if we decided against it, but I wanted it on file in case you changed your mind."

"Did you, now?" Monica's words were as sharp as any chef's knife.

"But you did send Barney links to videos?" I cut in.

Yale huffed, then began pacing the room as he spoke. "Barney and I got into a conversation, and he mentioned how he'd have liked to make a great big point against Julie's position. I told him I'd seen someone else do a pretty good job of that and sent him the links to a few videos. I didn't really expect him to act on it. I didn't even believe he hadn't seen something like it before. Julie told me these farmers gang up against her all the time. I didn't see the harm in it; I was just trying to get on his good side."

"She's dead, Yale." Monica's voice rose in pitch. "Where's the good side in that? What if he killed her?" She stood up from the couch and squared off with her husband. "What if you riled up the sheep farmers so much that they didn't just parade their flocks down the street—they killed her?"

"That's ridiculous," Yale replied, his voice pitching up to match Monica's.

"Not when you consider the warehouse door and its ventilation fans were jammed by shepherd's crooks," I said.

Monica's face went white. Evidently Frank had left that detail out. I might get a talking-to for that slip. But if whoever had done that had been going for shock value, I was staring at proof they'd hit it spot on.

"And I found another crook just like it on Barney's property yesterday," I added. The words flew out of my mouth before I had a chance to consider the wisdom of that addition.

Yale's face paled a bit at that news. Even if he hadn't meant to incite those farmers to murder, it was quite possible that he had. So far he had struck me as the kind of man who felt there was no such thing as "too far" in terms of publicity, so I was grateful to see the news hit him as hard as it had. Would that make him an accessory to murder?

Monica turned to me. "So they've arrested him."

"Well, no. I think we'd all agree he has motive, but there doesn't seem to be enough evidence to arrest him."

"You did this," Monica snapped at Yale.

"Oh, I think Barney hated Julie long before I came along," Yale shot back. "I'll admit I may have stoked the fire a bit, but the flames were already going strong."

Who uses so poetic a metaphor when talking about inciting someone to murder? Was that a crime? I knew "inciting to riot" was, but I wasn't sure a herd of spray-painted sheep counted as a riot.

When Monica's glare didn't let up, Yale added, "I didn't mean any harm by it."

Monica got up and went to the window as if she couldn't bear the sight of her husband at the moment. From behind, framed by one of the inn's beautiful old windows, she looked very much like her sister. Monica's hair was the same color as Julie's—a lovely chestnut brown—but Julie's had been an artistic long and wavy mane whereas the woman in front of me wore a sharp, efficient bob. They had the same medium build, and I watched Monica run her hand along the back of her neck in a gesture I'd seen Julie do several times.

An uncomfortable silence filled the room, and I wondered if I ought to leave.

"For Pete's sake, Yale. Did you even think to talk to me about this? Ask my opinion?"

This wasn't just a small spat. I got the distinct impression we were looking at the last straw in a long-simmering professional and perhaps even personal argument. Yale's "stoked the fire a bit, but the flames were already going strong" reflected back on his own marriage.

"It is *my* show, after all." Her icy emphasis spoke volumes.

They both looked like they were about to really get into it when I realized I had an opportunity here. "Yale, I wonder if you could show me one of the videos in question."

"The ones I sent Barney?" he asked, looking none too eager to do so.

I'll bet he wasn't eager.

"Yes," Monica shot back. "I'd like to see it myself."

Reluctantly, Yale walked over to his laptop on the

nearby desk and flipped it open. After a few clicks, he pivoted the screen so we all could watch, and he hit the icon to play. The video started off with a misty pasture somewhere outside a postcard-perfect small farm town. But it quickly transformed into a sequence of yelling farmers and unflattering stills of Julie speaking. Then it cut to clips of one farmer using red spray paint and a set of stencils to paint messages like *WOOL IS GOOD* and *SHUT UP, JULIE WILSON*. Their method was slightly different—these were painted on shorn sheep so the lettering was clearer—but it wasn't hard to see Barney's inspiration. Especially when this herd was shown clogging the streets outside a yarn shop with a sign promoting one of Julie's appearances.

"She's bad-mouthing our livelihood," one farmer yelled. "Shut her down and shut her up—that's what I say. We're all sick of it."

A chill ran down my spine as another farmer stepped into the shot and shouted, "She ought to watch her back, that one. Wouldn't surprise me if one of these days some farmer makes her really regret it."

The prediction in those words kept us all silent for a moment. Someone had made sure Julie regretted it. Permanently.

Monica whirled on Yale. "You *sent* that to the sheep farmers? *Here?*"

Yale pointed to the stats on the page. "Did you see how many views this thing got? You can't blame this on just me."

"I'm sure *you* took careful note of how many views it got." Monica put her hand on her forehead. "Why did it have to be against Julie? If you wanted publicity, there were other ways to go about it. Why is it always about what Julie does?"

It seemed to me she asked that last question to the world in general, not her husband.

I memorized the title of the video so I could show it to Frank. "Did you send this to anyone other than Barney?"

"No," Yale replied. "But he did tell me he was going to share it with some friends."

"Did you get the sense he was going to do something like it?"

Barney obviously had imitated the protest in the video. If Yale had known the protest was being planned and kept it quiet, everything looked much more suspicious.

"He told me how much he liked the idea, yes. And he also said we were welcome to come out to the farm and film whatever we liked." Yale turned to Monica. "Which was the whole point of my contacting him, I might add."

"Hell of a way to grease the wheel, Yale," Monica muttered, seething.

I took that as my cue to exit. Smart move, too, because even before I got halfway down the hall to the stairs, I could hear the beginning of a shouting match between Monica and Yale. *Dish Up Comfort* was going to have a long, hard stint in Collinstown—that was for certain.

I walked back to the shop and tried to calm my frazzled nerves with a few tedious shop tasks. It wasn't working. I was actually glad to see Mom waltz into the store with a wide smile on her face about an hour after lunch.

"I raised a brilliant daughter. Can I just say that?"

I was up for any compliment and encouragement I could find. "Of course you can. Any particular reason why?"

"I just came from the flower shop. I was walking by on my way back from lunch with the Gals and spotted your basket in the window." She winked and pointed a finger at me. "Clever."

"Well, it is one of the newest plant-based fibers. And did you feel it?"

"It's silky soft."

Mom reached into her handbag. Evidently she'd purchased one of the tiny dollar skeins I'd made and brought it into the shop for her discount. My mom does not need a discount from my store, but she's one of those coupon-hoarding seniors who can never pass up a sale.

"I'd have given you a whole skein. You didn't have to buy it at the flower shop."

She straightened up. "You're my daughter. I'm supporting anything you do. Especially something so smart as this." She waved the small lustrous skein in my direction. "I talked the two people behind me in line into doing the same thing. Where else do you have these around town?"

"I've got a basket with hemp at the hardware store and one with banana fiber at the grocery store and a pineapple one at Corner Stone."

It was working. I'd had five people come into the shop today alone—two of whom were brand-new to knitting. I was starting to think I really could give Margo's tiny tarts a run for their money in the clever-marketing-scheme department.

Mom set down her handbag on the store's center table and went to grab a cup of coffee. "The other ones I get, but the hardware store?"

"They used to use hemp to make rope and twine. It's kind of a thin connection, but I figure it couldn't hurt."

Mom gave a dubious grunt. "I'm not so sure how many knitters you're gonna discover among the garden tools and grass seed."

"Maybe I should send you over there."

"Not now. I'm due at the library at two."

I glanced at my watch. It was two twenty. "You're late. You should have come here after the library."

"Well, I need your card. I can't find mine again, and I'm too chicken to admit it to Theresa."

Theresa Porter was the nicest librarian I'd ever met. "She's not going to mind." Mom's sheepish look told me there was more to the story. "Um, how many times have you lost your card, Mom?"

Mom busied herself with the coffee creamer. "This year?"

It was barely April. Somehow I knew if I asked for a lifetime total, I wouldn't find the number reassuring.

Rather than wait for an answer, I continued. "Why don't you get the little plastic one you can add to your key chain?" Right after I said that, I found myself wondering how many times Mom had misplaced her keys so far this year. Maybe adding her library card to her key chain wasn't so great an idea.

Mom certainly didn't think so. "Those are silly," she replied, waving the idea off. "A library card should be a card, not some trinket dangling on your key chain. They don't make those for your driver's license or your credit card, now do they?" Mom held libraries in high esteem, and evidently that extended to library cards.

I ducked into the office and fished my library card out of my wallet. "Theresa will know anyway if you use my card."

"Not if I go to that other gal at the other desk. I'll just watch for when Theresa goes to help another person. Then I can pick up my copy of *Hunger Games* and get started while I figure out where my card is."

The title surprised me. "I didn't peg you for a *Hunger Games* fan."

"Well, it does sound rather angsty, but Jillian and I have this little two-person book group and it was her turn to choose. Want to join? We knit while we talk sometimes."

"I wish I had that kind of time. But no, I like that it's your and Jillian's thing."

"Suit yourself." Mom began sorting through the basket of rose fiber full skeins, picking out the mint green color. "Does this stuff wash up well? I want to make a chemo cap for Edna Anderson. She found out it came back last week." Mom made the *tsk*ing sound she always did for sad or bad news. "And she was just getting all that gorgeous hair back."

I walked over to join Mom at the basket. "I wouldn't throw it in the machine, but you're right, it would feel gorgeous and look great." I loved how Mom was always so generous with her knitting. In fact, I couldn't remember the last time she'd made something for herself. I pointed to the small pink skein in her hand from the flower shop. "You could use the little one to make rosebuds going around the brim."

"Edna would love that." She snatched up the green skein. "Put it on my tab."

I handed Mom my library card, wondering if I would ever see it again. "Sure thing."

Mom did technically run a tab at the shop, but I've never been able to bring myself to ask her to settle up. She was practically a member of the staff and the champion of my marketing team, and she had brought in more baked goods for us than she took home yarn.

"Edna's daughter decided to move up the wedding so Edna would have hair for the pictures."

This was a tender topic. Edna's daughter, Wendy, had been through a nasty divorce about the same time as mine, and her impending remarriage brought out Mom's competitive streak. I was in no mood to fend off some imagined race to the altar to prove I was putting my life back together with the same skill as Wendy.

"That's sweet of Wendy." I tried to keep my words neutral.

"Edna just wants to see her daughter happy." The unspoken "I do, too" practically echoed off the shop walls. She made a dramatic face. "None of us'll be around forever, sweetheart."

I pulled the skein from Mom's hand and went through the motions of recording the sale at the cash register. "Oh, Mom, we'll be celebrating your hundredth no doubt."

Mom was only seventy-one. She had plenty of time to see me happy the way I figured it. And quite frankly, I thought I was pretty happy now. Well, when I wasn't coping with recently deceased special guests, that is. That did feel like it sped up my aging process a bit.

"You could—" she began.

I cut her off instantaneously. "Nope. Don't go there."

"It's not as if . . ." she persisted.

I gave Mom my darkest glower. "We're not having this conversation."

She blinked at me with innocent who-me? eyes. "What conversation is that?"

My mother is a conversational ninja. If I told her to stop talking about Gavin and me, we'd *already* be talking about Gavin and me, wouldn't we? I deployed the biggest diversion I had.

"Frank has a new theory as to what happened to Julie."

It worked. "Ooh . . . what?"

This was going to require some conversational ninja skills of my own. "They found a nasty chemical on her skin and in her lungs. The common form is used in dyes—soda ash—but the high-potency industrial grade can do a number on your respiratory system. Nobody's sure, but we're thinking the industrial grade may have been part of Julie's secret dyeing formula."

"Like a chemical spill." I watched Mom connect the details, eyes narrowed in thought. "Industrial chemicals." She gave me a direct look. "Are you saying it wasn't an accident?"

"Well . . ."

Mom picked up on my hesitation instantly. "Frank thinks Julie Wilson was murdered, doesn't he?"

"It seems that's a possibility. Someone definitely set out to harm her."

I hated how frail and victimized I sounded. I was having a hard time not feeling like there was a target on my back.

Her shock was oddly comforting. "Honey, that's awful!". I wasn't so sure about the determination that filled her features when she added, "We've got to figure out who did it. And fast. This isn't the kind of thing you want to get around."

Rather late for that, I thought.

CHAPTER FOURTEEN

When Gavin asked me if I'd like to make another attempt at our quiet dinner that night, I said yes right away. I was fully ready to eat my feelings, and his suggestion of Lilly's by the Bay sounded like the perfect place to do it.

Gavin's eyes, closed in carnivorous bliss beside me, told me I was not alone as I sank my teeth into delectable fried chicken. We told ourselves we were just trying to attend as many festival events as we could, doing our part to support the town and not let Julie's death—now Julie's murder—derail the event. But mostly, we were trying to make ourselves feel better.

Lilly's was one of the newer local restaurants in town. Lilly Sorrington had recently moved her Southern-style restaurant here from the Delaware Bay, choosing to keep the name even though she was now on a river. She was one of those silky classic Southern women who could wield "bless your heart" as both a compliment and a curse, and managed to make pearls work with every single outfit, no matter how casual. I didn't know her well yet, but I liked her. She struck me as more of a needlepoint person than a knitter, but I could work with that. All needlecrafts were interconnected in my worldview. And heaven knew the woman could certainly cook.

Lilly wasn't doing today's cooking, however. She was hosting a guest-chef appearance by another woman with a dozen popular cookbooks to her name. Gavin and I were sampling a collection of classic Southern dishes from the chef's latest release. There was enough lard and corn bread in front of me to keep a cardiologist in business for decades, but all of it so delicious and soothing, I couldn't bring myself to care. After all, Julie had been an obsessively healthy eater, and here she was with a bright life cut short. The whole thing was succeeding in pushing me toward a less-than-helpful eat-another-dessert-today-because-who-knows-what-tomorrow-will-bring attitude I knew I'd have to curb soon or pay the price.

George's distinctive harsh laugh caught our attention, and both Gavin and I looked across the room to where King George was holding court. It struck me that this moment was a perfect illustration of the differences between George and me. I was attending this event to support my community, to make sure Lilly felt welcome, and to enjoy myself. George, on the other hand, was quite clearly "working the room." I'm not sure the man knew how to have a conversation that didn't contain an agenda—hidden or otherwise.

"Thanks," Gavin said without further explanation.

"For what?" I asked as I licked my fingers shamelessly. Bless my quickly coagulating arteries, this stuff was good.

He managed a startlingly charming smile. "You want the list?"

"Of course I do." After the last six days, I was ready to hoard all the gratitude I could find.

Gavin flushed just a bit as if he hadn't counted on being asked to elaborate. "For being here. For supporting the festival even though I know you didn't take to the idea at first."

Now it was my turn to feel my checks heat up. I thought I'd hidden my initial dislike of the See More Than Seafood Festival. I did come around, but I'll never tell Gavin how ridiculous I found the idea when he first proposed it. Who held a festival that was all about what it *wasn't* all about?

Evidently, Collinstown and its very clever mayor did. And rather successfully at that.

I surprised myself by feeling capable of a bit of flirtatious teasing. "That's only two. A list implies more than two."

Gavin smiled back. Every once in a while we allowed ourselves to toe up to the line between friendship and . . . something else. With all that romantic backstory between us, it came far too easily. It never seemed to be deliberate, just sort of creeping up on us—often under surprising circumstances, and usually when Mom and Jillian weren't around. We never could manage it for very long before it began to feel, well, risky. All the history between us simply refused to stay buried. Still, I'd be lying if I said I didn't enjoy it.

He nodded toward George, now pumping hands as if he'd start kissing babies the next minute. Truth was,

George always tried hard to be charming and failed miserably, while Gavin never tried to be charming and still succeeded in a million ways.

"For taking him on," Gavin said. He leaned in so close, I felt my breath catch a bit. "I can't say it publicly, but my life will be a million times better when you are Chamber president."

He said "when," not "if." I noticed the choice of words, and the corners of his eyes crinkled at my resulting smirk of delight. Even when we were young, there had always been something tremendously comforting in knowing Gavin Maddock was in your corner. I think his landslide election as mayor before he even turned forty had a lot to do with the fact that he seeped loyalty out of his pores.

I gave a sigh. "I can't decide if that was brave or foolish."

After all, it had been more frustration than aspiration that drove me to run against George. I mostly just couldn't take him and the way he strutted around Collinstown as if it were his own personal fiefdom. No matter what the initial motivation had been, I still found myself one hundred percent committed to the idea.

"A little bit of both," Gavin conceded. "Then again, I find most good things are."

I suddenly found myself wondering if he'd apply the same thinking to us crossing *that line* in our relationship. It would definitely be both brave and foolish. But staring into his changeable gray eyes, feeling the solid strength of the man and how nice it was to field a list of compliments from him, I was starting to think it might fall under the category of a "good thing."

"For being kind to Jillian," he went on, adding to his list as requested but getting more personal this time.

"I adore Jillian," I replied immediately.

I really did. Sure, I could go without the shameless matchmaking she and Mom seemed to delight in. But she had also hinted sadly during our knitting sessions about how much her mother's inattention stung. I took a personal, quasi-maternal pride in how much she trusted me with her friendship.

"It's not at all hard to be kind to her," I continued. "She's clever, talented, creative, and not afraid to think for herself. What's not to like?"

It was fun to watch fatherly pride gleam in Gavin's eyes. His adoration for his daughter was one of the most attractive things about the man. I'd known even back in high school that he possessed the kind of fierce loyalty that would make him a spectacular father. Had we married and discovered my inability to have children, I am certain he would have adopted. The guy was wired to be a family man.

Sterling seemed almost relieved we couldn't have children, although his mother was famously disappointed in my failure to produce a true family heir. The look my mother-in-law gave me when we learned the "fault" was in *my* genes stung for months and might never leave me.

I dragged my thoughts back to the present and continued my brave flirting. "Anything else? Evidently I'm fishing for compliments tonight. Must be the wine."

There was a long, poignant pause before he said, "For coming home."

Three words that had a hundred words behind them. Gavin couldn't have said anything more powerful. I was thankful myself for my return to Collinstown. Every single day. Even the tough days. The friends I'd returned to like Margo and the new ones I had made—like Linda from the shop, Paul from Corner Stone, and even tonight's host, Lilly—all reminded me how much a community made a rich life.

I had been rich—by economic standards, at least—when I was married to Sterling. But it had been an empty wealth, tangled up with expectations and distractions and outright lies. I was now living on one-third of the assets I'd had with Sterling, but it felt like ten times more. Even my blood pressure had gone down. No easy feat with Mom's antics and the challenges of the store.

I couldn't think of a safe way to respond to Gavin's words and his simmering tone. This wasn't the time or the place to go where we were heading. Still, I allowed myself to drink in the warmth of his gaze and tuck it away for another time. Maybe we would go there . . . someday. And perhaps it would be a very good thing. But there was a host of reasons—not the least of which was next Tuesday's debate, in which Gavin couldn't show any hint of favoritism—to avoid going there now.

As if sensing the precariousness of the moment, Gavin cleared his throat and adopted his mayoral voice. "I've been advised, by the way, that I can't coach you for the debate. The 'optics'"—he put the term in air quotes to show his distaste for such political buzzwords—"aren't good. As moderator, I have to appear impartial." He gave the word "appear" just enough emphasis to show me just how partial he truly was.

"Well, now what will I do?"

I wasn't eager to head into combat with King George without a good suit of oratorial armor. Speeches never have been my thing, and this event—even if it was my idea—seemed like a night filled with speeches George would be itching to pick apart.

"Relax. I've got you covered. Jillian's debate coach from school has offered her services. She's just as eager to take down George as you are. And she has the luxury of impartiality."

"Thanks. That'd be great."

That was pure Gavin. If he couldn't help you, he'd make sure he found someone who could. He'd made dozens of connections between businesses to solve problems in his term as mayor. I hoped to do the same as Chamber president. George always seemed to find ways to set businesses in competition with one another. It was a natural extension of his bone-deep need to always have the upper hand.

I, on the other hand, saw myself as a partnership builder, a connection maker both in knitting and in business. I thought of Paul and how he had welcomed the collaboration when I went to him with my baskets of mini skeins. I felt my shoulders straighten as I reminded myself that Deborah at the florist felt the same way.

"You know, I think I just figured something out."

"What's that?"

"I started out running against George. Since then I've been trying to figure out what I'm running *for*."

"And . . . ?"

"I'm running for collaboration. And community. And partnership."

Gavin's eyes practically sparked with a tenderness I felt all the way to my toes. "You didn't know that already?"

"I guess not."

"That's because it comes that naturally to you. You connect people." He paused for a potent moment before adding, "Something else for my list."

I resolutely put down the wineglass I was holding. At that moment I realized I was tipsy enough that if Gavin had suggested we go out back behind the restaurant and get a little connected ourselves, I might have said yes. We were most definitely toeing up to that line, and I had better figure out what I wanted to do about it soon.

I was saved, oddly enough, by Frank. He broke up our little moment by coming into the restaurant and making a beeline across the room to me. "Libby," he said, his voice alarmingly official.

"What is it, Frank?"

"I just got a call. Someone busted the front window of your shop"—his frown deepened even as I gasped—"with a shepherd's crook."

CHAPTER FIFTEEN

I didn't even bother to get in my car. Gavin, Frank, and I simply sprinted out of Lilly's and ran the two blocks down Collin Avenue to Y.A.R.N. The jagged edges of broken glass and cracks spreading out from the shepherd's crook thrust through one of my front windows stole my breath. Shards on the sidewalk and scattered over Julie's yarn and knitting still in the window display caught the police car's red lights, which looked like brilliant blood all over my precious shop.

We close at five on Wednesdays, so neither Linda nor any customers had been in the shop, thank goodness. I also said a dozen prayers of gratitude on the way here that I'd chosen to keep Hank at home tonight. I often let him wait for me in the store if I'm downtown for the evening, and I couldn't bear it if any harm came to him from something like this.

Such an attack didn't feel like a protest statement or a

crime against an agitating woman. This was directed at me. I reeled under a staggering collection of reactions: fearful at being targeted, wounded that someone would do such a thing, and angry at whoever had brought their fight with Julie to my doorstep. I never wanted Collin Avenue to feel like an unsafe place. My blatant refusal to install a security camera now felt naive and foolish.

I turned in a stunned circle to the small crowd now gathered around the shop. "Did anyone see anything?"

One of Frank's efficient young officers shook his head. "No, ma'am. It was the first thing I asked."

"How did somebody manage to do this in the middle of a food festival without anyone seeing?" I know I should have taken the edge out of my voice, but my current state wouldn't let me.

I felt Gavin's grip on my upper arm trying to hold me steady. "Has anyone called to board it up?"

"Ready and waiting," Frank replied, "as soon as we finish here, which shouldn't take long. We'll try the door and the window frames for prints, but I doubt there'll be anything to process. I have someone checking out the bank's security footage, but I don't think they're close enough to have caught anything."

He handed me a pair of latex gloves. "Door's locked. Use your key carefully to get us in and check to see if anything's missing."

I couldn't believe I was being asked to wear evidence tech equipment to get into my own shop. The mere suggestion that someone not only bashed in my window, but stole from the shop made me feel as if my lungs were filled with cement.

"Of course," I choked out.

The snap of the latex gloves stung my ears, as did the

horrible crunch of glass under my feet. Some overly optimistic part of me tried to argue that it could have been
just kids in on a foolish prank, but only a few people
knew of the shepherd's crooks in the warehouse windows. No, this had to be tied to Julie's death, and that
certainty sent ice down my spine.

A quick glance around the store showed nothing
missing. The store laptop was still on my desk, the cash
register was untouched, and the stock was undisturbed.
Only the glass of the window and the display behind it
had been damaged. Nothing appeared to have been
taken from the window. The display had been knocked
over, props and knitted samples of Julie's shawl patterns
toppled from their artful arrangements. The collection of
needles that had been standing in a glass vase were now
scattered like pick-up sticks, the vase cracked in its fall
from a small wooden pillar. And over everything lay a
glistening coat of broken glass, as if a malicious ice
storm had visited Julie's presence in my window.

"Nothing's gone," I informed Frank as he stood behind me. "It's just the window."

I can't explain why that felt worse—a robbery would
have felt less like a personal wound, I suppose. This was
pure violence aimed directly at me.

"Someone wanted to make a point," Frank muttered
as if he'd heard my thoughts.

Half of me wanted to grab a broom and start to clean
right this minute, while the other half was too shocked
to choose where to start.

"Loud and clear." My voice cracked on the words. I
was losing my battle to stay calm and composed.

Gavin caught the tone and put a hand on my shoulder,
which only made it worse.

My cell phone rang in my handbag.

"Do you want to get that?" Gavin asked.

I shook my head. Vandalism felt like an excellent excuse to let everything go to voice mail right now. Maybe this whole week. Not a minute later, Gavin's phone rang, and he fished it out of his pocket. As mayor, he evidently didn't have the luxury of letting things go to voice mail. He stepped away and I dimly heard him say, "No, no, she's okay. We're here now," as Frank and I moved to survey the ruined display window from the inside.

While it wasn't much more than a blunt, curved stick, the crook stabbed me like a broadsword. My chest physically recoiled as Frank's gloved hand extracted the crook from the jagged spiderweb of cracks and shards in my window.

"It's exactly like the one you found on Barney's farm, isn't it?"

"Yes, I think so. And the ones from the warehouse."

Frank turned the thing over in his hands, examining it with a policeman's keen eye for details. "Looks like the real thing. I mean, not a theater prop or anything like that. Any idea where you buy something like this?"

My mind conjured up the absurd image of Barney coming out of Costco with a bulk box of shepherd's crooks. "I didn't even know you could buy them anymore. Barney says no one uses them."

"Well *someone* does."

As weapons, my brain finished for him.

"If we could find out where these came from, that might help us discover who got them. And if they have any more."

We'd found only five. Did they come in eight-packs

like hot dog buns? Six-packs like beer? My brain chose to handle the shock by spinning through ridiculous ideas. Deciding on something more logical, I walked over to the office and opened up the laptop. I went to one of the largest online knitting and weaving communities—I belong to dozens—and typed "traditional shepherd's crooks" into the search bar.

Evidently people still *did* use these, because eight sales sites came up on the first page alone. Not to mention a collection of Pinterest pages showing decor ideas and construction techniques. I added "wooden" to my search criteria to weed out the many wrought iron garden items and still ended up with a hefty selection.

I turned the screen to face Frank. "I guess Barney's wrong."

Everything from European craftsmen to hobby woodworkers to Amish merchants—the selection of wooden crooks for sale surprised me. While all of them had the iconic curve on top—many with a little curlicue at the edge that once was meant to hold a lantern—most of them looked polished and had a decorative feel. More home accent than farm implement, and nothing so rough and rustic as the ones that had been used here in Collinstown.

"I wonder if any of these are local," I said, paging down through the items in search of one that matched our evidence. I added "made in Cecil County" to the criteria and still ended up with seven sources.

And there it was. At the bottom of the third source was a crook that looked exactly like the ones in Frank's evidence locker—and the one in my window. A friendly-looking woodworker about forty miles from Collinstown smiled back at me from amid a collection of shelving and furniture. How would he feel to know his handiwork had been used for such sinister purposes?

"He looks like the kind of guy who would remember selling a batch of these."

"I'd consider that a solid lead." Frank nodded. "I'll send a deputy first thing tomorrow morning."

"No, don't. Let me go."

"Libby . . ."

"He makes knitting needles and crochet hooks. He'll see me as a potential customer," I argued. "I'll get more out of him than you would."

Frank gave me an I-doubt-that look. But this guy really was a potential vendor, and I somehow wanted to be the one to break it to him that his crooks might have been used as a murder weapon. If the crooks could be considered a murder weapon. If nothing else, getting the purchase information might narrow down our vague list of suspects from the large collection of people who had lost no love for Julie Wilson.

Frank was taking a breath to argue back when a commotion rose up behind me.

"Elizabeth!"

How was it Mom couldn't find her checkbook but she could find her way to me the instant something happened?

Gavin, bless him, tried to head her off. "Rhonda, I told you there was no need to come over here."

"Nonsense. I was just up the street at poker night when Angie called me."

Poker night? Since when did Mom play poker? That seemed like the mother of all bad ideas—pun intended.

"I'm going to have to have a talk with Angie about protocol again," Frank muttered, trying to sound as if he treated Angie as just an employee when everyone in Collinstown knew differently.

Mom pointed at the crook, now encased in plastic in Frank's hand. "That is just like the one used to murder Julie Wilson, isn't it?"

Had I mentioned the shepherd's crooks to Mom? If I had, it was a mistake. The window of my shop was open to the street, and Mom's loud voice hit the small crowd like a douse of ice water. If Frank was ready to make the case's status as a murder investigation public, Mom had just done it for him. Collinstown's split-second gossip network adored a juicy bit of shocking news, and this certainly qualified.

"We've got things under control, Rhonda."

Mom glanced around. "Doesn't look that way to me." Admittedly, the shop looked a far cry from "under control." "I needed a reason to get up and leave anyway. I was losing my shirt tonight."

Mom was playing poker *for money*? I added that to the long list of issues to discuss with her and tried to keep my focus on the current crisis.

"That's the only set of crooks that looks like these," I said to Frank after I paged quickly through all the other sites the Internet search had returned. "I'll make an appointment to go see him."

Mom's glance bounced between the crook and the window. "Crooks using crooks. It'd be poetic if it weren't so awful."

I hadn't even thought of that. It *was* crooks using crooks. The only thing worse than the absurdity of it was the truth of it. I would have liked to laugh, but I just didn't have it in me.

* * *

For the second time in a week, Mom sat in my kitchen having a late-night cup of tea while we tried to make sense of a catastrophe. She was worried about me and hadn't wanted me to go home alone. In fact, she had insisted on following me home.

Granted, she also made none too subtle a plea for Gavin to take on that role, but after the warmth of our conversation earlier, both Gavin and I instinctively knew that wasn't the brightest of ideas. Stress, fear, and attraction rarely lead to rational decisions. Besides, if I ever chose to cross that line with Gavin, I wanted to do it with a clear head and my eyes wide open about the consequences.

So instead, my consequences were my mother's worries. And her comfort. Every time I closed my eyes, I saw the gaping wound of my shattered store window and the ugly plywood that now stood where all that beauty had been.

Mom poured me more tea as we polished off the tin of cookies we'd opened the other night.

"This is getting out of hand, Elizabeth. That loud-mouthed woman was one thing, but this was your property. Your store."

I cringed at Mom's description of impassioned Julie as "that loudmouthed woman," but part of me suspected Julie would have enjoyed the words. Julie wasn't the least bit afraid to say what she thought—a characteristic I sometimes dreaded in Mom but that part of me still admired. To be *that* sure of who you were and what you stood for? I didn't seem quite capable of such boldness yet, although I was proud of the progress I'd made this year. After all, Y.A.R.N. did stand for "You're Absolutely Ready Now," and that had a bold, assertive ring to it, didn't it?

Tonight, however, it also stood for "Yellow Alert— Random Nastiness." Maybe I'd get creative and have Arlene paint that phrase on the plywood. Anything was better than the hasty, rough-hewn cover-up look of that yellow board across what used to be my lovely window display.

I shared the same argument I'd been telling myself for the past hour, "If they really wanted to hurt me, they'd have robbed the store. They didn't take anything. This was another point to make. Another protest." I didn't fully believe that, but repeating it kept the full-on panic at bay.

She leveled me with one of her narrow-eyed looks. "Have you considered that you might be in danger?"

Way to soothe, Mom. "I don't think so." It would have been better if I'd had more confidence in my voice.

"There are worries for a woman living alone in this world. I watch the news. You can't just put up one of those fancy video doorbells and call yourself safe."

I had not, nor would I ever put up a video doorbell. "I'm not alone, Mom. I have Hank," I replied.

At the sound of his name, Hank rose from his place at my feet and laid his head on my thigh. I patted his head, again grateful that he'd been here and not at Y.A.R.N.

"I adore Hank. You know that. But Hank can't call nine-one-one if something happens. He can't go get help if you're knocked out cold on the floor or some goon comes crashing through your window."

I didn't like that Mom had been dreaming up drastic

scenarios of my doom. "That's not going to happen. Besides, you live alone and you seem perfectly fine to me."

Now there was a white lie if ever I'd told one. I hadn't believed that even before I learned about her kitchen fire. The way I saw it, the threats to Mom's well-being were an inside job.

Mom pointed at me as if my statement played right into her line of thinking. "Well, now, that's exactly what I mean. We're two women living alone. We can solve that, you know."

If my thought process had been a car, you would have heard squealing brakes. *Oh, no. No, no, no.* I did not like where this was heading. Not one bit. I tried to level Mom with a narrow-eyed don't-you-go-there look of my own.

She was oblivious, selecting the last cookie as if we were discussing the most sensible of subjects. "Really. It would solve a whole world of problems if I moved in here. I don't know why I didn't think of it sooner."

Think of it sooner? She'd been dropping hints left and right. I'd been tiptoeing around them like a minefield of bad ideas for half a year. Still, this was the first time she'd come out and openly suggested it. She clearly thought tonight's events played right into her campaign to cohabitate.

I opened my mouth to launch the torrent of objections building up in my chest, but Mom kept right on going. "I'm alone. You're alone. You've said you don't think my town house across the river is the place for me."

This was true, but I had another very different kind of place in mind. One with words like "independent living" and eventually "assisted living" and maybe even "memory care" in the title.

Mom went gaily on without skipping a beat. "And I'm

always heading back over the river to do something in town. I think it was a mistake to ever move across, actually. You're in the perfect spot. If I ever have to give up driving, I can walk to everything from here. It's an ideal solution when you think about it. You can't tell me you haven't considered it, because I raised a sensible girl and it makes *so much* sense."

Lord have mercy. She had really thought this through. I was about to come up against the immovable force that is my mother when she gets an idea in her head. Dread wrapped itself around my chest—and when I considered the night I'd just had, that was saying something.

"Wow, Mom." Not exactly the sturdiest of objections, but I was still in shock. This was not the night for me to be prepared for rigorous pushback against the Worst Idea Ever.

She smiled, eyes sparkling with a Best Idea Ever gleam. "I know. Brilliant, right?"

CHAPTER SIXTEEN

She said she ought to move in with you?" Margo's mouth dropped open. Hank and I had shown up at the Perfect Slice immediately after breakfast Thursday morning—a full hour before Y.A.R.N. was due to open.

Margo had called and offered to come over to the house last night. I had declined, seeing how eager Mom was to be the one to keep me company. Now I wished I had told her to join us. Mom might not have been so brave in her lobbying had Margo been there.

"She had a whole sales campaign laid out. If she knew how to work her computer correctly, I'm sure it would have come with PowerPoint slides."

Margo refilled my coffee. Clearly the fact that I hadn't slept well showed on my face. "What did you say? Did you tell her no?"

I sunk my chin into my hand. "I didn't tell her anything. I told her I was too rattled to even think about something like that. I'm worried that only made her point for her." My eyes wandered across the road to the ugly plywood patching my storefront like some horrid industrial Band-Aid. "I mean, I'm scared. Someone broke my store window. Just to be mean. I didn't feel like I could admit any of that to her after she told me she ought to move in."

"Of course you're scared," Margo replied. "Who wouldn't be? We got broken into once and I made Carl come to the kitchen with me every morning for a month. And you know what a morning person he is."

Carl was absolutely *not* a crack-of-dawn kind of guy. I hadn't even realized that had happened. "You were robbed?" I should have known if something that big had happened to her, shouldn't I?

"Some dumb kids back while you were still in DC with Sterling. They stole six pies and eighty-five dollars. Frank eventually caught them and they had to wash my sidewalk for a month and write the world's most reluctant letters of apology."

That sounded like something Frank would do. A wise mix of mercy for teenage stupidity and justice to teach them a lesson. The world needed more Franks in it. Collinstown was certainly fortunate we had him at the helm of our police department.

Margo's eyes widened. "She's not there now, is she? Tell me you didn't let her stay the night."

My friend knew what I knew: One night would transform into two more, then into a week, and suddenly a moving van would pull up in my driveway.

"No. It took nearly an hour of convincing, but I sent her home last night. She tried to pull the I-hate-to-drive-this-late ploy but I stood my ground."

Standing my ground. Suddenly I felt like the cover model for *Worst Daughters Monthly*. Guilt took advantage of my frayed nerves and welled up like a full-moon tide.

"Am I terrible for not wanting that? My own mother tried to help me and I shoved her out the door."

For a woman who has never been a parent, Margo had a mother's "eye of death" down to an art form. "Your own mother used an awful situation to try to get something she wants. Something that isn't healthy for a self-reliant thirty-eight-year-old woman of your brilliance."

I swallowed hard. "Thanks. I needed to hear that."

Margo sat back. "You know as well as I do that the two of you would last about four days—if that—before you got on each other's nerves. Your mom is a strong dose. You have a good relationship because that relationship has boundaries. And distance. Those would fly to pieces if you lived together. You know that."

"Yep."

"And then," Margo went on, clearly on her soapbox, "you wouldn't have a relationship. You'd just have a great big ball of manipulation and resentment. And when your mom gets to the point where she really does need your help, you won't have any compassion left to give her. Saying no is the healthiest thing you can do, not the least bit selfish."

"No, really, Margo, tell me how you truly feel."

It was something I often said to her when she got into speechmaking mode. Maybe I didn't need Jillian's debate coach. Maybe I had my speech coach right in front of me. Delicious snack incentives included.

She shook her head. "Honestly, I've been waiting for your mom to pull a stunt like this for months now. I'm sorry she picked last night—that was dirty pool, if you ask me." Her expression softened. "Although I do think she's right about one thing. It was a mistake for her to move across the river. She should be right in town so she can walk to everything. Just not right in your living room."

I managed a tiny laugh. "Maybe instead of luxury lofts, they'll turn the warehouse into senior housing."

Margo pointed at me. "Maybe you should bring it up with the mayor. I hear he has a soft spot for your ideas."

When I raised an eyebrow, she explained. "Lilly was in ordering some coconut cream pies early this morning, and she dropped a few hints about the two of you. I haven't heard someone use the phrase 'he's sweet on her' since junior high."

"Lilly said that?" I gulped.

Evidently the temperature rise I'd felt in the room wasn't just my hormones. Other people had noticed. I thought of the way people gossiped about Frank and Angie and felt my temples start to throb.

"Relax," Margo assured me. "The two of you can handle this. You're both grown-ups, even if your own mother doesn't always act like one." She rose, checked her watch, and gathered the pair of coffee mugs. "What we need is a good solid break in the case to divert everyone's attention."

I'd almost forgotten. "We have one of those."

She sat back down. "What?"

"I found the likely source of those shepherd's crooks. Not too far away. Whoever did this had to have bought at least six of them, so the woodworker is bound to remember them even if they paid cash."

"But didn't you say there were chemicals involved in Julie's death?"

"There were. But maybe if we find who planted the crooks, we can start piecing together who messed with Julie's formulas. I convinced Frank to let me make an appointment with the guy tomorrow morning."

Margo looked surprised. "You convinced Frank?"

"I'm Rhonda Beckett's daughter, remember. Sometimes I won't take no for an answer. This guy might be a dead end, but I'm hoping it's a start."

I need your journalism instincts," I told my friend and customer Caroline as we pulled into the drive that led up to Jameson Farm and Woodworks Friday morning. Frank still wasn't convinced I was a better choice than one of his uniformed officers, and I was determined to prove him wrong. And I wasn't kidding about the potential vendor tactic. Lloyd did have some exquisite needles and crochet hooks. If I didn't get any information, I was still likely to come away from today with new stock for the store.

Caroline smiled. "I'm glad to help. And anyway, you know I'm always up for one of your adventures."

I sighed. "I wish this adventure was a bit less . . . traumatic. We're about to tell some nice woodworker his art was weaponized. Not fun. My idea of an adventure is more like finding a new bakery or a great source for discount handbags."

Caroline laughed. "Or an Aran cable?"

Relatively new to knitting, Caroline had taken to it fast and furious, gaining skills at a pace that rivaled Jillian. Her latest project was an ambitious cable-knit stitch-sampler afghan that kept her coming into the shop with frequent cries for help. I didn't mind a bit. I enjoyed her company. Sure, she'd taken on a challenge, but who didn't want to encourage a brave knitting spirit? And while it sometimes took her a while or a few tries, Caroline always conquered her challenges.

"How's that afghan coming?"

"This block's coming along, but I'm gonna need more help on the next one, I'm sure."

"Count on it," I assured her. "Let's go in and see what we can find out."

I parked the car outside a picture-postcard rustic barn with a set of exquisite rocking chairs out front. The artistry of his Jameson Woodworks sign above the barn door was as beautiful as the Y.A.R.N. shop sign. A trio of stunning birdhouses hung from the branches of a large oak by the door. Despite the rough-hewn look of the shepherd's crooks I'd seen, this man was clearly an artist. I might come away from this visit with more than information and needles.

I'd called ahead—mentioning only the interest in the needles—so Lloyd knew I was coming. At the sound of my car, the barn door opened and a tall, handsome, rather intense-looking man walked out, wiping his hands on a blue bandanna. His well-built frame was clad in a dusty work shirt, jeans, and boots. He looked to be in his late twenties, and I couldn't help but think he looked like Barney might have looked in his prime—clean and earthy all at the same time. The bio on his website stated Lloyd had ditched his corporate job two years ago for a more authentic and artistic lifestyle. That gave him a lot in common with Caroline, which was the other reason I chose her as my partner today.

"Hello, Ms. Beckett."

Wow. The deep, resonant voice I'd heard on the phone was even more impressive in person.

"Libby, please." I extended my hand, charmed by his manners and silky tone. "Nice to meet you, too, Mr. Jameson."

"Lloyd," he replied, giving my hand a good shake. He had the rough, strong grip of a man who earned his living with his hands.

I watched his eyes stray toward my companion. "This is my friend Caroline."

In addition to being a wonderful person, a clever knitter, and a smart journalist, Caroline was also a knockout beauty.

Lloyd tipped the well-worn baseball cap on his head of dusty blond hair, his gaze still firmly on Caroline's friendly smile. "Pleased to meet you, Caroline."

Caroline motioned toward the beautiful chairs. "Are these your work?"

"They are."

"They're gorgeous. Do you deliver?"

He returned her smile. "Sometimes even personally."

We were off to a fantastic start. "If they're any indication, I'm sure I want to carry your needles. And maybe a few of those beautiful drop spindles as well."

Lloyd's website had also featured a small collection of drop spindles. Those were a throwback to how yarn had been spun back before spinning wheels. Imagine a sort of inverted spinning top that stretched out and wound fleece as you worked it through your fingers. It's quite calming and more than a bit mesmerizing once you get the hang of it. I gave high odds both Caroline and I were coming home with at least one of those each if not more. I was already calculating which corner of my living room needed to host one of Lloyd's rocking chairs and could feel Caroline doing the same.

Lloyd took us into the shop and showed us many examples of his expert craftsmanship. There was no need to feign interest in his products for sale. One rocking chair for Caroline, two dozen pairs of needles for me, and a drop spindle for each of us later, I finally circled around to the real reason for my visit.

"Lloyd, there's another reason for my visit today. I'd like to talk to you about your shepherd's crooks."

There was a small collection of them standing in a tall container in the corner, but most of them were the more polished and decorative versions.

"Thinking of taking up sheep farming?" he asked.

"Heavens no," I replied. "I have my hands full with the shop." *That and more*, I added in my head. "Actually, I want to ask you about a set of crooks you may have sold recently." I gestured toward the collection in the corner. "Much more rustic than these. I'm interested in this one." I pulled up a screenshot from his website on my cell phone. "Or more accurately, I'm interested in the person who bought them. Did you by chance have a customer recently who bought more than one of these crooks?"

Lloyd's face registered surprise and recognition. "I did. Six, actually." Then, with a touch of alarmed concern, he added, "Why do you need to ask?"

I opted for truth. "Because one of them was bashed through my shopwindow Wednesday night."

Surprise and recognition turned to shock. "Are you sure? That's terrible."

His shock was going to double when I told him everything. He seemed like such a nice guy. It would upset him to know why I was really here, and I felt for him.

"We're pretty sure. I was hoping you would lend us one to compare it to the others—if you've got any left."

Lloyd put his hand to his chest. "He cleaned me out. I do a lot of custom work, so there's not a lot of extra stock."

So they'd been purchased by a man. That was useful, but what we really needed was a name. My insides lurched at what I knew I was going to say next; we had to convince Lloyd how seriously we needed his cooperation.

"I'm afraid there's more." I motioned to a collection of straight-backed chairs arranged around a clean-lined coffee table. "Could we maybe sit down?"

"Sure." He looked nervous. The poor guy had every right to.

"As I said, we—meaning the police and I—think it was one of your crooks that was used to shatter my shop-window."

"I'm so sorry about that," he cut in. "Really I am. The guy was a bit odd, and I have to say I felt a bit—I don't know—weird about selling them to him."

"I'm sure you are sorry," I replied, "and please know that I don't in the least blame you. You're entitled to sell your work to whomever you like. I know it's not necessarily normal for me to be asking about one of your customers, and you don't owe me any information."

"No, no. I'll help in any way I can."

The man looked as if his art had been violated by its use in a crime. I'd have felt the same way if one of my creations had been used to hurt someone. That wasn't what art was for.

"I'm glad to hear that," I assured him, my own nerves winding up. "Because there is more. A rather serious more."

Lloyd gulped. I swallowed hard myself, and Caroline wrung her hands into a tight knot in her lap.

I pulled in a deep breath. "Lloyd, I'm so very sorry to have to tell you that we believe three others were used in a . . ." I found myself stumbling on the word. It seemed too unfair to have to pull Lloyd into this. "In a murder, actually."

Lloyd paled. "What?"

"They were used to jam the door and the ventilation fans in a room where a very vocal opponent of sheep farming was dyeing fibers for an event of mine."

Caroline and I had spent twenty minutes on the drive over crafting that sentence. Turned out, kind and compellingly frank was a tough balance to hit.

Lloyd yanked his cap off and pushed his hands through his hair. "A murder? My crooks were used to kill someone?" He looked devastated.

"Julie Wilson was in a warehouse dyeing fibers for a workshop that was to have taken place last Saturday. We found her two nights before, dead from inhaling toxic chemicals. The crooks were jammed into the door to block her exit, and into the ventilation fans that would have kept the fumes under control."

"My crooks? Why my crooks?"

"I don't think it was specifically your crooks," Caroline offered, her voice soft and kind. "Any crooks would have done, and I'm sorry they chose to use yours. It doesn't seem fair."

Lloyd shook his head, trying to get his brain around the awful idea. "I don't get it."

"They were making a statement of sorts," I tried to explain. "Julie was a fiber dyer and knitting pattern designer who was blatantly opposed to using animal fibers."

"She was against wool? Okay, allergic I can see, but against it? Like *morally* against it?"

"Loudly morally against it," I continued. "She made a career out of championing plant and other fibers as alternatives to animal ones. She was vehemently against animal shearing as cruelty. And she trashed sheep farmers. Often. You can imagine they don't like what she does."

"She was murdered by sheep farmers?" I couldn't blame Lloyd for the I-don't-believe-this look on his face. The whole thing was as outlandish as it was tragic.

"We don't actually know that," I corrected, even though I had sound doubts about Barney's innocence. "But whoever did it used the crooks to make it clear—or at least make it look—as if sheep farmers were behind it. A calling card, I suppose."

Lloyd stood up and began pacing the room. "I got a bad feeling about the guy. I should have not sold them. I should have seen it as a red flag when he paid cash. When he didn't give his name." He stalled for a second to look at me. "I mean, I asked for his info so I could put him on my mailing list—he bought six, after all—but he declined." Lloyd began pacing again. "I was so excited to sell six of them that I just looked past what I should have seen."

His steps sped up with his distress until Caroline got up and touched his shoulder. "It's not your fault. You couldn't possibly have known."

"We don't blame you, Lloyd, really," I said, adding to her consolation.

I wouldn't say I wasn't disappointed. I had been hoping for a receipt we could track down, a name we could connect to our suspects, but we weren't going to get that. All we had was that the crooks had come from here and had been purchased by a man. Which made me think of something. I picked up my cell phone again, pulling up Jillian's videos of the sheep protest. I hit pause at a frame where you could see Barney and his buddies.

"Were any of these men your customer?"

Lloyd scanned the shot. "No. He wasn't the farmer type. That's what made it so odd. Usually the city people go for the more polished pieces. You know, decorative, not functional."

I tapped on to the Internet icon and searched through the images of *Dish Up Comfort* until I found one of Yale Wagner. "Was it him?"

"Nope. I'm sorry. Closer to this guy's age, but this isn't him."

We'd hit a dead end. I was so sure we were on to something—and I suppose we were now that we were almost certain the crooks came from here. I wanted to bring Frank back a solid lead, but our visit didn't really gain us anything. We weren't any closer to identifying our killer. Still, I didn't feel right just walking away from Lloyd after having dumped this terrible news on him.

"Do you think you could come to Collinstown and examine the crooks the police have in evidence? Maybe there's something you could tell them that we're missing."

"Absolutely. Anything you need." He gave me a mournful look. "I'm so, so sorry."

"We all are."

"I'll come tomorrow." He looked at Caroline. "I can stop by on my way into DC to bring you your chair."

Caroline waved his offer away. "You don't need to deliver it so quickly."

"No, I do. It's the least I can do."

I swear he held her gaze just a moment longer than necessary. There really was something sparking between those two.

I felt myself starting to say, "Why don't the two of you have dinner while you're in town?" but gulped the words back down in horror.

Why? Because that was something Mom would have said.

CHAPTER SEVENTEEN

While I never claimed to have a full social calendar, I felt ridiculous that night standing behind the small podium the shop used when guests gave lectures. I was spending my Friday evening at Y.A.R.N. after hours, and my only "audience" was Paula Nelson, Jillian's debate teacher and my new public-speaking coach. Linda and Margo were also here for moral support, bless them, so I suppose it could have been called a small social gathering.

"I'm not sure I really have time for this," I confessed to my "audience."

Being knee-deep in a murder investigation tended to eat up a lot of a person's free time. And energy. And ability to focus. Lately it felt as if between the campaign, the murder, and Mom's continuing full-court press to move in, I was getting hit from all sides.

"You're *smart* to make time for this," Paula advised.

I'd found her to be a pleasant mix of encouraging and straightforward. "The town hall is both a great idea and a bit of a minefield. It's George, after all."

"So he's bound to say something egotistical and annoying," Margo said from one of the three chairs currently placed in front of my podium. "You're giving him enough rope to hang himself."

I grimaced at the wording of the cliché, even though I'd had the thought myself. Anything involving death struck a raw nerve with me lately.

Paula frowned. "You're also meeting George on his home turf. This is a man who loves a podium. You can have the best ideas in the world and it won't mean a thing if you don't look comfortable and prepared up there."

"And you *do* have the best ideas," Linda chimed in. "I was over at the florist shop yesterday and Deborah went on and on about your brilliant mini-skein promotion. I kid you not. She actually said, 'George would never think of something like this.'"

George *would* never think of something collaborative like that. I'd been hearing it from every business where I set up a mini-skein partnership. The notion that I would make a good—maybe even a great—Chamber president was starting to settle into my bones. And after all, the town hall debate had been my idea.

"He's going to bring up the murder—you know that," Margo said. "Would it be fair to ask Frank if he can have it solved by Tuesday night?"

I leaned against the podium. "It won't matter. Solved or not, George will see it as my fault. And of course he's going to bring it up."

"Bev at the inn said she actually heard him saying your shop seems to attract 'an undesirable element' to town." Linda gestured around the shop, filled to the brim with color and texture and beauty. "Can you imagine?"

Paula set her jaw with a determined pride. "Collins-town's a better place because your shop is here, and we all know it. Well, all except for George."

"I bet even he knows it," Margo muttered. "He's just too stubborn to admit it."

"So let's go over how to handle Julie's murder. What do we know so far? Just like we talked about, list the facts for me."

I tried to channel my inner Frank and do as Paula advised—list facts confidently and clearly without making assumptions. I took a deep breath and tried to discover my own mayor voice—or in this case, Chamber president voice.

"Julie Wilson's death was not an accident. We know there was industrial-grade sodium hydroxide involved. It's a dangerous version of a substance commonly used in fiber dyeing. We don't know if she used the chemical deliberately—Julie always claimed to have private formulas that made her success possible—or if someone sabotaged her supplies to include it. The ventilation system where she was working was intentionally jammed by two shepherd's crooks, increasing the danger of the chemical. Her exit from the building was blocked as well. Frank is currently investigating, and I have every reason to believe whoever is responsible will be brought to justice."

Paula nodded her approval while Linda smiled wide.

"Do you have any idea how presidential you sound?" Margo asked, applauding. Even Hank woofed his endorsement. "It should stop George in his tracks."

"I doubt that," I replied. "But it does feel good to have

a response crafted and ready." I offered a smile to Paula. "You're right. Preparation does matter."

Linda pointed to the newly replaced shopwindow. "Should Libby talk about that?"

"Only if George brings it up," Paula said. "And I don't think he will. He wouldn't want you to get any sympathy for it."

"Unless he wants to use it as an example of this so-called undesirable element," Margo continued. "That sounds like something he would do."

I was surprised by Paula's mischievous grin. "Then you bring up the yarn bombing."

Collin Avenue had indeed been yarn-bombed last year. Mom and her friends had decorated nearly every tree on the street as part of an event I'd done. Everyone had loved it. Well, everyone except George, who naturally thought it gave me an advertising advantage and therefore demanded it be taken down immediately.

"Ask him if he thinks of art as an undesirable element since he demanded its removal last year."

"Ooh," whispered Margo, "I like that. You're good."

We went on through the other questions and strategies until Paula declared tonight's rehearsal finished. Best of all, I sent Paula home with two skeins of very good alpaca yarn and a simple scarf pattern, along with an appointment for three knitting lessons. All in all an excellent trade if I did say so myself.

"What did that Lloyd fellow tell you about the crooks?" Linda asked as we put away the podium and tucked the chairs back in their places around the shop table. "I feel so bad for him."

I grabbed my list of talking points—a term that made me a bit queasy, I confess, because it sounded so political—

and slid them into the bag with my other work papers. "I kept telling him we don't blame him, but he's being hard on himself."

Margo sighed. "To know your beautiful art was used for something so awful—that would upset anyone. I'd be beside myself if I discovered someone put poison in one of my pies to kill someone."

Linda picked up a pair of Lloyd's handcrafted needles, which we now displayed in a glass vase on the table. "His stuff is great. I suppose it's nice that at least you get a new vendor out of all this mess."

"That's true." I was always glad to have Linda's efficient optimism around. "As for the crooks, Lloyd is coming tomorrow to confirm the ones Frank has in evidence are definitely his. But that doesn't help us much if we can't identify who bought them."

"So it's like two different murder weapons?" Margo asked, wrinkling her brow in thought. "The strong chemical and the blocked ventilation?"

"That's one way to look at it. The blocked ventilation we know was deliberate. The door, too. The chemical, we're not so sure about." I shut off the store lights and grabbed Hank's leash. "Like I said, it may have been her secret ingredient and she somehow slipped up in her handling of it. Or someone put it in with her usual ingredients in order to make them toxic."

Linda's eyes narrowed. "Redundant systems. Sounds kind of complicated for a criminal."

"Huh?" I asked.

"If they were both deliberate—meaning the chemical thing wasn't a mistake on Julie's part—the killer had a plan and a backup plan. Two systems meant to do the same thing. Redundant systems. It's a software term."

"You mean like a fail-safe?" Margo asked as we walked out the door.

I stopped on the sidewalk, struck by a thought. "Or not." Margo and Linda halted beside me. "What do you mean?"

I faced both of them. "What if two different people meant to kill Julie, and each aided the other without realizing it?"

Frank sat back in his chair after I told him my unsettling theory the next morning. "I considered that myself, actually." He gave me a sad smile. "You aren't thinking about running for county sheriff instead of Chamber president, are you?"

I balked at the very idea. "Not on your life. The only thing I want to investigate is why the dye lot numbers don't match on my most recent yarn shipment." That sort of problem seemed like a vacation next to the knots I was untangling these days.

"I don't much take to the idea of us having to identify two suspects to the DA to charge. But we do have to consider it. We do know one is male, thanks to Mr. Jameson." Frank grunted. "I'd be happier if we had the name of that man, though."

"And just because he bought the crooks doesn't mean he was the one to use them," I added. "Lloyd didn't recognize Barney or Yale as his customer."

"So all we have is a cold lead."

He got up, walked to his office door, and shut it. I got the sense he was considering breaking a rule, which was very unlike our Frank.

"I'm going to ask you a question. In confidence. Because I think the answer will shed some light on the case."

His serious tone sank to the bottom of my stomach. "You know I'll do anything to help."

"What if Julie was pregnant?"

A sense of shock—and a jolt of horror—ran through me. "Was she?" That seemed too awful to consider.

"Actually, no. Not according to the medical examiner's report. But Monica came to me and asked if the autopsy would say if she was."

That was certainly a new twist. "Monica thought Julie could be pregnant?" It seemed such an odd thing not to know for sure. And an even odder thing to ask a police chief. "I don't get why she asked you."

"Evidently, Julie told Monica she was pregnant. Monica didn't believe her—or at least had reason to doubt her. At least that's what she told me."

"What did you tell Monica?"

"I told her that wasn't the kind of information I was able to release." Frank folded his hands on the desk. "Regulations are pretty strict about that sort of thing. The executor of Julie's estate will have access to the reports eventually, but we don't even know who that is yet."

"So why are you telling me? Why ask me about it?"

"Because we can't assume Julie was lying. She may have thought she was pregnant. And if she did, would she knowingly use the sodium hydroxide? It's a slim connection, but it might help tell us if that chemical was intentionally used or added without her knowledge."

"I . . . don't know." I knew a great deal about yarn and knitting, but not that much about dyeing. "I can look it up, I suppose. Or call one of my vendors."

"And not just the sodium hydroxide, since we don't know if it was Julie's secret ingredient. What about any of the normal dyeing ingredients? Can you find out if there's any danger to a pregnant woman using the dyes you said people normally use?"

"I'll try."

My brain was scrambling to connect the dots of this new information. It did seem a slim connection—if Julie knew she wasn't pregnant, the dangers of sodium hydroxide on a pregnant woman wouldn't tell us much. But we had no leads to follow, and I agreed with Frank that the information would be useful to have.

"Did Monica say if Julie told her who the father was?"

"I didn't ask her that."

Was there someone out there walking around thinking that not only his lover, but the mother of his unborn child had been killed? It made my stomach knot to think of it. Really, could there have been anything sadder?

"Wouldn't it have been kinder to let her know Julie wasn't pregnant?"

"I'm crossing enough lines as it is asking you, but I need your expertise here. I'd want to figure out why Julie was professing to be pregnant before I go releasing that information anyway. It could be pertinent to the case."

The investigation seemed so much more personal now, so much more unnerving. "It's all just terrible."

"She wasn't pregnant," Frank reassured me. "But she told Monica she was, which means Julie may have told other people as well. There's something behind that, and it could be connected to why she was murdered."

My urgency to see this case solved doubled. The twists and turns were starting to feel as if they were wrapped around my lungs, making it hard to breathe. I didn't know why it seemed worse for Julie to be murdered for personal reasons than for her ideals, but it did.

I pointed at the computer on the credenza behind Frank. "Want me to look it up right now?"

Frank vacated his chair and gestured me into it. I suppose he could have just as easily gone to a search engine and typed in "okay to dye yarn while pregnant?" but I appreciated that he asked for my help instead.

I sat down, went to the websites of three of my favorite small independent yarn-dyer vendors, and emailed them the question. While we waited, I went to two online knitting forums and typed in my question there.

For reasons I've stated before, I've never had the privilege of needing to ask such a thing. I found it ironic that Julie's death foisted such a tender question on me, and I wondered what drove her to say something like that to her sister. Sibling rivalry didn't go that far, did it? There was a girl in our high school class who had gotten married and then pregnant at blinding speed just to be the first of her three sisters to do so. It hadn't ended well, as you could imagine.

I took a minute to scan through what I found on the forums. "I've asked some dyers I know, but as far as what's here, there's no consensus. Some people say it's fine if you take sensible precautions. Others advise against it. Of course, that's all assuming the usual household substances are used, not the high-grade chemical stuff."

Frank grunted. "That doesn't tell us much. Julie Wilson does not strike me as a sensible-precautions person. If sodium hydroxide is the chemical in her formula and she was intentionally using it, maybe she knew she wasn't pregnant."

"But if someone messed with her formula and put that chemical in there, it's anyone's guess and we're back where we started." I stared out the window of Frank's office in the direction of the Riverside Inn. "We need to find who took those formulas from her silk recipe folder. It's probably the same person who has the room key— Bev still hasn't found it." I sighed. "If we could see her recipes, we'd know so much more."

Frank's gaze followed mine. "But who would know where Julie hid them?"

The proverbial lightbulb went off over my head. "Monica might. She had a recipe folder just like Julie's. It was a gift from their mother. Monica would know what she was looking for."

I started to wonder if Monica was more involved in all this than she'd let on. A sister relationship that complicated could make anything possible—but murder? I couldn't fathom it.

There was still one thing that didn't make sense. "What I can't work out is, don't you think using that folder seems too obvious? Julie was so secretive about those formulas. Why put them someplace easy to find like that?"

"If her mother gave it to her, then maybe it's just sentimental. People do illogical things for emotional reasons all the time."

Sterling had called my opening of Y.A.R.N. "a rebound ploy." He would have classified the shop as emotional and illogical. And being Sterling, he framed it all in terms of himself. I, on the other hand, think it is the most logical thing in all the world to reach for your dreams. Most especially when you realize life has distracted you from them. Is Y.A.R.N. emotional? Absolutely. Emotions like joy, satisfaction, happiness, bliss, and a host of others. Y.A.R.N. is the most sensible thing I've done in a very long time, so it's not one bit illogical to me.

I felt my brow furrow. "I don't know. The envelope doesn't add up for me. Julie liked schemes. She doesn't strike me as the hide-it-in-plain-sight type."

"But maybe it was hidden. We found that fabric envelope out in plain sight, but that doesn't mean she kept it there. Someone could have surprised her before she had time to hide it. Or someone knew what they were looking for."

I thought of the hurtful things Monica and Julie had hurled at each other that first day. Did that hurt go deep enough for murder? And why would that have had anything to do with whether or not Julie was pregnant?

"Could it really have been Monica?" My question sent ice down my own spine.

Frank's nod felt just as cold.

CHAPTER EIGHTEEN

Gavin took a massive gulp of coffee and stared at me. "I'm exhausted."

It was Sunday, the final evening of the festival, and everyone was worn out. The extra effort to try to keep things upbeat taxed everyone. While Julie wasn't officially part of the See More Than Seafood Festival, her murder had cast a shadow that was hard to shake off and was too large to ignore.

We were in Esther's Dockhouse restaurant, which had happily been restored to serving capacity the morning after the fire and had enjoyed a good run of Monica's cooking. It hadn't enjoyed a calm run of her personality, but chefs being who they are, perhaps that would never have been the case even without Julie's death.

The spot was one of four stops on a progressive dessert tour, the grand finale event of the festival. Monica's star offering here was her signature apple cobbler, but she had also set out carrot cake, rice pudding, and some very decadent-looking chocolate chip cookies for attendees. An event where you were encouraged to eat multiple desserts—who could have asked for more?

I selected a little dish of the rice pudding, complete with a tiny cookie garnish and a miniature spoon. The dessert portions were in little cups roughly the size of shot glasses—small enough that I declared it perfectly reasonable to sample all of them. "Monica seems hard to handle right now."

Gavin slid a cookie onto his saucer and looked across the room at Monica. She looked stressed-out and strung tight as she talked to one of the waitstaff. "Who wouldn't be? It's understandable, of course."

I know Gavin was thinking the same thing I'd been thinking: Monica's decision to stick with her events hadn't been a wise one. "She's the one who insisted on staying," I answered his unvoiced thought. "I don't think you could have shut her out of it without a big scene."

"We had a big scene anyway, though, didn't we?"

"True enough," I agreed.

There was little comfort in the *Dish Up Comfort* star's demeanor. Dark circles lurked under Monica's eyes, and she seemed to find every conversation intrusive. The rice pudding was delicious, and I found myself rather in awe that she could cook such exquisite food while in such a dark place.

I felt for Gavin. I had the luxury of my event being canceled during all this trauma, but Gavin had needed to soldier on despite the fact that a murder investigation was putting everyone on edge. And making his star chef rather cranky. I opted to change the subject.

"How is Jillian?"

"She was on cloud nine with all the attention she got from the Julie Wilson interview. 'Gazillions of hits,' whatever that means."

I laughed. "It means a lot, I'm sure." I polished off my tiny rice pudding and moved on to the apple cobbler, which had won me over the first night of the festival. "I thought Jillian handled the posting of that interview really well, Gavin. I mean, what a tough balance to strike, given the fact that Julie has died. I don't know many adults who could have pulled it off with grace."

It was fun to watch Gavin's eyes light up anytime anyone complimented his daughter. "It was the last interview Julie gave. Did you realize that? Jillian told me it's why it's gotten so much attention. By the way, what do you know about Sheepsake Yarns?"

"I never heard of them, but there are hundreds of yarn companies and independent vendors. Clever name, though. Why do you ask?"

"They approached Jillian about being a teen influencer. She's over the moon about it. I told her she had to check it out with you before she said yes."

It made me happy to know Jillian's good work was getting noticed. "I'll be happy to check it out. It probably just means they send her free yarn so she can knit with it and post about it."

"Shouldn't she be buying her yarn from you?"

I was about to tell Gavin that nothing would have made me happier than to share Jillian with the rest of the yarn world when Lilly Sorrington moved swiftly up to Gavin and tapped him on the shoulder. "Drama's a-comin', sugar. You might want to get over there."

Lilly pointed across the room, where it seemed Monica and Yale were on the verge of an argument. They'd been short with each other most of the festival, just barely holding it together in public. Based on what I had seen during my conversation with them about the sheep videos, I could only guess about the rows they'd likely had behind closed doors.

Suddenly Monica gave out a mournful cry as an older dark-haired woman and man swept into the room. "Mama!"

"Monica, baby!"

The two women dissolved into tears and hugs. My heart broke for the mother mourning such a tragic loss with her surviving daughter. How on earth did you get through something like that?

"I'd best get over there and offer my condolences," Gavin said as the crying went on at full strength.

No one begrudged Monica and her mother a tearful reunion, but perhaps the festival party hadn't been the best place to have it. I was truly glad Monica now finally had the support of her parents, but I also couldn't escape the fact that it meant more drama. We were almost succeeding at a happy finale until Mrs. Wilson's appearance, and now the room took on the atmosphere of a highly caloric wake.

"I should go over, too. Julie was here at my invitation, after all."

I wasn't especially eager to intrude on that scene, but I did feel as though I ought to at least offer my condolences.

Gavin and I walked over to the grieving family. "Mrs. Wilson," Gavin began, "I'm so very sorry for your loss."

"This is Mayor Gavin Maddock," Monica said as

Gavin extended a hand. "The festival was his idea. Everyone's been so very kind to me."

It was the nicest thing I'd heard Monica say all day. Maybe the whole festival. But I couldn't say I'd have been especially gracious under these circumstances, either, so I was ready to cut her a little slack.

Mrs. Wilson, however, was clearly not in a gracious mood. As the woman's eyes shifted to me, I swear the room temperature dropped ten degrees.

"This is Libby Beckett," Monica said. "She's been just as nice."

"The yarn store owner," Mrs. Wilson said with unmistakable ice in her tone.

There are certain people in this world who can do polite and hateful at the same time with vicious expertise. I was looking at one of them.

"I'm deeply sorry about what happened to Julie."

It felt like a cumbersome greeting, but I didn't have time to think of anything better to say. And I was deeply sorry. I had hoped her appearance here would bolster her career, not end her life.

"Yes, I expect you are," the woman said.

No one needed to tell me how she felt. It was crystal clear she held me responsible for what had happened to her daughter. It dawned on me that somehow she still believed Julie's death was an accident. And there were no doubts where she placed the blame.

"So sorry you had such a time getting here, Dorothy, Hugh," Yale said, shaking what I assumed to be Mr. Wilson's hand. "Difficult stuff all around."

"How can I help make things easier for you?" Gavin said. He was trying to break the chill of the cold glare

Dorothy continued to cast my way. "I assume Bev is taking care of you at the inn?"

"We have an appointment to see Chief Reynolds in an hour, but of course I wanted to see Monica first." Dorothy reached out and grasped Monica's hand, eyes brimming over again.

"Monica, there's no need for you to stay."

Gavin gestured around the room. There had been pockets of cheery conversation over the collection of desserts, but all talk had halted as the eyes of the entire room shifted to us.

"I'm sure you want to spend time with your parents."

Monica's chin rose. "No. I've seen my way through all the other parts of the festival. I'll do this, too. I'll see it through."

"Really, dear," Yale offered. "No one would blame you—"

"No. We're staying." Monica's tone was final.

"May I get you both some coffee?" I offered to Mr. and Mrs. Wilson, trying to make any kind of peace.

"Thank you, no."

It was easy to see the roots of Monica's sharp edges. Dorothy didn't actually say "not from you," but I expected half the room heard it in her tone anyway.

Gavin knew a no-win battle when he saw one. "Your daughter has been extraordinary under such terrible circumstances, Mr. and Mrs. Wilson. You should be proud of her. Please do let me know if there's anything I can do while you are in Collinstown."

Hugh Wilson simply nodded while Dorothy's frown deepened into a near sneer.

Gavin and I walked away even as most of the room

continued to stare at the family. I found myself extra glad Gavin had insisted none of Yale's nosy television crew be here. The last thing this dramatic family reunion needed was a film crew. I kept waiting for the chatter to return to the room, but instead the uncomfortable silence refused to leave. The most the guests could manage was a low, tense murmur. So much for ending the festival on any kind of an up note.

"I don't think they know," Gavin said as soon as we were out of earshot of the Wilsons. "Seems like they still think it was an accident."

"And one that was clearly my fault," I gulped. "I felt that glare clear to my bones."

"Don't worry, Libby. They said they were meeting with Frank. He'll set them straight."

I risked a glance back at the Wilsons, only to see Dorothy staring daggers at me from across the room. It wasn't hard to see where Julie got that fierce intensity and those piercing eyes.

"I'm not so sure it will help."

Ten minutes later Mom and the Gals walked in from their journey through the other three dessert locations. "I heard that woman gave you a ton of dirty looks," she said as she rushed up to me. "Hardly fair. You okay?"

The speed of gossip in this town never ceased to amaze me. "She's just an upset and grieving mother." It was what I'd been telling myself. Monica was shooting me looks that waffled between "what she said" and "I'm sorry you had to hear that." Part of me wanted to go over to her and ask, "Why on earth haven't you told your mother Julie was murdered?" Another part of me thought not only was it a pointless question, but this was entirely the wrong place to ask it.

"She'd better not lay into my daughter," Mom said.

"I'd like to think she won't in front of a horde of people, but . . ."

Gavin didn't finish the thought. The celebratory air really had gone out of the room, and I felt bad that his much-deserved finale had fallen flat. His last thirty minutes hadn't gone any better than mine, and we were both feeling stung.

"She's just been cold to me," I said. "I'll be okay. I just . . . didn't see it coming, that's all."

Mom picked up one of the rice puddings. "You shouldn't have seen it coming because it shouldn't have happened. Frank will set her straight. And if she has any sense at all, she'll come back and apologize."

"She didn't say anything outright . . . yet."

Mom stared at Dorothy Wilson, as if the sheer force of her maternal protection could stave off the frost coming from that side of the room. For a moment I was worried Mom would actually stomp over there and make yet another scene.

"I should just—" Mom began, proving me right.

I grabbed her arm. "No, you shouldn't. Please, Mom, just let it be. The woman just lost her daughter. I can handle a cold shoulder from her." I stepped in front of Mom, blocking both her path and her view of the icy glare Dorothy continued to throw my way. "Just enjoy your rice pudding. It's very good."

Mom looked at the artful dessert and set it down. She gave me a sideways glance.

"Well, that doesn't mean you have to sit here and take it. No offense, Gavin, but I've had enough of that woman's looks and of these froufrou goodies. I've got a sudden itch for one of Tom's cheeseburgers and a shake." She leaned in. "Let's get out of here."

"I can't," Gavin said, sounding like the idea had tremendous appeal.

I had to agree. The back of my neck was starting to hurt and it felt as if I was carrying my shoulders up around my ears.

Mom raised an eyebrow at me. "Maybe he can't, but *you* can."

Gavin gave a long-suffering sigh. "Go ahead. Save yourself."

Now that Mom had planted the idea, a gooey, greasy cheeseburger along the peaceful river suddenly looked way better than all the confections in the room. Still, I felt bad abandoning Gavin.

"No," I replied. "I can wait it out. It's only thirty more minutes." Thirty minutes that would feel like two hours, actually.

"Go," Gavin said.

"See?" Mom insisted.

"But . . ." I could feel my resistance dropping with every stare from Dorothy. And now even Hugh was giving me dark looks.

Gavin nudged me toward the door. "I'll feel better knowing you're out of the spotlight here. And maybe those two will simmer down."

After a few more assurances, I let Mom lead me in the direction of Tom's Riverside Diner and a culinary rescue. A deep breath of the gorgeous spring evening air made me feel as if I'd been underwater back in that restaurant.

"Thanks," I said as we turned the corner off Collin

Avenue. "I didn't want to leave Gavin, but I won't say I'm not glad to get out of there. The way Julie's mother looked at me . . ." I shook off the lingering chill.

"What's a mother for if not to stage a rescue? And besides, you can get away with stuff like that at my age. Or you don't really care what other people think—either one works."

I walked with Mom for a quiet minute or so, enjoying the space and the evening and the lack of accusatory parents before Mom said oh so casually, "I measured my bed the other day. I think it's just small enough to fit in that back bedroom at your house. I might not need most of the other stuff."

I shut my eyes. Why had I forgotten walking with Mom might be trading one aggravation for another? "I really don't want to get into that now."

"It fits. That's all I'm saying."

That's not all you're saying, and you know it, I yelled in the silence of my mind.

"I could probably pay off half your mortgage with what I'd get from selling the town house. It's got such a nice river view. Those go quick, you know."

I tried not to grit my teeth. "My mortgage is just fine, and you should keep your money."

She huffed. "Whatever for?"

Even though I thought, *Long-term care,* I opted for "Getting up there in years can be an expensive business."

She huffed again, louder this time. "Nonsense." Her tone changed immediately when she said, "Oh, look, there's Caroline. And who's that handsome man with her?"

I followed Mom's gaze to see Caroline sitting at one of Tom's outdoor picnic tables with Lloyd Jameson. They looked very happy to be in each other's company. And I was very happy for a diversion to steer Mom off the tender topic.

Mom hurried her steps to greet the pair. "Hello, Caroline dear. Who's your handsome friend here?"

Lloyd looked away in embarrassment, and Caroline's face flushed even as I felt my own heat up.

"Hello, Rhonda. This is Lloyd Jameson. He . . ." She seemed to realize—as I did—that there was no polite way to say, "He created the shepherd's crooks used in the murder and attack on Libby's store." Instead, Caroline shrugged and said, "Libby introduced us."

Mom seemed utterly thrilled at that. You'd swear she saw this as delightful proof I was taking up the family matchmaking business. Which I absolutely was not. Sort of. I gave myself stern orders to ignore the little glow of satisfaction sitting in my chest that my instincts about those two had been right.

"Caroline bought me a ticket to the dessert thing as a thank-you for delivering her rocking chair," Lloyd explained. "We got sidetracked and ended up here."

Lloyd cleaned up very nicely. It wasn't hard to see that "sidetracked" translated to "wanted to be alone."

"Us, too!" Mom said gleefully. "Good choice. Great burgers. And *such a pretty view*." She was all too obvious in her efforts to cast the spot as romantic, falling just short of a knowing wink.

"Yeah," said Lloyd, looking a little lost for words. "It's nice."

I tugged Mom toward the diner door. "Come on, Mom, I'm hungry." Not at all true, but I knew the windup to a Mom session of matchmaking when I saw it.

"There's the sweetest little gazebo down beyond the bend in the river," she called as I continued to tug her away from the happy couple. "Just perfect for a quiet conversation. The sunset is *so pretty* from there."

"See you later," I called over Mom, fully intending not to see Lloyd and Caroline again tonight.

I rushed Mom in through the diner door, hoping I hadn't ruined the evening for the one set of people in town who seemed to actually be enjoying themselves.

CHAPTER NINETEEN

R ats, I lost count again," I grumbled, and recounted the shipment of double-pointed needle sets for the third time Monday morning.

We still didn't know who had bought the crooks, who had set them at the warehouse, or who—if anyone—had messed with Julie's formulas. The long list of unknowns was playing havoc with my focus. Y.A.R.N. felt like it stood for "You Aren't Really Noticing" this morning. For the whole time since the murder, actually. I know stretching brings out the beauty in any lace pattern, but I was feeling stretched in every direction without any beauty coming from it. I was downright cranky lately, and that was no way to live.

Linda walked up and took the box from me. "You. Sit. Knit." She commanded me like a disobedient puppy, eyebrows furrowed. "For ten minutes, at least. Get yourself centered before we find the lace weight in with the extra chunky."

I picked up a cheery cotton washcloth I'd been working on that sat in a wicker basket on the table. The bright red square had a design of knit-and-purl stitches that created a trio of little hearts in all four corners. I rolled my shoulders, let out a long, slow exhale, and stitched a row. I told myself to let the stitches soothe my spirit, to make the beauty I'd always known as my best defense against chaos.

My quiet didn't last long. "Is it Barney? Someone Barney knows? Someone we don't even know?" I asked Linda after only two rows. I was bone weary of such questions.

Linda continued counting out needle sets against the shipping invoice. I tried not to be humbled by her ease with the task. "Maybe nobody meant to murder Julie," she offered, checking off a line with a pen. "Maybe someone just wanted to scare her and things went too far."

"I suppose that's possible. If people thought she was using ordinary dye chemicals, she'd just maybe get nauseated from the fumes without the ventilation, right? Or light-headed or some such thing?"

It bothered me that I considered those a lesser evil in this case. And blocking her exit? This wasn't some harmless prank. *You don't sicken people for fun. Ever.*

From what I gathered from Frank, buying the crooks wasn't in itself a crime, but using any object for homicidal or harassment purposes definitely was. And if the lack of ventilation had contributed to Julie's death— which I'm sure it had—whoever had put those crooks in place could be charged with murder.

I didn't like the idea of being afraid of yarn dyeing. It was a way colorful fiber came into the world, not a lethal process. This wasn't biological warfare, for crying out loud; this was fiber dyeing. And Julie was an expert at it. That woman was as competent as she was creative. I understood that she could be as caustic as her chemicals, but nothing about what she had done should have placed her in harm's way.

And then there was this pregnancy business. Had Julie believed herself to be pregnant? Or had there been some reason to lie about it to Monica? I had a million questions about the Wilson family dynamics, only none of it seemed to be any of my business. I certainly wasn't going to bring it up with anyone. I felt weird knowing it myself, although I understood why Frank sought my opinion. I didn't like the weight of such secrets dragging around behind me. I wondered how Frank coped with all the troublesome things his job must hand him. Maybe I *should* teach him to knit.

The sun came out from behind the veil of clouds that had darkened the morning, and I reveled in the light. The shop had looked so dark while the plywood covered the broken window. I'll never take my big beautiful sunny shopwindows for granted ever again. Had one person wielded all the crooks? Or had it been a gang of them? Frank couldn't solve this fast enough.

"There's just so much we don't know," I moaned to Linda as I finished off a row and turned my needles.

I was sitting, I was knitting, but I wasn't calming or centering. Calm and centered felt beyond me this morning.

"Seems to me," Linda said as she sorted more needles, "somebody had to have inside information. With how carefully Julie guarded her formulas, the only person who'd know about the sodium hydroxide was either Julie or the person who put it in her supplies. We should be paying more attention to that, maybe, than the crooks."

I voiced the thought that had kept me awake half of last night. "Unless they were the same person. Someone truly bent on ending Julie's life."

Linda nodded seriously, using the term she'd brought up earlier. "Redundant systems. For something you want to make absolutely sure happens no matter what."

We both shivered at that thought. If you want to talk about malice and forethought, a redundant murder system most definitely applied.

I was just shaking off the chill of that dark notion when the bell over the shop door rang. I looked up from my stitching, hoping to see Frank, but instead I saw Dorothy Wilson. She was the last person I expected to be visiting Y.A.R.N.—today, or ever.

I rose and set down the yarn. "Hello, Mrs. Wilson." I normally called people by their first names, but she looked like the formal type who didn't take to that sort of thing. "I'm surprised to see you here," I ventured.

She stood just inside the doorway, looking around the shop. It's a beautiful shop if I do say so myself. Bins of color and texture, samples of all kinds of needlework, and the great big blackboard with all the meanings for Y.A.R.N. I love to watch people take it in for the first time.

Normally. Not so much in this instance. In fact, I could see the exact moment when Dorothy Wilson's gaze found her daughter's handiwork. A sad shock, a jolt of grief pressed down her shoulders and tightened her jaw. She stood still for a moment or so, hands clasped tightly in front of her. I thought maybe it pained her to be so close to Julie's yarns. She surprised me, though, by walking straight over to the display of Julie's collection. She hesitated at first, then reached out to touch it with a cautious care. As if it stung. Given the circumstances, wouldn't it?

I didn't know whether she'd appreciate it or not, but I still felt compelled to say, "I am very sorry for your loss. It's so tragic." After her statement to me last night, I regretted those last three words.

And yet those three words knocked Dorothy out of her momentary stupor. "Yes, it is," she said, turning to look at me. Her expression bore little resemblance to the sharp glares she'd given me the night before.

"You've talked to Frank," I said simply. It was the only explanation for her change in attitude.

"Yes."

I couldn't imagine what that would have been like. To come thinking your daughter had died in a horrible accident only to learn it hadn't been an accident at all. I'd felt undone by the malice of my broken window—how much worse must it feel to learn your daughter was murdered?

Dorothy stood erect, tight and closed like a clamshell pulled from its tidal home. "It seems I owe you an apology."

Her tone was both clipped and weary. A handful of words carefully doled out by a woman barely hanging on.

I hadn't expected that. Sympathy twisted my heart as I pointed to the table. "Please, sit down."

She turned toward the table, then doubled back to pick up one of Julie's skeins and hold it tight between white-knuckled fists.

I began in the only way I could. "Monica tells me you taught both of them to knit."

"I did. Monica never had the patience for it, but Julie took to it like . . ." She glanced around the shop, "Well, like I suppose you took to it as a girl, too."

"My mother taught me," I offered. It seemed a silly detail in light of all that had happened. "I admired your daughter's work very much."

Dorothy met my eyes as she sat down. "Not everyone did."

I sat down opposite her. "Oh, I think most people liked her yarns and patterns. They were extraordinary. I suppose it was"—I searched for a kind way to put it—"the sharp edge of her opinions that put some people off."

She nodded in appreciation of the wording. "That is a good way to put it." She sighed. "She did always speak her mind."

I was wondering, as I'm sure Dorothy was, if Julie's speaking her mind had incited the violence against her. Mom always spoke her mind, and I liked to think I did as well. I didn't like the idea that it led to murder in this case. I knew Julie had held her values dear, but they seemed nowhere near important enough to kill over.

I dared to ask, "Why didn't Monica tell you?" It seemed a cruel thing to have to hear from a chief of police, even though I'm sure Frank was as compassionate as possible.

"Couldn't bring herself to do it, I suppose."

Dorothy set the skein on the table, unleashing her grip but still touching it with the fingers of one hand. I made up my mind right then to give her any skeins of Julie's yarn that she wanted. It seemed the least I could do.

"Monica is a fragile sort of soul," Dorothy said.

How different siblings could be. Fragile was the last word I'd have ever used to describe Julie. "I'm sure it must bother you how much they fought."

Dorothy's eyes got a faraway look. "They weren't always like that. As little girls, they were inseparable. But as they got older . . . Julie always seemed to skate through life while nothing came easily to Monica. Monica was such a peacemaker, where Julie lived for trouble. Whatever one of them did, she knew just how to throw it in the other's face."

I'd certainly seen that. "How is Monica?"

Dorothy's shoulders seemed to sink down at the question. "How are any of us? Shocked. Numb. Wanting to know who'd do this?" Her voice pitched up on those last words as she fought off tears.

"I have no doubt we will know the answer to that."

It seemed the only true assurance I could give. What would Barney and his friends have said if they could have seen this woman in front of me? This grief-stricken mother?

"I have some questions," I went on. "Would it be okay if I asked them?" When she raised an eyebrow as if she hadn't been expecting an inquiry from me, I explained, "I've been trying to help Frank with the investigation, and I think there are some important things you could tell us."

"I'll try."

"The silk pouch—the one like an envelope that said 'Recipes.' Do you by any chance know if that is where Julie kept her dye formulas?"

Dorothy seemed shocked at the question. "She still kept that?"

My heart warmed at the fact that she seemed so

touched by the news. "We found it in her room. Monica told me you made one for both of them."

"I didn't know Julie kept hers. Yes, I made them. A long time ago."

"So you don't know if she used it to store her formulas?" I continued. "A lot of people wanted to know how Julie created the incredible colors that she did. We found the pouch open and empty in her hotel room."

Dorothy shook her head. "She never told me much about what she did. I was never all that in favor of how she promoted her views. She was so talented. I can't understand why she felt she had to be so mean. She could have been even more successful than Monica if she had just *toned it down*."

There was a touch of anger in Dorothy's words. Understandable, given the circumstances, but the sharp comparison brought an echo of "Mom likes you best!" to my imagination. It seemed that Dorothy, knowingly or unknowingly, had pitted her daughters against each other.

"Can you think of anyone else with whom Julie might have shared her formulas?"

"Sharing was never one of Julie's strengths. Why would you ask that?"

Dorothy seemed to be missing a lot of details. "Didn't Chief Reynolds tell you any of this when you met with him?"

"I'm afraid I became quite . . . emotional . . . once I learned that her death was not an accident. I cut the meeting short. We have another meeting with him later today, but I felt I ought to come and apologize to you for the way I treated you last night."

"It's a very emotional time. I understand. About the

formulas . . ." I tried to find an easy way to explain it.
"There was a particular chemical—a dangerous one—
involved in Julie's death. A household version of sodium
hydroxide is often used in dyeing—"

She cut me off with a lift of her chin. "I know what
sodium hydroxide is. Mr. Wilson is in the adhesives
business."

I didn't know that sodium hydroxide was an adhesive
ingredient. I made a mental note to look further into that.

"I'm quite sure Julie didn't use sodium hydroxide.
She used soda ash like every other yarn dyer."

I found that awfully specific for someone who
claimed her daughter hadn't talked about what she did.
And exceedingly important to our investigation. It was
crucial that we figure out if Julie was knowingly using
that chemical.

"You know that? For certain?"

Dorothy backpedaled. "Well, no. Not specifically
about Julie's dyeing formulas. But I did try to learn a bit
about her work. A mother should show an interest, after all."

"Mrs. Wilson, an industrial version of sodium hydroxide was in her dye vats and in her body when we
found her. I—"

"You found her?" Dorothy cut in again.

"The paramedics, the chief, the mayor, and I, yes." I
didn't really want to admit the next part. "I'm afraid we
were coming to ask her if she'd been involved in the fire
where Monica was cooking."

Dorothy's eyes narrowed and most of the sorrow left
her eyes. In its place was the cold, hard stare I'd first seen
at the reception. "They thought my daughter set her sister's kitchen on fire?"

"Julie predicted it, actually. She told me just hours before the fire that I should be careful of a fire breaking out in Monica's kitchen." When a how-dare-you? look began brewing in Dorothy's eyes, I added, "We did discover the wires shaved on the standing mixer Monica was using. And we found wire strippers in one of Julie's pans of yarn. And she was in the kitchen alone that afternoon."

The hands gripped the skein again. "What are you implying, Ms. Beckett?"

"I'm not implying anything," I said, even though the evidence seemed rather clear. "We're all just trying to piece together what happened that night. Your daughters argued pretty fiercely earlier in the day. They'd been arguing since they got here, actually."

"A sister's relationship is always complicated. And I'm afraid Yale hasn't helped in that department lately."

"Yale?" I asked. It seemed telling that she'd bring him into this.

"He got along with Julie at first. Acted as a bit of a go-between. It's why I liked him, even before he did so much for Monica's career."

I noticed she said "liked"—past tense. "And now?"

"Lately he was just as bad with Julie as Monica." Dorothy put the skein down again, smoothing it out like a child's unruly hair. "It's not hard to imagine. Julie was always irritating the very people who could have been a help to her."

"How could Yale have been a help to Julie?"

Dorothy looked at me, surprised I didn't know. "He'd been trying to get her a show of her own. There had been a lot of interest. She might have been even more successful than Monica until"—she shook her head—"until Julie threw it all away a month or so ago by being . . . Julie." Exasperation cut an edge into her words.

"And Monica was okay with that?" Given how competitive the sisters were, I could hardly see Monica letting her sister outshine her.

"Like I said, Monica is always pleasing everybody. I'm sure Yale thought their rivalry would either make both of them try harder or just make for great drama." She frowned. "Yale loves nothing more than drama."

"He certainly had no shortage of it with Monica and Julie here."

"I have no doubt he planned it that way."

"Actually, he did," I replied. "He contacted some of our local sheep farmers, sending them videos of other farmers protesting with anti-Julie messages painted on their sheep."

Dorothy's frown deepened. "That sounds like Yale."

"Did Frank tell you we found the door and ventilation system blocked in the building Julie was using the night she died?"

"He did. Monica only told me the ventilation system had failed."

Monica's wording had made it sound like an accident. I could easily see how Dorothy could have come into town ready to blame me. After all, I was the one renting the warehouse, and it was my event.

I felt as if I was driving a painful point home when I replied, "It didn't fail, Mrs. Wilson. It was sabotaged. The fans—and the exit door—were intentionally blocked. By a trio of shepherd's crooks just like the one that was used to break my display window Wednesday night. We're not talking about an accident here." After a moment I dared to add, "Do you think Yale loves drama enough to do something like that?"

"Yale?" There was something about her surprise. It didn't strike me as genuine. "It's absurd to think Yale is behind this!"

"He has admitted to stirring up trouble with the sheep farmers. Maybe he thought a scare would encourage Julie to be less confrontational. Teach her a lesson about stirring up hate. Maybe he didn't intend for this much harm to come from it, but—"

Dorothy stood up, the skein still tightly in her hand. "I *do not* like what you're implying." It wasn't hard to see where Julie had gotten her ability to intimidate.

I don't like it, either, I thought, but didn't reply. I wasn't thrilled to be spending my days trying to figure out who had wanted my celebrity guest dead. "I don't mean to upset you."

"Well, you have. You've got a lot of nerve. How dare you? How dare you whip up notions that my family is somehow involved in this when anyone can clearly see it's those filthy sheep farmers? How can you even think such a thing?" She stalked toward the door. "My daughters would never harm each other. What's the matter with you people?"

Funny how selective a mother's vision can be. Dorothy could easily see, and perhaps even encourage, the wedge between her daughters. But she couldn't grasp the idea—even in the face of Julie setting the kitchen on fire—that such fierce friction had driven them to hurt each other. Maybe that was just an impossible thing for a mother to grasp.

I tried to salvage the moment. "I'd like you to have

that," I said, pointing to the skein of aquamarine yarn, "and anything else of Julie's that you want."

Dorothy seemed to wake up to the fact that she was about to walk out my door with a skein of my yarn in her hands. She looked down at her hand, still in a vise grip around the skein. "Oh, heavens." It seemed to derail her anger. "Just this, thank you."

"Mrs. Wilson," I began, keeping my voice soft, "I'm sure Frank has asked you this, but can you think of anyone other than the sheep farmers who would want to hurt Julie?"

She waved her free hand in exasperation. "Julie? I can think of dozens of people. She lived to rile people up. Julie reveled in the scorn. I told her over and over that one of these days her agitation was going to . . ." Her hand went to her mouth and she shut her eyes for a moment, composing herself. "So yes," she continued when she was ready, "lots of people wished Julie harm." She fixed me with a direct look. "But none of them is from this family."

With that, she put her hand on the door handle and resolutely pulled it open. "Arrest those horrid sheep farmers and stop casting shadows on Julie's own flesh and blood."

CHAPTER TWENTY

I had the most interesting conversation with Dorothy Wilson this morning," I said when I stopped into Frank's office as soon as I could get away.

"Lot of that going around," he grunted. "Some family, huh? It's been a long time since I've had that much drama in my office. I barely got half of the information out to her, and we never got to the questions I wanted to ask."

I sighed my agreement. "Well, I managed to get some information from her. And tell her most of what she didn't know before. But it wasn't fun. I'm actually startled she's talking to me at all."

"You don't need to play police chief, Libby. In fact, you shouldn't even be trying. I can handle it."

If I felt a little bit like I was being chastised, I was. Frank still hadn't quite forgiven me for going over to talk to Yale and Monica after he'd warned me off.

"I know, Frank. But I did learn some things from her. Before we get into that, please tell me we know who bought the crooks?"

The chief pressed his lips together. "We don't. And I don't mind saying I'm annoyed at that."

I sat down in his guest chair. "You and me both, Chief. Okay, so if we don't know, who do you *think* bought them?"

"My money is still on someone Barney sent over. I expect he thought the obviousness of shepherd's crooks would do double duty. It'd make the statement he wanted while being too foolhardy to let most people believe it was him. He was right about one thing—it was like signing his name to the deed. But it could just be hiding in plain sight."

"If that's true, why leave one on his own property?"

Harmless, grumpy old Barney out to murder Julie Wilson? Even with the facts lining up, I couldn't believe it.

"That way he looks like a victim rather than an instigator. But he had to have had help. Lloyd said it wasn't Barney who made the purchase and I can't see him getting up on that roof and pitching the crooks into the fans. Those were way up there. But he could have easily done the door. Or your window, for that matter." He leaned his elbows on his desk, looking a little weary. Weren't we all? "And then there's still the matter of the chemicals in the formula. Did Dorothy tell you anything about that?"

"As a matter of fact, she did." I was pleased to be able to give Frank substantive information. Playing police chief did have its advantages, you know. "Hugh Wilson is in the adhesives business. And Dorothy knows what sodium hydroxide is because it's used in adhesives."

Frank looked reluctantly impressed at my investigative find. "Well, what do you know?"

"And if you ask me, Dorothy seems to have a great talent for pitting her daughters against each other. She may have been half the reason they fought, from the looks of it." I paused for a thoughtful moment before adding, "Heaven knows Mom's a handful, but I'd never put her in the same class as Dorothy Wilson's parenting. That woman has mean, sharp edges. Even for someone in grief. At least Mom's just a loving sort of foggy."

Frank shook his head. "I gotta admit, I do find I have to take what Rhonda tells me with a grain of salt these days."

Leave it to Frank to say he had doubts about my mom's clarity in the kindest way possible. He'd always been so sweet with her. Even when she tried to text me and ended up dialing 911, he gently advised her to "leave texting to the kids"—and then told me never to text her.

Thanks to Jillian, Mom is now a champion—if inaccurate—texter. Some of my greatest laughs these days come from the field day autocorrect has with Mom's arthritic thumbs. Knitting dexterity does not translate to texting prowess. But it makes for some highly entertaining typos.

"She's trying to move in with me."

I don't know what made me blurt the words out like that. Maybe I wanted Frank's endorsement that it was a terrible idea. He was closer to Mom's age than to mine, and far more sensible about it.

He paused, taking in both the weight of my words and the not-so-hidden panic in them. "Sounds like something Rhonda would do."

"She's talking like it's the answer to everything."

For all his former brusqueness, his eyes took on a gentle understanding. "It's not."

It felt so good to hear someone else say that. "You know that, I know that, but how do I get Mom to see it?" I shifted my weight in the chair. "I'd last a week—maybe less—with her in that house. I love her—really I do—but . . ."

He held up a hand. "Rhonda can be a bit much, I know. Is she lonely over there across the river? Those town homes are nice, but I was never sure that was the best of ideas. Then again, you can't talk Rhonda out of anything once she gets it in her head."

I gulped. "That's exactly what I'm afraid of. She can't move in with me, Frank. We'll end up hating each other." I wanted to treasure—or at least enjoy—the time I spent with my mother. Her being around 24/7 seemed like the fastest way I could think of to kill that. "How do I explain that to her?"

Frank sat back in his chair. "Maybe you don't. Maybe you get one of the Gals to do it. Arlene."

I hadn't considered recruiting Arlene, but Frank's idea made a lot of sense. Arlene had a daughter my age who had a lovely family and lived about an hour from here. I'd never heard Arlene talk about moving in there.

"Anything's worth trying."

He nearly winked. "I thought those campaign posters were a hoot, by the way. Angie made sure we had one up here, although I wouldn't let her put it in the window." He chuckled.

"I have to go over to the theater later for a town hall rehearsal," I groaned.

"A town hall needs a rehearsal? Why are you having that thing in the big theater anyway?"

I groaned again. "George feels we're going to have a packed house. He wanted to be certain the sound and lighting were top-notch." I leaned in. "Now I wish I'd just kept the posters up and never suggested this. It's going to be awful."

"Oh, no," Frank refuted. "It's going to be fun. I'm going. Most of the department that isn't on duty will be there. Who doesn't want to watch you take George down a peg? We've all wanted to."

"That's just it," I replied. "I feel like everyone is expecting me to do what they've wanted to do for years. I mean, I know that's why I ran at first, but I want it to be about more than just everyone's annoyance with George."

"It is." Frank's voice had some of the grandfatherly assurance I always liked about him. "Gavin says you have some great ideas. You've got nothing to worry about, Libby."

I shook my head. "I'm debating King George and my celebrity guest was murdered and we don't know by whom or why. I've got lots to worry about."

A re we finished?" I said for what felt like the tenth time as I stood on the stage at one of three podiums set up for the coming debate. "I really don't think this is necessary."

I had a store to run and a murder to solve. It was almost dinnertime, I'd skipped lunch, and I felt little need to be wasting time checking lights and sound as if this were a national press conference. Our town's vintage theater, lovely as it was, felt enormous and empty. Anyone could see it was far too large a venue for the event. You'd have thought George was running for governor for all the fuss he was making.

"Speak into your microphones," the soundman, a local volunteer from our community theater troupe, said from his booth. He sounded as irritated to be there as I was.

"Hello, I'm Libby Beckett," I said, bending closer to the microphone until I heard Paula's voice in the back of my head reminding me not to do that. I adjusted the microphone so that I stood up straight, cringing at the feedback that filled the room as I raised it.

"More words," the voice said.

"Hello, I'm Libby Beckett and I think we're making far more of this than is necessary," I replied, indulging in a sideways glance George's way.

"It was your idea," George snapped back, but he evidently hadn't adjusted his own microphone. George's whine along with earsplitting feedback boomed throughout the room.

"One at a time, you guys" came the weary disembodied voice.

George's podium squeaked across the floor as he moved it a few inches toward the center. I found myself fighting the ridiculous urge to move mine as well. George was trying to position himself center stage and me off to one side. I expect even our poor sound technician could see that.

"I had a much smaller venue in mind. Town hall or even Corner Stone would have been nice. Not this."

I rather liked the idea of a friendly discussion at the local coffee bar. It would certainly be less nerve-racking than this business up on a huge stage in front of what was destined to be a tiny crowd. Was it too late to reinstate the Give Me LIBBertY posters?

"George now" came our technician's voice, sounding seriously put-upon.

"I asked to be addressed as Chamber President Barker," George huffed.

I gaped at my pompous opponent. "Oh, come now, George, really? Perhaps you'd feel more respected if your podium was center stage instead of the moderator's. I'm sure Gavin doesn't care where he stands."

Okay, that was a trifle petty, but George deserved it. I didn't have many calm nerves left and he was stomping all over them.

It quickly became clear that drawing this out any longer would likely result in a squabble. George might have wanted it, but I didn't need it, nor did our poor sound volunteer.

I closed my folder of notes and called brightly to our anonymous booth operator, "Thank you for your time. I'll be going now."

I could hear a glass of wine calling to me from the inn's bar across the street. Maybe I could even talk Bev into joining me and bringing something delicious from the kitchen. Since most of the festival guests had left or were on their way home, maybe she was ready for a bit of a victory celebration, too.

Leaving King George to his theatrical tendencies, I crossed the street. A group of men I recognized as Yale's camera crew was ferrying crates and suitcases out of the inn into a truck parked just outside the door. I offered a friendly wave as two of them recognized me. They'd been intrusive and annoying throughout the festival, but that wasn't their fault—they were just doing their jobs, pointing the camera where Yale told them.

I tried to edge around them, but one of the larger crates caught the edge of my tote bag and sent it to the ground. Some of the crew were quick to help me gather up the cards and notes that spilled onto the sidewalk and I waved another goodbye and ducked into the bar.

Inside, I found myself smiling at a small victory of my own. Lloyd and Caroline were tucked into a corner, leaning into each other in postures that had "second date going very well" written all over them. Two dates, two nights in a row. I beamed. It was nice to see something wonderful come out of all this nastiness.

Caroline caught sight of my entrance and waved a sheepishly happy hello. I waved back and started walking toward them when someone caught my elbow.

"You missed this," one of the camera crew said, handing me another card that must have escaped from my tote bag.

Lloyd's face changed immediately. He straightened up out of his chair. "Hey!"

He wasn't talking to me. He was glaring at the man beside me. "Hey, you!" Lloyd called. "Wait a minute. I need to talk to you."

The stocky cameraman took one look at Lloyd trying to make his way through the maze of cocktail tables and headed out of the bar.

Lloyd took off after him, yelling, "Stop! Wait!"

Caroline and I started to follow them both into the lobby.

"You're him," Lloyd declared, pointing a finger at the man.

"Him what?" the man replied. "Who are you?"

"You know who I am," Lloyd fired back. He started walking toward him. "I sold you those shepherd's crooks. You're the one who bought them."

Caroline and I stared at each other, then at the man, who was holding out a hand and shaking his head at Lloyd's accusation.

"Hey, I don't know who you think I am, but you got the wrong guy." He started back toward the truck.

Lloyd pursued him onto the sidewalk. "No, I don't. You're him. Admit it."

"I'm not gonna admit anything because we've never met. Lots of people look like lots of people, dude. I've got work to do, okay? Take your gripe somewhere else."

He joined the rest of the crew, who grumbled their annoyance and resumed work as if this happened all the time. It made me wonder just how much Yale put them up to on a regular basis.

Lloyd stomped back to us. "That's him."

I gaped at Lloyd. "You're sure? He bought the shepherd's crooks? One of Yale's camera crew?"

"Positive."

Lloyd turned back toward the truck and glowered at it as if his eyes could burn holes through it to the men working inside. I watched his hands fist at his sides and hoped a fight wasn't about to break out. Four to one wasn't good odds, even for someone as fit as Lloyd.

"I don't care what he denies," Lloyd said. "He's the one who bought the crooks."

"Well, then, you *should* take it somewhere else," Caroline said, putting a hand on Lloyd's tensed arm. "The police."

"I can't prove it." Frustration pulled Lloyd's tone short and low. It had truly wounded him to know his craftsmanship had been used in such an awful way. To have seen the man who had done it must have made the whole thing worse. "But it's him. I know it's him."

"Caroline, can you go in and settle up the bar tab while I walk Lloyd down to Chief Reynolds' office? You can meet us there."

The crew climbed out of the truck and walked past us, presumably back upstairs to get more things to load into the truck. I resisted the urge to tug on Lloyd's arm as the accused and the accuser glared daggers at each other. Lloyd was right. He had no proof, but his eyewitness account had to be valuable to Frank in looking for other clues. Still, Yale's crew? Why? As I got out my phone to dial Frank, I realized we might never have learned this if I hadn't brought Lloyd and Caroline together. Maybe the Beckett brand of matchmaking really did have its advantages.

Do not *ever* tell Mom I said that.

CHAPTER TWENTY-ONE

Tuesday morning, I tried to keep my head in the shop and let Frank do his job with Yale, Lloyd, and the crew. The crew truck—and I assume the crew—had not left despite packing up yesterday. That meant Frank must have made some progress. I was dying to know what had happened, and it was taking all my discipline not to walk down to his office and request an update.

Fortunately, a very pleasant distraction showed up. "What do you think?" Jillian said as she came in and held up her finished striped tank.

Evidently it was one of those school institute days. Her coming in to show off her work was the perfect way to take my mind off police matters.

"You're done? Already?" I didn't have to fake one bit of the admiration in my voice. I'd made a similar pattern and it had taken me twice as long.

She beamed. "I binge-watched a whole series and just

kept going. It's mostly stockinette stitch and I hardly even have to look down for that anymore."

While stockinette is one of the easiest of knitting's stitches, it usually takes a new knitter some time before it becomes that automatic—and that fast. I realized I had to stop thinking of Jillian as a new knitter. In her short time with the craft, she'd surpassed half of my customers.

I examined the garment she handed me. "Nice work, kiddo. That striping idea really worked."

"I know. I think I'm gonna wear it to the Corner Stone with Mark."

Her eyes went wide, as if she hadn't meant to let that slip. On the other hand, she also looked as if she was bursting to tell someone, and I knew as well as she did that someone probably shouldn't be Gavin. He'd blow a gasket. The least I could do was learn a bit more on his behalf.

"Going to the Corner Stone with Mark?" I tried to make sure my voice was dripping with friendly curiosity rather than a your-dad-might-go-nuts inquisition vibe.

"It's not a *date*," she shot back, emphasizing that last word. "We're studying. Mark is so busy on the lacrosse team, he's kinda flailing in history class." She tucked a strand of her wavy hair behind one ear with just the hint of a dreamy look in her eyes. "I'm just helping him."

A lacrosse player. "Did you know your dad played lacrosse?" I hoped that would earn poor Mark some lenience from the mayor's fatherly eagle eye.

"Kinda."

Kinda nothing. The only time Gavin waxed nostalgic about our high school days was when he talked about lacrosse. I suspect the trophies were still somewhere in his house—not that I'd ever been over there to snoop.

"He was really good," I offered. "I've always thought lacrosse players were nice guys. Just the right amount of athlete without the whole jock factor."

"No kidding?"

I'd meant it more about Mark's prospects, but the resulting expression on Jillian's face told me she was all too eager to interpret this as a compliment for her father.

"So when is this study session with Mark?" I tried to ask casually.

"Why? Are you gonna tell Dad?"

I allowed myself a dubious look. "Aren't you?"

She rolled her eyes. "He'll go bonkers. He'll make a huge deal out of it."

I handed Jillian back the tank top. "He might. But I can almost guarantee you he'll go even more bonkers if he finds out you kept it from him." I carefully waded into the dangerous current of quasi-parental advice. "Trust is a big deal for someone your age. You want more freedom, but your dad has to learn he can trust you with it. Hiding the fact that you're studying with Mark will do just the opposite."

She threw her hands up in the air, a touch of teenage drama pitching her voice higher. "There'll be three other kids there. It's a whole group of us."

"Well, there you go. Lead with that. It'll make it a whole lot easier for your dad to know that up front." I couldn't resist adding, "But that doesn't mean you can't make sure you sit next to Mark."

"Is that Julie's yarn?" came a voice from behind me.

I turned to find Monica staring at the top Jillian had made. I'd been so caught up in Jillian's social adventures, I hadn't even noticed her come in the shop. I certainly hadn't thought I'd be seeing her today.

"It is," I answered her with as much warmth as I could. "Didn't Jillian do a wonderful job with the pattern?"

"Jillian," Monica said, eyes narrowed in thought. "You're the girl from the YouTube channel, aren't you? The mayor's daughter."

Jillian didn't seem to know if Monica found this a good thing or a bad one. I have to confess, I didn't, either.

"Yep, that's me," she replied, fingers tightening a bit around the knitting. For a split second Jillian's grip reminded me of Dorothy Wilson. So many people were trying to hold on to a bit of Julie.

"You did a nice job with that interview. My sister is— *was*"—her words hitched on the correction—"a handful."

Jillian shrugged. "She was nice to me. I'm sorry about what happened. I came in to show Ms. Beckett what I'd made and to buy more of Julie's yarn."

Monica swallowed hard. "Funny, that's why I'm here, too."

In the time since I opened the shop, I've learned to spot when someone says they've come in for yarn, but they're also here to talk. Usually it's customers I know well, but not always. I suppose the comfort of the craft and all the cozy textures open people up. Monica's expression, and whatever I suspected was swirling around Yale and the crew this morning, gave the woman the air of someone who needed to talk.

This wasn't playing police chief. There were things I could do that Frank couldn't, and this morning a woman-to-woman conversation with Monica was one of them. Here was my chance to ask Monica the dozens of questions buzzing around in my mind about her family.

"Julie's pattern books are over there," I said to Jillian,

pointing to the bookshelf on the back wall of the shop. "Pick what you like and I'll ring you up when you're ready."

"Yep." Jillian picked up her bag and her garment and trotted back to the pattern books.

Even at her age, she needed very little guidance from me about choosing a pattern. Choosing a boyfriend? Well, I said a small prayer she'd come to me when that question arose whether it was Mark or not.

Monica looked after Jillian. "Clever girl. I don't think I had it all together like that when I was her age."

I managed a soft laugh. "I find myself saying the exact same thing around Jillian a lot."

"She was Julie's last interview."

"I know."

We let the finality of that sit between us for a moment. I expected her to say something about the camera crew thing, but she didn't. Maybe she didn't want to. I couldn't believe she didn't know.

I was just trying to figure out how to bring it up when Monica squared her shoulders and said, "Mom said you gave her a skein of Julie's yarn. I'd like one, if that's okay."

The sadness in her tone reminded me that whatever else was going on, the woman in front of me was still in deep grief over losing a sister. "You and your mother can have as much of Julie's stock as you'd like. On the house. I feel like it's the least I can do after what's happened."

Monica's eyes glistened. "That's very kind of you. I just want to make something small. A scarf perhaps. You know, just something to . . . have."

I touched her shoulder gently. "Of course. I think she's got three or four patterns to pick from. Let's start with a color and go from there." I brought her to the shelves Jillian was just stepping away from with an armful of the Riverbank color.

Despite an altered formula or a botched process—we'll never actually know what the process should have been—the Riverbank yarn had still turned out beautifully. Despite the yarn sitting in the dye water far longer than I imagine Julie had planned, I was still able to salvage it from the warehouse, rinse it, and hang it out to dry. The blues and greens softened as the skeins dried, bringing the white touches out and showing off a shimmer that reminded me so much of water, it was pure genius. We should have had so much more of the exclusive color. It saddened me that now we never would. Julie had never finished the multiple batches she planned to make.

"What are you going to make with that?" Monica asked.

"The cardigan. The one with the big collar." Jillian looked at me. "Is it okay that I use this color?"

I knew exactly which sweater Jillian was talking about. It was one of Julie's most beautiful patterns in my opinion. I'd been hoping to carve out enough time to start one myself.

"I can't think of a better place for those to go than with you. I'd like to think Julie would agree. Don't you, Monica?"

Monica swallowed hard and simply nodded at the skeins in Jillian's arms.

"You've got enough skeins?" I asked, a little sad to see them go but happy they were going with Jillian. "Was that all of them?"

We all paused for a moment, snagged by the thought

that there would be no more amazing fibers—in River-bank or any of her legendary colors—from Julie Wilson. What we had would be all we'd ever get. There seemed so much wrong about that.

"There's one left." Jillian shrugged. "I'm pretty sure I have enough and it wouldn't be fair to take them all."

Without a word, Monica took the last remaining Riverbank skein and placed it in Jillian's arms. Neither Monica nor I said anything, because I think we both worried we'd burst into tears if we tried.

"Thanks," Jillian said tentatively, as if not sure that was the right answer in the awkward moment. "Grandma Rhonda would say it was meant to be, huh?"

I smiled. "That's what Mom always says, doesn't she?"

I rang up her purchase while Monica looked around the shop and explored the baskets of Julie's fibers. She seemed to need a bit of time alone with Julie's work, and I was glad Jillian's purchase gave her that space without it feeling awkward.

Jillian walked over to Monica before leaving. She held out an impressively polite hand for someone not old enough to drive a car, and said in earnest, "It was nice to see you again and I really am sorry about your sister."

I made a mental note to tell Gavin about her poise and manners. Monica and I both gazed at Jillian as she nearly skipped down the street, delighted with her purchase.

"Remarkable young lady," Monica said. She then turned to me. "Your mom is her grandma?"

I could tell she was trying to work through the illogical family tree on this one.

"My mother decided Jillian could adopt her as her

grandmother. I can't give her the precious commodity of grandchildren, and let's just say biology didn't deal Jillian a good hand in the maternal resources department."

Something flashed in Monica's eyes. "No family of your own?"

I sighed. "Not for want of trying. Well, on my part. Sometimes I wonder if my ex wasn't secretly relieved. Our divorce was nasty enough as it was. But Gavin is doing an all-star job as a single father, wouldn't you say?"

"I can't seem to get pregnant," Monica blurted out. "I never know how to tell people that. And it's always the insensitive ones who grill you about it, isn't it?"

Suddenly things made a lot of sense. If Julie was an expert at pushing Monica's buttons, fate had handed her a very large and painful one to push. It seemed cruel for Julie to flaunt even the possibility of her pregnancy—wanted or unwanted, which we'd never know—to her sister. But why lie about something like that to the person it hurt the most?

It would probably be classified as Mom-class nosiness, but I couldn't help myself. "Frank told me what you said Julie told you." When Monica's eyes shot wide in surprise, I added, "Frank had to ask me questions about which dye chemicals Julie would avoid if she was pregnant. It was pertinent to the case, and he asked me in strictest confidence. Please don't be upset."

Monica blinked back tears. "Isn't it obvious?"

The pain these two sisters had flung at each other stunned me. How could their mother have sat there and watched this kind of warfare between her children?

"Did you want Frank to give you proof? Did you think she might be lying about that? I mean, it's not the kind of thing you can . . . fake. Not for long, at least."

Monica rubbed one arm. "I don't know if you realized this, but my sister had a . . . shall we say *casual* relationship with the truth. She's very good at finding whatever facts will support what she wants to say." Her tone took on an edge. "I mean, look at your sheep farmers. She's made every farmer out to be a villain. But maybe in this case they are, huh?"

I chose not to answer that. "Still, a *pregnancy*?"

"Two weeks ago Julie and I got together and tried to . . . resolve . . . some things. Well, *I* tried. Of course, it failed miserably. It always has. I made the mistake of telling Julie the show was in talks to be picked up for national syndication. *Dish Up Comfort* is in a position to take a great leap forward. Product branding, a whole new line of cookbooks, the works. Yale's been working on this for months."

She picked up the same golden-hued skein for the third time—as if she loved the color but couldn't bring herself to take it home. It was a lush mixture of butter-yellow and honey-toned hues, with just the tiniest bit of sheen to make it glow when the sunlight caught it right.

The hue was the exact opposite of the dark flash in Monica's eyes as she looked at me. "She'd been on the brink of her own success, you know? I actually thought maybe now she could be happy for me." Her tone was sharp and sour, wounded to the core. "I was hoping this festival might just be the turning point for us. Can you imagine?"

"I'm sorry." Really, what else was there to say?

"So of course she went out and cooked up her worst to hurt me. Say *the one thing* sure to hurt me the most. Who cares whether it was true? When did she ever care if anything was true? As long as she got the upper hand over me, nothing else mattered."

"I'm so sorry," I repeated.

And I was. So much bitterness. Things ought to have been so different between them, and now there was no chance for that to ever happen. Monica was going to have to make peace with the lack of peace between them all on her own. Much more had died that night than just one fiber artist. Hope and any chance of reconciliation were gone, and maybe even a whole family was going to dissolve in the process.

I nodded toward the yarn in Monica's hands. "That will make a lovely shrug." I reached for one of the pattern books. "It's a little sort of sweater that just goes around your shoulders. And it's simple to knit. You'd only need that one skein." I held out the page in the book like a peace offering. "It's even called the Honey Shrug. Fits the color you chose, don't you think?"

She had chosen the color—three times—but she just wasn't ready to realize it. People think I help customers pick out yarn. Many times, however, I'm just helping them act on the choice they've already made. Or want to make. It never ceases to amaze me how so many people need permission to be nice to themselves.

"Please let me give this to you."

I meant every word of my plea. Even if I discovered Julie's killer and brought them to justice an hour from now, so much of this tragedy could never be made right. This one little thing, this one tiny bit of reconciliation, was within my grasp.

"I don't deserve it." Her voice was soft and so very wounded. "The things I said over these past days . . ." Her words trailed off.

Monica's shrill voice shouting insults in the Riverside Inn hallway echoed in my ears.

"One of the saddest things in life is that you never know the last time is the last time." I don't know what made me tell her my story, but I went on. "My dad was one of those people who was never afraid to tell me how proud he was of me. For even the tiniest things. And what I remember is not so much the words, but the way he'd hold my shoulders when he said them." I felt my own voice grow thick with the threat of tears. "Take the yarn. Knit the shrug. And tell yourself this is Julie holding your shoulders in the way she should have."

A tear ran down Monica's cheek. "You think I should?"

I sniffed myself. "I know you should."

Her shoulders, so slumped in sorrow and anger when she had walked into the shop, straightened just the tiniest bit. "Okay."

CHAPTER TWENTY-TWO

Sometimes pie for lunch is an excellent strategy. Actually, I believe pie for anything is a worthy tactic, but after the emotionality of my morning in the shop, I headed across the street the minute Linda arrived to hold down the fort. Between Mom, Monica, and George, my stress level was somewhere between lemon merengue and chocolate pecan. Maybe even both.

Margo, the practitioner of pies, prescribed cherry à la mode, which I didn't even think of but was absolutely the perfect choice. Cold ice cream, warm cherry pie, and the ear of a good friend are some of life's best stress busters, and I was fortunate enough to find myself sitting in Margo's with all three.

"Julie really would do that to her sister, say she was pregnant just to get under her skin?" Margo gave the same shiver I'd been feeling since my conversation with

Monica. "That's some weapons-grade sibling rivalry right there."

I swirled my forkful of pie in the delectable pool of melting ice cream. "I know. But evidently Monica was about to have a big success with the show. I guess Julie chose the most painful weapon she had—even though it doesn't make much sense."

Margo pulled a set of pies out of the oven. "Not really a smart choice. Can't really fake something like that for long, can you? The truth would come out sooner or later."

"I know. I thought just the same thing. But Frank was just telling me people do illogical things when their emotions get the better of them."

Margo pointed at me with an oven mitt still on her hand. "And he ought to know, being police chief and all. I mean, let's talk about Angie."

"What about the police chief—and Angie?" came a deep, familiar voice from behind us.

Margo and I traded glances. Neither one of us had seen Frank coming in the shop, and we would never have said a word if we had known he was right there.

"What?" Frank pressed.

I opted for diversion. "I was just telling Margo something Monica admitted to me and remembering how you taught me that emotions make people do illogical things."

Frank wasn't being diverted. "What's that got to do with Angie?"

"Nothing," Margo piped in. "That's what we were saying."

Sometimes you can almost see Frank's police evidence radar go up. He's like a dog with a bone when he sees something he has to uncover. Rather like me when

I discover my stitches are off—it can be eleven thirty at night and I'll stay up until I find the error and correct it all the way back to where I was. But less life-or-death.

The chief's steady gaze told me we were about to broach the subject of Frank and Angie. Margo and I exchanged you-say-it/no-*you*-say-it glares. Why was the world asking so much bold bravery out of me this week?

"Frank," I said, trying to match his talent for delivering startling news with compassion, "no one thinks your relationship with Angie is illogical."

He froze for a moment, stuffed one hand in his pocket, and shifted his feet nervously. His rebuke of "What relationship with Angie?" was about as useless as they come. "Who thinks I have a relationship with Angie?" he demanded.

It probably was unfortunate that Margo and I answered, "Everyone," in immediate unison. The man's face went nearly as red as my cherry pie.

"It's sweet," Margo said. "You're perfect for each other."

Frank looked utterly, adorably exposed. His eyes went everywhere around the shop except to meet the smiles we were trying to give him. "I . . . but . . . we . . ."

"That's almost the best part," I said. "You two are trying so hard to hide it. But you don't need to. We're all for it. Really."

He looked as if that shocked him. "Really?" He paced the shop for a moment, trying to reconcile the fact that his secret wasn't a secret at all. "We were . . . so careful."

"What you *are* is so *adorable*," Margo replied.

"You've been the model of discretion," I offered, looking for a way to soothe his agitation. His don't-play-police-chief chiding aside, he'd been a support to me about Mom. I wanted to return the favor. "But this kind of thing gets to be pretty obvious—when two people are so perfect for each other, I mean."

Margo's directness got the better of her. "Mercy, Frank, stop fussing and just *date* the woman. Take her to a lovely dinner. Buy her flowers. Hold her hand as you walk down the street. Be *happy*!"

Frank looked as if Margo had just challenged him to jog down Collin Avenue in his boxer shorts. His mouth opened and shut twice as if he couldn't for the life of him figure out how he was supposed to reply to that.

"Why wouldn't we want our chief of police—and our friend—to be happy? This is one workplace romance not a single person I can think of will object to. Really." I swear Frank actually flinched at my use of the word "romance." "Please don't think you need to be careful. You don't." I tried to add my warmest smile. "Most of us figured it out a long time ago anyway."

The chief struggled with this epic failure of secret keeping. I suppose he probably prided himself on his ability to keep information under wraps. After all, my short time in helping him with investigations—even when I wasn't supposed to had taught me Frank always knew way more than he ever revealed. About a lot of people. Part of the job, I imagine.

"I . . . suppose," he bumbled, at more of a loss for words than I had ever seen the man.

Margo, master anticipator of needs, leapt to action. "Start with something small. Take her some chocolate tarts. Right now. On the house as my endorsement." When Frank hesitated, Margo gave him a do-as-you'retold glare. "Frank Reynolds, you are the bravest man I know. Do it."

To drive her point home, she began boxing up a trio of her small tarts with a conviction that told us this baker was not taking no for an answer.

"I can't," Frank protested.

"You *can*," Margo insisted.

"No, I mean I can't right now. I came in here to give Libby an update."

"Will you take these tarts to Angie right after you give Libby an update?" Margo's middle name isn't Relentless, but it should be.

I was getting my long-awaited update! Frank walked to the small table where Margo and I had been sitting. When his quick glance Margo's way indicated a need for privacy, Margo found something to do in the back kitchen. But not before making a grand display of placing the box of tarts in front of Frank on the table.

We sat down. "You got something out of the crew member?"

If I'd wanted a distraction from my need to know this morning, life had certainly delivered it in Jillian's and Monica's visits to Y.A.R.N. But I was more than ready to learn the truth now.

"No. He insists it wasn't him. Of course, his alibi is that he was with the crew, and they back it up. I'd expect them to."

I hadn't made an important connection until just this moment. "Did you ask him if he was the one to put the crook through my shopwindow?" I'd been so busy thinking about the crooks as a murder weapon, I'd momentarily forgotten they'd harmed Y.A.R.N. as well. "Lots of people look like lots of people, dude." I felt my fists tighten as much as Lloyd's had.

"He denies he has anything to do with any of it." Frank's frown was filled with the same frustration I felt.

"I don't believe that for a minute," I muttered.

"Neither do I, but I can't prove it. Yet. Someone had to give him the money to do it—I don't think he was acting on his own. I wouldn't be surprised if we find out he has Bev's missing hotel key, either."

"But don't forget, Barney said his nephew worked at the inn." I thought some more. "Yale? The crew members are his employees."

"Wagner's denying it all. And even if he did admit to the crooks, buying them isn't a crime any more than you buying a steak knife makes you Jack the Ripper. The purchase is suspicious, but it isn't illegal. We have to prove one of them used the crooks with intent to harm, and that might be a challenge."

"Of course they intended to harm. Blocked exits? Jammed fans? Hardly *decorative* uses."

"True, but it doesn't tie anyone to the sodium hydroxide, either."

"So we are looking for one person who had access to both the crooks and the sodium hydroxide." It was a sad commentary on the state of affairs that I considered one culprit better than two.

"Which points to the Wilson family," Frank replied. "Their company would have the stuff on hand. That'll take some digging, but there might be some shipping records or supply documents we could get our hands on. In the meantime, can I count on you to press charges if I can nail the crew guy for destruction of property?"

"Oh, count on it." A realization shot through me. "Wait. . . . There were six crooks. We found five. Where's the last one?"

He scratched his chin. "Well, that's the problem."

I stared down at my ice cream, now fully melted all over what was left of my cherry pie. I confess it looked more like a bloody mess than a delicious dessert at the moment. "So there's one more crook out there and we don't know where it is or who has it or what it will be used to do next?"

I took no comfort from Frank's worried look. "I'm afraid so."

"The debate's tonight," I complained. "How in the world am I going to keep my mind on that challenge with all this going on?"

Frank shrugged. "Another slice of pie?"

CHAPTER TWENTY-THREE

It was six fifty-nine p.m., and I couldn't remember the last time I had been so nervous. I kept looking out over the audience in the theater seats, imagining some goon waiting in one with a hidden shepherd's crook poised for harm.

I knew that was ridiculous. A shepherd's crook is far too large to hide, I doubted it could do much harm to me from that distance, and I'd already been the target of one attack and was unlikely to be the target of another. None of those sensible facts did a thing to the legion of butterflies in my stomach. Ninety percent of me wanted to call this off, but the other ten percent knew I'd never hear the end of it from George if I did. It had been my idea, and it was time to see it through.

George stood in the wings on the opposite side of the enormous stage. For the tenth time in as many minutes, I regretted agreeing to George's choice of venue. When

Gavin walked onstage for his role as moderator, he looked like he'd have rather been doing anything else. I couldn't blame him.

"Well, folks," Gavin began, "welcome to the first ever Collinstown Chamber of Commerce Candidate Event." Despite George's strong preference, Gavin refused to call it a presidential debate. "George and Libby will each read a short statement and then answer an agreed-upon list of questions. After that, we'll take questions from all of you. With any luck we'll be out of here by eight thirty and you can all get on with your evenings."

As we took our places behind each of two podiums, I looked out into the audience to see Mom and Jillian; Margo and her husband, Carl; and Arlene and all the Gals in the front row. Directly behind them on the aisle was Frank, with Angie sitting next to him.

Good for you, I thought. *Go be happy.*

In fact, the first few rows were filled with YARNies and Collin Avenue business owners. I caught sight of Mom nudging the bank manager next to her and mouthing, *That's my daughter,* as if he didn't already know.

My nerves eased a bit as I reminded myself most of these people were all friends eager to see me succeed. If I lost the election—even by a landslide—I'd still be able to count every one of these smiling faces as friends.

Gavin gave each of us a "Ready?" look and cleared his throat again. "George, your opening statement."

How the event went from there wasn't a surprise to anyone. George gave a long list of his perceived accomplishments and business genius. I set forth my vision for how Collinstown businesses could work together. George clearly saw me as an unfortunate nuisance of democracy, just a hoop he had to jump through to earn his next term as president.

When I admitted, "I've never been a Chamber president. In fact, before last year, I hadn't even been a shop owner," George made such a derisive grunt, I hoped everyone heard. True to Paula's prediction, George's own bombastic style felt as if it was winning the debate for me.

The first audience question came from Paul, who owned the Corner Stone. "What, in your opinion, is Collinstown's greatest challenge in the coming years?"

I was ready for something like this. "Our greatest challenge is to keep being Collinstown. To keep our charm and sense of community as we grow and as tourism grows. Oh, I know technology gives us new ways to advertise and communicate, but it will always be who we are that attracts visitors and sustains our businesses. We're knit together. We care for one another, and there are so many ways we can support one another."

Paula gave me a big thumbs-up, Margo beamed, and Mom nudged the bank manager again.

"George, your rebuttal?" Gavin said. I could tell George's insistence on the procedural formality of this whole thing was getting on his nerves.

"What's our biggest challenge?" George declared with a theatrical flair. "We've learned the answer to that now, haven't we?" He indulged in a dramatic pause. "Crime," George bellowed into his microphone. "It pains me to say that crime has come to our quiet little town. *Murder* has come to Collinstown."

There was a collective gasp from the audience as both Gavin and I gave disbelieving looks of shock to George.

George, of course, ignored us, giving a jam-packed speech that stopped just short of accusing me of busing homicidal maniacs into town. He somehow made the shepherd's crooks look like the mob's pitchforks in *Frankenstein*, and Barney's sheep protest seem like a violent riot. And laid all of it at my feet.

Here I'd always thought my challenge was that I was only running against George and not for anything concrete. I was suddenly looking at the transformation of George's campaign into an anti-Libby diatribe rather than any solid defense of his own service to our town. Paula was right. All I had to do was be me, calmly state my ideas, and stand back to watch George work himself up into an unreasonable lather. And hope he failed to bring anyone over to his viewpoint.

After our concluding statements, I let out my breath. Home stretch. Job done. George and I gathered on either side of Gavin to bid good night to our long-suffering audience. I was just daring to believe I might have come out on top of this when a strange metallic clang rang out above our heads. The lights flickered for a second, and I looked up to see the shadow of something swinging down out of the scaffolding. Before I could take a breath to scream, I felt Gavin grab me and pull me back out of harm's way, but not before a shepherd's crook plummeted to land with force on Gavin's right shoulder.

Gavin sat on the edge of the stage and winced as I handed him the ice pack Bev had rushed over from the inn. He rolled his shoulder carefully as if to confirm it still worked.

The paramedic nodded to the shepherd's crook Frank

was sliding into an extra-large evidence bag brought over from the station. "That thing could have broken your collarbone if it had landed another few inches toward your neck. Or given you a concussion if it had hit your head."

Frank sealed the bag. "This had better be the last of them."

Our chief had been impressive. While the rest of the audience was frozen in shock once the staff of wood landed with a sickening thud on Gavin's shoulder, Frank had sprinted from his seat and leapt onstage. With a speed belying his years, the chief darted through the backstage area in search of whoever had rigged the crook to fall. When they lowered the fly rigging, we learned why there was no one to find. There, attached to the bar that held various lights and theatrical hardware, was a latch system and a timer set to go off at eight twenty-three p.m. I wanted to shout either "Who would do something like this?" or "Someone go arrest the *Dish Up Comfort* camera crew!" but with Mom and Jillian nearby, we were all trying to keep things from escalating here.

"Are you sure you're okay?" I asked Gavin for the tenth time.

Three people had asked me if I was okay. No one had asked George, but he kept assuring people, "I'm fine. I've not been injured."

"I expect I'll be sore in the morning," Gavin replied, "but I'll be fine. Nothing's broken." He finished off the sentiment with another shoulder roll and a nasty glare at the timing device.

I had never seen Frank this angry. This blatant attack—yes, I was choosing to use that word—combined with George's none-too-subtle knock at Collinstown's rising crime rate, was already enough to get Frank's goat. George's reaction to the whole situation was only making things worse. Rather than show any concern for Gavin's well-being, George stalked around the auditorium with an unspoken "I told you so" radiating off him like a heat wave. For a moment I think he actually considered that I'd rigged the crook to take him out of the running—can you think of a more absurd notion? Had Gavin not been injured, I think he would have physically dragged George out of the building. Mom and Arlene looked as if they might actually try it.

"Not to worry, folks," Frank said to all of us as the officers expertly removed the release mechanism from the theater rigging and bagged it alongside the crook. "I'll get to the bottom of this."

With no evidence to hold him, the *Dish Up Comfort* camera crewman had been released with the rest of the crew to head on to the show's next project. As for Yale, I had little doubt he'd be getting a visit from Frank within the hour.

The stunned silence was broken by a quiet, nervous question from Jillian. "Can we go home, Dad?"

The poor girl was rightly scared by the whole thing. She'd always been so proud of Gavin as mayor, I hated that she now had to associate that honor with danger.

Gavin rose. "Of course, sweetheart. It'll all be okay. Don't worry."

None of us was sure it would be okay, and all of us were worried. But there was Gavin trying to be the reassuring father, the stalwart mayor, and my dear friend.

I went over and gave Jillian a big hug. "Everyone is okay or mostly okay. Chief Reynolds will do his job and in no time we'll be thinking up another festival."

I paused for a moment before putting my arms carefully around Gavin and his ice pack. "You're my hero," I said quietly in his ear. Then, on pure impulse, I left a small kiss on his cheek. Surely being saved from assault by a shepherd's crook deserved more than an ordinary thank-you.

I had meant for it to be a small thing, but it wasn't. I think on some level I knew it never could be—not with all that history between us. I like to think that we hid the significance of it, that no one noticed the seismic shift occurring between Gavin and me. Based on the look I got from Mom, I expect we were no more successful than Frank and Angie had been. We made a hopefully none-too-flustered flurry of small talk as everyone gathered their things and made their way out of the theater.

I wasn't surprised Mom followed me to my car. She was parked next to me, after all. I was surprised when she popped her trunk, pulled out a suitcase, and tossed it onto my backseat before planting herself in my passenger seat.

"That's it," she said. "I'm moving in."

CHAPTER TWENTY-FOUR

I was in the shop by eight the next morning. Two hours early, but I needed to get out of the house before Mom could launch back into the nonstop argument I hadn't been able to squelch last night. Somehow Mom's brain simply could not accept the words "No, you're not moving in."

Of course, the fact that I'd been too jittery and exhausted to stop her invasion last night wasn't helping. I'd made a colossal mistake in allowing her that inch, and she was already calculating her next mile. Plotting my countermeasures, I made a hasty morning exit and told her I'd swing back with her car to pick her up for lunch and further negotiations. No, not negotiations—there was nothing to negotiate. This was boundary enforcement. Mom was *not* moving in.

By nine the lack of information was making me fidgety. What had Frank learned? Who was behind the crooks? Could we prove yet that the *Dish Up Comfort* cameraman had bought them? And who had put him up to his crimes? I had lost patience for uncovering who had harmed Julie, scared my town, and bashed my window.

There had to be something I could do to move this investigation along. So despite the fact that I knew it would likely earn me a lecture from Chief Reynolds, I hatched a plan. Armed with a selection of scones from Corner Stone and two large coffees, I once again walked up the stairs of the Riverside Inn to where Monica and Yale, and now Mr. and Mrs. Wilson, were staying.

As I rounded the landing, déjà vu hit me as I heard Monica yelling, "You and mother! I can't believe my ears. Did neither one of you ever think to talk to *me* about this?"

"Something had to be done. She was getting out of hand. You tried talking to her, and you saw where that got us. No one was supposed to get hurt."

I heard a click and the door to Monica's room was flung open. I ducked back down the stairs far enough to be out of sight but still close enough to hear any further conversation. Not exactly noble of me, but I couldn't resist.

"And we all see where that got us. She's dead, Yale. You and Mother decided she needed a good scare and now your stupid prank killed her. I hope you're happy."

The door shut again. "Lower your voice, Monica. People will hear you."

"They should hear me," Monica shouted. "I should go to the police right now. They already think your crew did it. Imagine how fascinated they'll be to learn you *told* them to!"

I found it *fascinating* she referred to the workers as

"your crew." Weren't they her crew as well if it was her show? I heard a few thumps and wondered what was being slammed to the floor. A suitcase? Cookware?

"Monica honey, if you can just stay calm—"

"I will not stay calm. Don't you 'Monica honey' me. Not after what you've done. Don't you *ever* 'Monica honey' me again. Do you hear?" More thumps of things hitting the ground—or the wall. "Get out of here, Yale. Take Mom and Dad with you for all I care. Right now I can't stand the sight of any of you." There was a pause, and then Monica's voice returned, tearful. "God, Yale, how could you? This on top of everything else you've done to me? To us?"

What else had Yale done? My mind calculated a dozen options, all of them chilling. I pulled out my phone and texted Frank: INN NOW YALE. I figured this deserved all caps.

I heard a door click open again and saw the corner of a suitcase being launched out into the hallway. Yale and Dorothy were trying to find a way to frighten Julie into toning down her behavior? That was ironic. Dorothy had sounded so sad and sorry at the shop, but evidently that had all been an act.

"I know you're upset . . ." Yale sounded a bit desperate not to get kicked out and likely turned in, but Monica did not sound as if she was going to give him any choice.

"Upset? *Upset?* Burning my caramel is upset. I'm *livid*, Yale. Get out of my sight. I mean it. Would you like me to take a knife to your pretty little sports car to show you how much I mean it? Because I swear to you, if I don't watch that car pull out of the parking lot in ten minutes, I'll . . ."

Wow. Monica was showing a rather violent tendency

here. This was a far cry from the mournful sister from my last visit. This was sounding closer to "like mother, like daughter." Was she going to turn Yale in or send him packing?

I typed HURRY to Frank. Forget "playing" police chief. I was on the verge of needing to make a citizen's arrest here.

I heard Yale pick up his suitcase, followed by his footsteps heading toward the stairs. He stopped on the landing three stairs above me, startled by my presence and what he must have known I'd heard.

I stood my ground on the stairs below him, cell phone in one hand, coffee and scones still in the other. We eyed each other for a tense moment.

"What did you hear?" He didn't ask the question; he growled it.

"More than you'd like," I said, trying to buy time. "Is Monica okay? She sounds really upset."

I watched Yale's eyes calculate the space on either side of me on the stairs, as if he'd push me aside if that was what it took. "She's hysterical," he said too calmly. "Like I said, she lets her emotions get the best of her."

He motioned for me to move over so he could continue down the stairs. I did not. I tried not to think about how he loomed over me from that landing. Would he push me down? I put my phone in my pocket and grabbed the railing to steady myself.

That was when I saw it. On the left side of one shiny brown loafer was a pair of small scuffs. Pale yellow paint and something black. Like tar.

I froze. The side panels of the warehouse roof were that exact color. And the flat portions just outside the ventilation fans were black tar. Yale Wagner had been on the warehouse roof. He might have ordered his crew member to purchase the shepherd's crooks, but he'd been the one to use them to block the fans. And the door. Monica was right—his efforts to scare Julie had ended up killing her.

Yale's face paled. I felt a gush of relief as I heard Frank's voice from behind me.

"What's going on?"

No point in beating around the bush. "I just heard Monica accuse Yale of arranging for the crooks and putting them in the fans and door to scare Julie."

Frank raised one eyebrow. "Perhaps you and I should have a conversation before you go wherever you think it is you're going, Mr. Wagner?"

"I don't have to talk to you if I don't have my lawyer."

Yale was starting to look nervous. I didn't pose much of a threat evidently, but with Frank involved, he seemed to realize things were about to come apart.

I wasn't sure Frank could take Yale in just based on what I had overheard. But thankfully, I was pretty sure we now had physical evidence. I pointed to Yale's shoes.

"Look at those, Frank. Those scuff marks are the color of the paint on the warehouse walls, aren't they? Wasn't the warehouse roof tarred outside where the ventilation fans were?"

Yale looked down at his shoes. "We were up on the roof getting some wide-angle shots of the town. B-roll and all."

The chief crossed his hands over his chest. "Seems to me you were up there doing a lot more than that."

I turned to Frank. "I heard Monica accuse Yale of killing Julie when he only meant to scare her. He and

Dorothy were scheming to frighten Julie to back off her confrontations."

The blatant message of the crooks made sense now. Who better to frame than the people she regularly bad-mouthed?

The staircase of the Riverside Inn obviously wasn't the place to have this interrogation. Frank reached to his belt and took out a pair of shiny handcuffs.

"You can call that attorney of yours from the station while I get a statement from Libby about what she heard. But you *will* be coming with me. Will you walk out of here nice and calm, or do I use these in front of everyone?"

Yale?" Gavin's eyebrows shot to his hairline when I barged into his office and told him how I'd spent my morning. "Yale and Dorothy did it?"

"Well, yes and no," I explained. "It's both and neither. Their actions are sort of murder adjacent if the cause of death is the sodium hydroxide."

His brows descended into an agitated furrow. "That can't be a real thing."

"Well, I don't know if Dorothy telling Yale to scare her own daughter *is* criminal, but—"

"Who does that?" Gavin cut in. "What monster of a parent does that?"

Being the outstanding parent that he is, Gavin had every right to call out Dorothy. His outrage made me feel justified in my own. I'd like to think any compassionate person would be outraged at what Dorothy had asked Yale to do. What Yale had agreed to do, for that matter.

That whole family seemed to be one nonstop carnival of dysfunction.

"She told Yale only to scare Julie. It sounds like Julie's behavior killed her chances for her own show, so maybe they were afraid she'd take it out on Monica if the show went big. Sibling rivalry. Or just plain Julie being Julie."

Gavin looked repulsed. "So he figured if Julie got to thinking some of the shepherds were ready to make good on those death threats, it might give her the fright she needed to tone things down." He looked out the window of his office down Collin Avenue in the direction of the warehouse. "He probably got the idea from being up on the roof to get those wide shots he and the crew took the first day. I'd forgotten they were even up there."

"Me, too. But he could plant those crooks at the warehouse, knowing someone would find them when the fumes filled the room, and blame the shepherds. Honestly, if she really was using standard dyeing materials, it might have made her only a little nauseous or woozy." I thought of something else. "I bet he was planning to happen to walk by in time to unblock the door and save her so he'd have reason to give her a big lecture."

"But the fire at the restaurant delayed his arrival," Gavin added.

"No wonder Monica was beside herself. To know the person you were married to was capable of such scheming—and in league with your own mother, for that matter." Suddenly Mom's over-the-top behavior seemed tame by comparison.

"Only what they ended up doing was paving the way for whoever messed with Julie's chemicals to be the one to kill her."

It sounded so needlessly tragic to hear Gavin put it that way. I sank into the chair opposite Gavin's desk, the tangle of the thing getting to me—until I came up with another, even more upsetting thought. "Unless he was the one to mess with her chemicals, too." Suddenly it went from being needlessly tragic to downright evil. A redundant system to ensure death. It chilled me just to think of it.

"But why would Yale be so intent on killing Julie? It doesn't make sense."

"I know. There's got to be more to it." I thought about the whole scene between Monica and Yale I'd overheard. "Monica said 'on top of everything else you've done to me? To us?' We're missing a piece of this whole thing. I'm sure of it."

Gavin rose and walked around his desk to where I was sitting. "Dorothy, Yale, Monica . . . was this entire family trying to kill off one of their own?" He shook his head. "I don't get it. Each of those sisters had their own success. They had everything they wanted. Why try to destroy each other like that?"

Julie's and Monica's shrill shouts at each other that first day rang in my ears. Families seemed so talented at hurting one another. I watched Gavin's hand travel unconsciously to a photo of Jillian on his desk, one of those paint-it-yourself ceramic frames that read *Best Dad*.

It hit me. Like my first entrelac pattern, it suddenly all made sense. The way you knit the woven-look blocks of entrelac makes no sense at first. You can't see how the steps you're taking will achieve the end result. And then suddenly it all fits together and you can't imagine how you missed it earlier. The sensation I felt as I stared at the picture frame was exactly the same.

"You're wrong," I said, a little breathless from the revelation. "They didn't have everything they wanted. They each had what the other wanted." I shot out of my chair. "I've got to go back to the inn."

"I don't think you should do that." He looked ready to drop everything and come along as my bodyguard if I was going to be foolish enough to go play yarn-shop cop again.

Only I was certain I'd solved the case. And just as certain I was the only person who could get the proof we needed.

"No, I absolutely should," I replied. "I've got to go talk to Monica."

CHAPTER TWENTY-FIVE

For the third time, I walked up the Riverside Inn stairs to the sound of Monica yelling. Only this time, it was general grunts and shouts of anger as I heard the crashes and thuds of things being thrown. For Bev's sake, I dearly hoped Monica was flinging her own objects about and not trashing the room's furnishings. I had the split-second image of chef's knives embedded in Bev's colonial wallpaper. I hoped I wouldn't have to worry about them flying in my direction.

The door to Dorothy and Hugh's room was open, the room empty. I suspected Mr. and Mrs. Wagner were down at the police station. The eerie knowledge that Frank was probably booking Dorothy and Yale right now for "conspiracy to frighten that became murder"—or whatever legal charge amounted to that—made my insides wobble.

The missing piece was that I couldn't for the life of me figure out what could have catapulted this sibling rivalry into the realm of murder. Everything between these two was serious and sad, but my gut knew that only something catastrophic would have taken things to the level that got Julie killed.

I was taking a whopping risk knocking on Monica's door and asking what I was about to ask, but I was almost certain my hunch was right. And if I was right, I might be the only person Monica would tell.

She didn't answer on the first or second knock, but when I called out, "Monica, it's Libby. Please let me in," the noises stopped. After a few moments, she opened the door.

She looked terrible. Red-rimmed eyes, messy hair, no makeup, clothes thrown on as almost an afterthought. I recognized the look immediately and felt even more confidence in my hunch.

"Sorry about the noise." Her accommodating voice sounded as if it was coming from a different person. The comfort food chef emerging for a moment from inside the deeply wounded woman.

"May I come in?"

She didn't answer, but simply stepped aside to let me enter. The room wasn't trashed in a rock-star-smashing-the-furniture kind of way, but things were thrown everywhere. I was glad not to see any knives embedded in walls. Her cookbooks were tossed in a dozen different places, clothes were flung everywhere, and even the bed linens and couch cushions had been yanked from their places. Monica had pitched a first-class fit in here. I didn't feel entirely safe, but I also saw the spent look in her eyes and knew I was coming in on the tail end of the storm.

"I'm sorry your family seems to be coming apart at the seams."

I felt I owed her the acknowledgment that everything in her life had come completely undone. I knew what that felt like. I also knew either you found a way to push up off the bottom or you watched yourself drown. I was pretty sure Monica had chosen the latter.

"Are you?" she asked with a touch of hysterical bitterness. "'Cuz I can't decide if I am or not."

"Yale is down at the police station. Your mother is, too." When she didn't answer, I continued. "Did you know what they did before now?"

She was still holding a scarf—a knitted one, actually, that looked like something out of Julie's designs. I saw the yarn I'd given her earlier lying at the far corner of the room, where she'd clearly thrown it.

Monica continued to glare at the scarf in her hands. "I knew they were at the end of their ropes. We all were. But . . ." She let the thought trail off, never really answering my question. "Julie took so much effort. Everyone was always talking about how to control Julie." She began twisting the scarf, working herself up into the anger I'd heard earlier. "'What terrible thing has Julie done now? Why does she do that to herself? We can't let her ruin *Dish Up Comfort*'s chances. What are we going to do about Julie?' As if the success was *hers* to ruin, not mine to have earned."

"I heard what you said to Yale earlier," I said.

Surely she must have realized that by now, but she was distant and agitated. I'm not sure she was paying attention to anything but the storm of her own feelings. She kept twisting the scarf.

"At first I thought it was about the shepherd's crooks, but I don't think that's true anymore. You weren't just talking about the crooks, were you?"

She wrapped the scarf around one hand and pulled. Hard. A stranglehold.

I stepped a little closer and tried again, pretty sure I already knew the answer. "What did Yale do, Monica?"

I nearly shuddered when she finally raised her eyes to me. Pure hate isn't something you see very often, and it's chilling.

"Not what, *whom*. Julie. Yale and Julie were having an affair. Oh, he said it meant nothing and they'd broken it off, but it doesn't go away like that, does it?"

"No." I could speak from experience. A she-meant-nothing-I-swear claim from Sterling about a vapid but pretty sales rep had taught me that. But a sister? One everyone claimed to barely tolerate? It would have been hard to come up with a deeper wound.

I was sorry to have to take the proverbial knife in her chest and twist it. Because while many a woman had been wronged by a straying husband, I knew this one had gone further.

"Julie told you she was pregnant by him, didn't she?"

"She flung it in my face the first day here. She lied that she was pregnant by him. She *lied*." The scarf stranglehold was turning her one hand pale. "She lied. About that. *About that*."

"She knew the one thing you couldn't have and flung it in your face to hurt you." There aren't many things in life I'd categorize as unspeakably cruel, but Julie's deliberate lie qualified in my book.

The waters were all clear. The dye had been extinguished, and the colors had been cast. The sense of completion was heavy and fragile at the same time. "You put the lethal level of sodium hydroxide into Julie's formula, didn't you? You got it from your father's company and slipped it in while the ingredients were still in her hotel room."

Monica's head cocked to one side as if she still hadn't come to grips with what she'd done. "I swiped her formulas. That one time when we got together and she thought they'd gone missing. At first I was just going to publish them, leak them out over the Internet so anyone could make the colors she did. She wouldn't be special anymore."

She paused—perhaps expecting me to comment, I suppose—but I was too sad and stunned to say anything.

"Then I found out about her and Yale. Then just putting the formulas on the Internet wasn't good enough. I figured out which chemical to swap. It wasn't hard to get it from Dad's company. No one watches what I do over there, and why would they? I'm just the sister who cooks. It's Julie they think they have to worry about, isn't it?"

Again, I didn't answer, just let her slowly spill out all the bile she'd been holding in for so long. A chill ran through me as I spied a key on the floor in the corner amongst all the other things hurled about. The missing one to Julie's room?

"I was never really planning to use the stuff, you know. I just wanted to know I could. To have that power over her. I could make her a little bit sick or a lot sick or . . . But when she told me the baby was Yale's, I couldn't . . . I wanted to hurt her. I had to hurt her as badly as she'd hurt me."

Monica met my gaze and I nearly shivered. "She would never stop, you know. Never. Just kept pushing and pushing and pushing . . ." She let the scarf fall to the ground.

"Did you want her to lose the baby?"

An eerie clarity glistened in her eyes. "I did. Oh, Mom would have been furious at first, but she would have found a way to love that baby no matter how disappointed she was. Julie could disappoint her in a hundred other ways but *this*? This would make up for everything. Julie would have this, this thing I couldn't do no matter how hard I tried." Monica's tone sharpened to vengeful edges. "And she'd lord it over me. Always. It was so unfair. I couldn't live with that. Not knowing the child was Yale's."

She grabbed her own chest with both hands as if she were physically coming apart. "Yale is *my* husband. I couldn't let her steal all that from me. I couldn't."

If I had been looking for darkness deep enough to enable murder, I'd found it. Sometimes being right about a hunch is a frightening thing. Monica was coming undone right in front of my eyes. I wondered if I needed to have Frank here to record this confession, but I didn't dare disrupt her outpouring.

There was an even sadder level to this. "But the baby wasn't Yale's. Julie wasn't pregnant at all."

"I didn't believe Yale when he told me he was sure she was lying. Why should I? I thought he was trying to get out of it by insisting the doctors said it wasn't just me. It was both of us who couldn't . . ."

Her words fell off as she seemed to cave in on herself. The full weight of what she'd done had come down upon her, and it was a hard thing to watch.

Now it made sense that she had gone to Frank and asked if the medical examiner could tell if Julie was pregnant. She'd had to go to such extremes because she couldn't believe her own husband's denial. And it meant she had killed her sister for nothing. Well, not for nothing. For years of festering competition and envy. That wasn't nothing.

I couldn't come up with a gentle way to put it. "So while she was setting up the equipment, you got into the room with the key you took. You swapped the chemicals Julie used so that they would harm her."

That seemed just the smallest bit kinder than to say, "Kill her." Although I'm not quite sure why I felt any need to be kind. Maybe it was just the overload of cruelty I'd been witness to recently.

"I didn't really mean to kill her. I just wanted to make her see. I just wanted to make her *pay*."

I expected each of them—Yale, Dorothy, and Monica—had had a similar intent. I found it utterly sad that the unwitting combination of all of them had done what none of them had intended to do: end Julie's life.

CHAPTER TWENTY-SIX

After the police left Monica's room, I should have gone to the station to give a statement. I should have gone to the shop.

Instead, I walked home in a bit of a stunned daze, sank down at my kitchen table with Hank at my side, and cried.

It all seemed such a horrid, tragic ball of hate and envy and cruelty. Wrong on too many levels to count. And I couldn't stop thinking about all the beauty Julie had created that now would end. Monica had told me she had burned the formula copies she had stolen. Maybe someone somewhere would find Julie's original formulas. Or some new artist would discover the secrets Julie hadn't lived to tell.

All that felt like too slim a hope today, an unbearable loss. I have always liked to think of families as knit together, but Julie and Monica's family seemed knotted together in an ugly tangle that choked everyone.

I heard Mom rush downstairs in a flurry of concern. "Oh, Elizabeth honey, what's wrong?"

I let the whole thing pour out of me in a gush of tearful words. I managed to finish with "You drive me nuts some days, Mom, but you're so much better than that."

Mom slanted me a look. "While Dorothy Wilson sets a pretty low bar, I think that was a compliment."

When I half laughed, half cried in response, Mom wrapped her arms tightly around me and said, "I'd never, ever hurt you, sweetheart. I couldn't, no matter what you did to me. That's who mothers are supposed to be."

I clung to her with all my might, even as I blurted out, "I love you, Mom. But you can't live here."

She pulled back and caught my gaze with sad, brimming eyes. "I know."

Surprise filled me. "You do?" I sniffed and wiped my eyes on a napkin from the place setting at the table—place mats and napkins Mom had sewn for me when I first moved in here.

"The thing about Arlene is that she tells it like it is, whether you want to hear it or not. And Frank may have given me a none-too-subtle hint. But when Gavin said something . . . Well, your father had a saying. 'When the third person tells you you're drunk, go lie down.'"

"I'm sorry." It seemed like the right—and the wrong—thing to say.

She took both my shoulders. "Don't you dare be sorry about being the independent, opinionated daughter I raised you to be." She pushed herself up off the chair with considerable effort. "I don't mean to shock you, but not every idea I get is a gem."

I managed a good laugh at that one. "Lots are." Funny how it took a monster like Dorothy Wilson to get me to see the many good things my mother was to me. Oh, she still was a pile of frustration and meddling, but she knew what love ought to look like.

Mom opened my refrigerator door and pulled out a box from Margo's. "Pie, on the other hand, is always a good idea."

Right now a cup of coffee and a slice of pie with my mother sounded like the best idea ever. "Agreed."

She set the buttermilk pie down on the table with two plates, a pie server, and a pair of forks. "What about next door?" She nodded out the window to the little colonial house just across my side yard.

I cut two generous slices. "Absolutely not."

Frank, Gavin, and I watched the district attorney's office van drive away with Monica and Yale inside. While Dorothy's actions ought to have been criminal—and in my mind and most definitely Gavin's they *were* criminal—evidently she couldn't be charged with anything other than hideous parenting. After all, while she and Yale might have agreed Julie needed a good scare, it was Yale who had chosen to make the shepherds' threats come to life. Dorothy probably thought of it as tough love, reining in the monster her favoritism had created, but Yale had meant harm.

One of the saddest parts was Hugh. It seemed tragically clear that he had no idea what the other three had been doing. His life had come unraveled through no fault of his own—although Gavin held some strong opinions about the favoritism Hugh should have stopped. The Wilson family was forever torn apart, everyone's aspirations destroyed by everyone else's.

"Explain this to me again?" I asked Frank as the three of us walked back toward the shop. I still didn't quite understand how the DA had brought the charges he had.

"Murder is about intent," Frank explained. "If you intended to harm and you ended up killing—even if it turned out to be a joint effort—that's still murder. Both Monica and Yale were actively involved in things designed to hurt Julie."

"But not Dorothy?" I asked. "I mean, she suggested Yale scare Julie, right?"

"If she had known about and sanctioned harming Julie, they might be able to pin her with conspiracy to commit murder. But the way I see it, the harm was all on Yale and Monica." He gave me a piercing look. "They'll both go down for murder."

I noticed Gavin had used the arm opposite his injured shoulder to pull the shop door open. "And the cameraman? There was intent to harm there."

"Yale came clean that the man Lloyd ID'd bought the crooks for him. But like I said, buying them isn't a crime. Not coming to us when he saw how they'd been used, well, that's another story. Guess paying that well buys you a lot of loyalty. What's the world coming to when a man like Yale can have that much leverage over those guys?"

"Enough to send them after my shopwindow, too. *And* Barney's farm. *And* the theater rigging." I didn't care for how long that list was. "Only, why?"

"Barney's easy. . . . It made him look guilty. And while it's sneaky and underhanded, it's not illegal. Your window and the theater were supposed to make things less about Julie and more about the festival. A pretty poorly thought-out batch of red herrings in my opinion."

"Or scare tactics," Gavin added, "to stop you from asking so many questions." Gavin gave me an irritating I-told-you-not-to-do-that look. "You ask a lot of questions, Libby."

Seeing as how that crook would have landed on me had Gavin not been there, I chose to let that slide—for now.

"So what does the crew get charged with?" I asked.

"Vandalism, criminal mischief, maybe even reckless endangerment if the DA is feeling cranky," Frank said. "Good thing they won't need a clean record, seeing as how they're all out of jobs. *Dish Up Comfort* is officially off the air."

"I still can't figure out how they broke my window without anyone knowing." I stared at my beautifully restored window. Linda had filled it with gorgeous summer yarn in a beach bag with a little chair and umbrella. "Glass is loud when it breaks."

"One of them told us how they did it, thinking it would help get him off easy."

"It won't, will it?" Mom asked from her place at the shop table. She was knitting and paging through the local paper at the same time, circling things in red marker.

Frank grunted. "Not if I can help it."

"So how?" I asked.

Frank gestured out the window. "Two of them parked the truck in front of your shop while the other two got in an argument down the street to draw everyone's attention."

"Hooligans," Mom muttered. I had to agree.

Frank peered over Mom's shoulder. "Real estate listings?"

She looked up at him. "You don't think I'm going to

hire George, do you? I wouldn't trust that man to find me a doghouse much less a good place this side of the river."

When Frank looked at me, I said, "We're collecting options."

Well, mostly Mom was collecting options and I was finding reasons why they were unreasonable. She'd nixed everything I'd suggested so far, but I remained hopeful we'd come to some kind of agreement one of these days. Yesterday she added, "You Are Residing Nearer," on the shop chalkboard, so evidently she felt the same.

"How's your shoulder, Gavin?" Mom asked. "Healed up from saving my daughter's life yet?"

While I was indeed grateful Gavin had saved me from harm, I didn't classify his act as lifesaving, as Mom insisted on doing. She hadn't stopped citing Gavin's heroism every time they were together. It was sweet in an irritating kind of way. Just like Mom.

"I'm doing just fine, Rhonda," Gavin said with endless patience. "Looking forward to a calm couple of weeks."

Mom looked around the room and rolled her eyes. "In this town? It'll never happen. The election's Friday, isn't it?"

"Next Tuesday," Gavin and I said in unison.

Mom nodded. "A whole week from today?"

"Mom, it's Wednesday."

"Is it?" Mom checked her watch. "Well, in that case I'd better get going. I'm due at the library book club. By the way," Mom continued ever so sweetly, "I'll need to borrow your card again."

CHAPTER TWENTY-SEVEN

Six days later, the mood in town hall was optimistic. Everyone seemed to breathe easier with the mystery of Julie Wilson's death behind us. The See More Than Seafood Festival, while more dramatic than anyone would have liked, had been a relative success. Local restaurants were happy, and businesses were glad to start the high season off with an extra boost. Collinstown was ready to launch into her glory days of spring and summer.

We just had one more hurdle to get over: the election. All of the Chamber of Commerce members were present—a first for a presidential election in recent memory. Of course, no presidential election in recent memory had boasted the drama and attention my challenge to King George's reign had caused.

While technically not Chamber members, Mom, Jillian, and several of my customers were here. Even Caroline and Paula showed up, saying how they wanted to be "witness to my historic victory." I was simply hoping that if I did win, we all weren't witness to a historic rant from George.

"Think he'll pitch a fit if I win?" I asked Margo as we waited impatiently for the votes to be tabulated.

Up until this year, voting had been done by a simple raising of hands. George had insisted it be by anonymous written ballot this year, and I eagerly agreed. The man knew how to hold a grudge, and I didn't want to put any of my friends and colleagues in his mean-spirited sights.

"*When* you win," Margo corrected, "because you will. Seriously, do you think anyone is going to vote for George after the way he acted at the debate?"

Margo's husband, Carl, gave me a grin. "You're a shoo-in, kiddo. I predict a landslide."

"That'll sting," I replied, mustering up a surprising dose of pity for George. "Maybe he has enough business sense to be a gracious loser."

"You're gonna win," Jillian said with charming certainty. She was standing with us while Gavin was locked in his office with two witnesses doing a ballot by ballot count. "Everybody knows it."

"Maybe the sheep farmers will join the Chamber of Commerce after this," Mom suggested.

I'd gotten more than a few jokes about sheep advertising in the days since Barney's flock had trotted down Collin Avenue. I still hadn't had a chance to talk to Barney about all that had happened. I felt better knowing that someone I considered a friend and vendor hadn't had it out for Julie or me, even if he had taken Yale's bait to stage a sheep protest march. I made a mental note to take a trip out to his farm and close the whole thing up on a friendly basis. That, and I truly wanted to know how the other sheep farmers viewed what Yale and his crew had done. Those farmers didn't deserve to be in my crosshairs any more than I deserved to be in George's.

Just then the door to Gavin's office opened, and our mayor and his two vote-counting witnesses emerged. I wanted to be able to read the results in Gavin's eyes, but he did an excellent job of keeping his expression neutral. We hadn't yet talked about how the two of us would handle the new roles tonight might give us, but I felt confident we'd figure it out. We'd been through so much already—what was a little civic awkwardness if you'd survived murder and vandalism?

Everyone turned to look at Gavin, then gathered in a semicircle around the podium Gavin had set up on the far side of the room.

"Hello, everyone," he began, setting the ballot box on the podium in front of him. "Thanks for coming and for participating in the voting. It's always good to make sure everyone's opinion is heard."

I scanned his face again for any sign of the result, but Gavin kept his eyes straight ahead, not looking at either George or me as we stood on opposite edges of the group.

"And I want to thank our two candidates for their dedication to Collinstown and its continued success."

"Get on with it—who won?" someone yelled from the back of the crowd, resulting in a flutter of tension-easing laughter.

"Get on with it" was a favorite phrase of Gavin's, so it was amusing to have it turned back on our mayor at a time when he was clearly trying to be as diplomatic as possible.

"Our next Chamber of Commerce president"—no one appreciated his dramatic pause—"will be Libby Beckett." Then and only then did Gavin allow himself to look at me. "Congratulations, Libby."

I felt the round of applause and cheers sparkle under my skin. This was a victory on so many levels. An affirmation of my store, my ideas, and my abilities. Oh, I knew this wasn't global commerce, but I dearly loved Collinstown and wanted all of us to succeed in ways that didn't need George's competitive appetite.

I walked to the podium and gave a short speech about how grateful I was for this town and how it had welcomed me back as a business owner and now as their Chamber president. I meant every word of it—even my thanks to George. Looking out over the crowd, I saw a heartwarming collection of friends with care and support in their eyes. I'd had a lot of money when I was married to Sterling, but I never felt as rich as I did at that moment. It struck me that I wouldn't have felt that much different if I had lost, and that seemed a treasure in itself.

No one was talking to George and Vera. I walked over and solemnly shook his hand. "It's a big job that I know you made look easy. I hope you'll allow me to turn to you with questions if I have them."

"Of course."

He said the words, but his eyes wouldn't quite let me believe him. I had the feeling it would be a long time before George forgave me for this. The look Vera gave me as they turned and left the room—half resentment, half apology—would stay with me for a long time.

Most of that dark cloud walked away as Gavin appeared at my elbow with a glass of champagne and a glowing smile. His eyes were as brilliant as George's were cold. I accepted the glass and we clinked them to toast my victory.

"Never had a doubt," he said as we each took a sip.

"Good for you. I did."

"Nah," he said, scanning the room after another healthy swig of bubbly. I could feel the relief pouring over both of us. "Everybody thinks you're great. They always have."

Gavin had a tremendous talent for keeping me guessing if he was talking personally or mayorally. It was our way of toeing up to that line we kept daring ourselves to cross. We hid our growing—or perhaps returning—affection for each other in deniable hints and double meanings. I wondered, as I stood there enjoying the feeling of him next to me, all proud and supportive, how long we could linger close to that line. We'd have to choose whether to cross or not eventually. Most likely sooner than later. The kiss on his cheek I'd given him after the crook fell still sparkled in my memory, and I expected in his as well.

I stole a glimpse at Frank and Angie. Frank had his hand on Angie's back with a look that was half astonishment and half embarrassment. A holy-cow-is-this-okay? expression that belonged more on someone Jillian's age. Had Frank had the nerve to ask anyone that very question out loud, he'd have received a landslide vote in his favor, I was sure. If Frank and Angie could pull it off to everyone's approval, could Gavin and I? And as two consenting adults, we didn't really need anyone's approval anyway, did we?

I knew the answer to that, but I was also wise enough to know things would become even more complicated now that he was mayor and I was Chamber president. One of these days we were going to come down on opposite sides of a civic argument. Maybe several. Would we know how to do that?

In any case, tonight wasn't the night to ponder the complexities of mayor-Chamber relations. Or even Gavin-Libby relationships. Tonight was a night to celebrate a new chapter in my new life. The dye had taken to the yarn and the water was clear.

Time to start knitting with it.

Three weeks later, I sold the last of Julie's yarn to Caroline.

"That's it," I said as Caroline walked out the door with the last skein of all the stock we'd brought in for Julie's appearance. "That's the final skein. I'm happy it went to her. I wouldn't have wanted it to go to just anyone."

Linda wore the same smile I did. "What's she going to make with it?"

Caroline had purchased a sturdy blend in a rich chocolate brown deep enough to make your mouth water.

"A hat for Lloyd."

Linda put her hand over her heart. "Sweet. I'm glad you didn't have to talk her out of a sweater."

There is a myth among knitters that you should never knit a sweater for a boyfriend you want to keep. To many who love yarn and needles, knitting a sweater spells instant doom for a relationship. I have customers who won't do it, even if the man they love begs for a sweater. One of my customers flat-out refused to cast on until the day after they were married. Sterling never asked me for a sweater, and I never knit him one, so I can't speak to the truth of that myth. But why tempt fate? I would have talked Caroline out of it not only for that reason, but because she wasn't ready to knit a sweater. But who knows? By next spring Lloyd could have a new title—groom-to-be.

Linda closed the register drawer. "Speaking of sweaters, did you see Jillian's? It's gorgeous. That kid is talented. And fast."

"I did. She wore it to dinner the other night. I think it's sweet that she has the one and only garment made from the Riverbank color Julie created. A bright spot of good in all that mess."

Linda raised an eyebrow, her attention snagged by a single detail. "Dinner?"

I rewarded her nosiness with a dark look. "We went out for pizza to celebrate her YouTube channel hitting ten thousand subscribers. Gavin's a little nervous about the whole thing, but I think she'll do fine."

"More than fine. I predict bright things for our Miss Jillian."

Linda returned to her file of tasks we were scheduling for our next big event. I'd fired up my bravery and gone totally upscale by booking Vincenzo Marani for a holiday event. Vincenzo was known as the Gallant Herdsman; his prize vicuña yarn—arguably the most expensive and exclusive yarn in the world—was as admired as the dashing man himself.

I cut open the box to reveal the single skein of vicuña Vincenzo had sent along with his press kit. Wow. I'd have never spent the three hundred dollars a skein this stuff cost, and he sent it out as an advance gift? If this guy was half as charming in person as he was on video and the phone, tickets would sell themselves. Vincenzo was bringing a few animals from an East Coast zoo for a one-of-a-kind shearing demonstration. Y.A.R.N. was getting a holiday vendor trunk show no one could match.

"Gavin should be more worried about Mark if you ask me," I said, recalling the fourth guest at our dinner table that night. "Jillian's new friend looks pretty smitten."

I'd stopped short of saying "boyfriend," but that didn't stop Linda.

"Oooh," she cooed with a fascinated expression. "A boy? And Gavin let him be there? At dinner?"

I smirked. We both knew that was a massive step for someone with Gavin's protective nature. "I may have helped Gavin see that including Mark in places where he could keep an eye on the guy was a better choice than banning him. Poor Gavin. Nothing will make you more leery of high school boys than having been one of them."

Linda laughed. "But Jillian's not in high school yet."

"Tell that to Gavin. I think he'd put off fall for a decade if he had the option. Mark seems to be a nice boy. I think Jillian'll be fine."

"After all," Linda teased, "I seem to remember you met a nice boy in high school. Maybe . . ."

I was about to toss a skein of chunky alpaca at my shop assistant when Caroline burst back through the door. "Libby, you need to see this!" She threw her bags down on the counter and grabbed my hand, pulling me toward the door.

Once on the sidewalk, I noticed everyone on the street was looking up the block and pointing. My first thought was that George had done something. He still hadn't quite surfaced out of his pout from losing the election.

When I turned in the direction of everyone's gaze, I

could only smile and burst out laughing. There, coming down the street in a parade of cuteness, was a collection of ewes and lambs. Each one bore the message "I ♥ Y.A.R.N." in pink spray paint. At the head of the flock, with a shepherd's crook to boot, walked Barney. His wrinkly old face split into a wide grin. Who knew there was a heart of gold hiding under that crusty curmudgeon shell?

"Maybe protest sheep aren't such a bad thing," I said, grinning myself as I walked up to Barney.

An adorable lamb and ewe walked up to me as if to say, "Remember us?"

"Pleased to see you again," I greeted Barney and his fleecy friends. "Congratulations on your little one there." I found it a nice reminder of the good things a mother could be.

The ewe gave the only appropriate reply: *Baa*.

I laughed and ducked back into the store to get my cell phone. It was time to post a video of my own.

ACKNOWLEDGMENTS

Some book plots are more complicated than others. They take unplanned twists and turns no matter how much an author "thinks" she's in charge. The creative process behind Julie's story was just as complicated as the woman herself, and just as surprising as her secret techniques.

I should start out by emphasizing that Julie's unique dyeing process for plant-based fibers is entirely a work of fiction on my part. No such secret formula exists. But getting to play "what if?" is the particular pleasure of novelists, and was grand fun while I wrote this book.

Still, one has to plant fiction on a firm ground of plausibility, and for that I had wonderful expert help. Michele O'Reilly lent me her vast knowledge of dyes and dyeing, making sure that while my story strayed into the realm of the imaginary, it never (hopefully) jumped the track into the impossible. Jim Hickey again patiently answered law enforcement questions while prosecutor Nancy Nazarian lent me both her legal expertise and a fantastic talent for spotting plot holes and questions of motivation. Any mistakes on any of these subject matters fall solely on me, and not these experts who generously offered their assistance.

I could not do what I do without the terrific support team that keeps me up and writing. My husband, Jeff; agents Sandy Harding and Karen Solem of Spencerhill Associates; editor Michelle Vega; and assistant Michelle Prima all provide the support and encouragement that keeps the words flowing.

Amy Kaspar created the charming washcloth knitting patterns that are included at the end of this book. If you do knit these, by all means send me a photo at allie@alliepleiter.com.

The digital world gives us many opportunities to connect, so please come find me on Instagram (@alliepleiterauthor), my Facebook page (Facebook.com/alliepleiter), Twitter (@alliepleiter), BookBub (Allie Pleiter), and Ravelry (@alliewriter).

I am indeed blessed to be able to do what I do. For that, my deepest gratitude goes to you, the readers who eagerly follow Libby into yet another Collinstown adventure. Get ready to "cast on" another later this year!

SISTERS WASHCLOTHS

by Amy Kaspar

ABOUT THE PROJECT: Ahh, sisters. We love one another, we hate one another, and there are still a few common threads holding us together when we are a bit off-center. These washcloths are designed with that in mind: They are just different enough to be engaging for a few hours, but similar enough to form a set.

DIFFICULTY: Easy (If you can knit, purl, and count, then you can do it!).

YARN REQUIREMENTS: One ball (50g/115yd) DK-weight organic cotton in Color A, and one ball (50g/115yd) DK-weight organic cotton in Color B. You can use any two complementary colors.

FINISHED SIZE (BLOCKED): 8.5" x 8.5" square before border, which adds approximately 0.5" per side.

NEEDLES: US 5 (3.75mm) straight needles.

OTHER SUPPLIES: A blocking mat and pins, a needle for weaving in ends, and scissors.

GAUGE: Approximately 5.5 sts per inch in pattern. If you don't feel like making a gauge swatch, go for "tighter than average."

Stitch Abbreviations:

WS: wrong side

RS: right side

K: knit

P: purl

SEED ST: Over an odd number of stitches, *(K1, P1) to last st, K1 on every row. After you K or P more than one in a row, start Seed st with the opposite stitch.

K FBF: A two-stitch increase where you knit in the front, back, and then front of the same stitch before sliding the loop off of the left-hand needle.

PATTERN NOTES: *DK-weight yarn will get you the approximate finished size, but you can make them in worsted weight for larger cloths or hand towels. You can also repeat rows 27 and 28 on Washcloth 1 more times, or the plain Seed st rows at the beginning and end of Washcloth 2 if you want to make them the shape of rectangles. The edging may take you longer than the main washcloth, but be patient. It's pretty when finished!*

WASHCLOTH 1 INSTRUCTIONS:

With Color A, Cast on 49.

Rows 1 and 2: Seed st

Row 3 (WS): Seed st 3, P3, Seed st 17, P3, Seed st 17, P3, Seed st 3

Row 4 (RS): K1, P1, K5, Seed st 15, K5, Seed st 15, K5, P1, K1

Row 5: K1, P7, Seed st 3, P3, Seed st 7, P3, K1, P3, Seed st 7, P3, Seed st 3, P7, K1

Row 6: K1, P1, K2, P1, K2, Seed st 3, K5, Seed st 5, K3, Seed st 3, K3, Seed st 5, K5, Seed st 3, K2, P1, K2, P1, K1

Row 7: Seed st 9, P7, Seed st 3, P3, Seed st 5, P3, Seed st 3, P7, Seed st 9

Row 8: Seed st 10, K2, P1, K2, Seed st 3, K3, Seed st 7, K3, Seed st 3, K2, P1, K2, Seed st 10

Row 9: Seed st 17, P3, Seed st 9, P3, Seed st 17

Row 10: Seed st 6, K3, Seed st 7, K3, Seed st 11, K3, Seed st 7, K3, Seed st 6

Row 11: Seed st 5, P5, Seed st 5, P3, Seed st 5, P3, Seed st 5, P3, Seed st 5, P5, Seed st 5

Row 12: Seed st 4, K7, Seed st 3, K3, Seed st 5, K5, Seed st 5, K3, Seed st 3, K7, Seed st 4

Row 13: Seed st 5, P2, K1, P2, Seed st 3, P3, Seed st 5, P3, K1, P3, Seed st 5, P3, Seed st 3, P2, K1, P2, Seed st 5

Row 14: Seed st 12, K3, Seed st 5, K3, Seed st 3, K3, Seed st 5, K3, Seed st 12

Row 15: Seed st 11, P3, Seed st 5, P3, Seed st 5, P3, Seed st 5, P3, Seed st 11

Row 16: Seed st 10, K3, Seed st 5, K3, Seed st 7, K3, Seed st 5, K3, Seed st 10

Row 17: Seed st 9, P3, Seed st 5, P3, Seed st 9, P3, Seed st 5, P3, Seed st 9

Row 18: Seed st 8, K3, Seed st 5, K3, Seed st 11, K3, Seed st 5, K3, Seed st 8

Row 19: Seed st 7, P3, Seed st 5, P3, Seed st 13, P3, Seed st 5, P3, Seed st 7

Row 20: Seed st 6, K3, Seed st 5, K3, Seed st 15, K3, Seed st 5, K3, Seed st 6

Row 21: Seed st 5, P3, Seed st 5, P3, Seed st 17, P3, Seed st 5, P3, Seed st 5

Row 22: Seed st 4, K3, Seed st 5, K3, Seed st 19, K3, Seed st 5, K3, Seed st 4

Row 23: Seed st 3, P3, Seed st 5, P3, Seed st 21, P3, Seed st 5, P3, Seed st 3

Row 24: K1, P1, K3, Seed st 5, K3, Seed st 23, K3, Seed st 5, K3, P1, K1

Row 25: K1, P3, Seed st 5, P3, Seed st 25, P3, Seed st 5, P3, K1

Row 26: K3, Seed st 5, K3, Seed st 27, K3, Seed st 5, K3

Row 27: K1, P3, Seed st 3, P3, Seed st 29, P3, Seed st 3, P3, K1

Row 28: K3, Seed st 3, K3, Seed st 31, K3, Seed st 3, K3

Rows 29 to 51: Repeat row 27 on odd rows, and repeat row 28 on even rows

Rows 52 to 63: Work rows 15 to 26 in *reverse order* (26, then 25, 24, etc.)

Row 64: Seed st 6, K3, Seed st 3, K3, Seed st 5, K3, Seed st 3, K3, Seed st 5, K3, Seed st 3, K3, Seed st 6

Row 65: Seed st 5, P5, Seed st 3, P3, Seed st 5, P3, K1, P3, Seed st 5, P3, Seed st 3, P5, Seed st 5

Row 66: Seed st 4, K7, Seed st 3, K3, Seed st 5, K5, Seed st 5, K3, Seed st 3, K7, Seed st 4

Row 67: Seed st 5, P2, K1, P2, Seed st 5, P3, Seed st 5, P3, Seed st 5, P3, Seed st 5, P2, K1, P2, Seed st 5

Row 68: Seed st 16, K3, Seed st 11, K3, Seed st 16

Row 69: Seed st 11, P3, Seed st 3, P3, Seed st 9, P3, Seed st 3, P3, Seed st 11

Row 70: Seed st 10, K5, Seed st 3, K3, Seed st 7, K3, Seed st 3, K5, Seed st 10

Row 71: Seed st 3, P3, Seed st 3, P7, Seed st 3, P3, Seed st 5, P3, Seed st 3, P7, Seed st 3, P3 Seed st 3

Row 72: K1, P1, K5, Seed st 3, K2, P1, K2, Seed st 5, K3, Seed st 3, K3, Seed st 5, K2, P1, K2, Seed st 3, K5, P1, K1

Row 73: K1, P7, Seed st 13, P3, K1, P3, Seed st 13, P7, K1

Row 74: K1, P1, K2, P1, K2, Seed st 15, K5, Seed st 15, K2, P1, K2, P1, K1

Row 75: Seed st 23, P3, Seed st 23

Row 76: Seed st

Bind off next row in Seed st. Use Color B for Optional Edging (see Optional Edging).

WASHCLOTH 2 INSTRUCTIONS:

Using Color B, Cast on 49.

Rows 1 and 2: Seed st

Row 3 (WS): Seed st 23, P3, Seed st 23

Row 4 (RS): Seed st 22, K5, Seed st 22

Row 5: Seed st 21, P3, K1, P3, Seed st 21

Row 6: Seed st 20, K3, Seed st 3, K3, Seed st 20

Row 7: Seed st 19, P3, Seed st 5, P3, Seed st 19

Row 8: Seed st 18, K3, Seed st 7, K3, Seed st 18

Row 9: Seed st 17, P3, Seed st 9, P3, Seed st 17

Row 10: Seed st 16, K3, Seed st 11, K3, Seed st 16

Row 11: Seed st 15, P3, Seed st 5, P3, Seed st 5, P3, Seed st 15

Row 12: Seed st 14, K3, Seed st 5, K5, Seed st 5, K3, Seed st 14

Row 13: Seed st 13, P3, Seed st 5, P3, K1, P3, Seed st 5, P3, Seed st 13

Row 14: Seed st 12, K3, Seed st 5, K3, Seed st 3, K3, Seed st 5, K3, Seed st 12

Row 15: Seed st 11, P3, Seed st 5, P3, Seed st 5, P3, Seed st 5, P3, Seed st 11

Row 16: Seed st 10, K3, Seed st 5, K3, Seed st 7, K3, Seed st 5, K3, Seed st 10

Row 17: Seed st 9, P3, Seed st 5, P3, Seed st 9, P3, Seed st 5, P3, Seed st 9

Row 18: Seed st 8, K3, Seed st 5, K3, Seed st 11, K3, Seed st 5, K3, Seed st 8

Row 19: Seed st 7, P3, Seed st 5, P3, Seed st 13, P3, Seed st 5, P3, Seed st 7

Row 20: Seed st 6, K3, Seed st 5, K3, Seed st 15, K3, Seed st 5, K3, Seed st 6

Row 21: Seed st 5, P3, Seed st 5, P3, Seed st 17, P3, Seed st 5, P3, Seed st 5

Row 22: Seed st 4, K3, Seed st 5, K3, Seed st 19, K3, Seed st 5, K3, Seed st 4

Row 23: Seed st 3, P3, Seed st 5, P3, Seed st 21, P3, Seed st 5, P3, Seed st 3

Row 24: K1, P1, K3, Seed st 5, K3, Seed st 23, K3, Seed st 5, K3, P1, K1

Row 25: K1, P3, Seed st 5, P3, Seed st 7, P3, Seed st 15, P3, Seed st 5, P3, K1

Row 26: K3, Seed st 5, K3, Seed st 15, K5, Seed st 7, K3, Seed st 5, K3

Row 27: K1, P3, Seed st 3, P3, Seed st 7, P7, Seed st 15, P3, Seed st 3, P3, K1

Row 28: K3, Seed st 3, K3, Seed st 15, K9, Seed st 7, K3, Seed st 3, K3

Row 29: K1, P3, Seed st 3, P3, Seed st 5, P11, Seed st 13, P3, Seed st 3, P3, K1

Row 30: Repeat row 28

Row 31: K1, P3, Seed st 3, P3, Seed st 5, P5, K1, P5, Seed st 13, P3, Seed st 3, P3, K1

Row 32: K3, Seed st 3, K3, Seed st 15, K3, Seed st 3, K3, Seed st 7, K3, Seed st 3, K3

Row 33: K1, P3, Seed st 3, P3, Seed st 29, P3, Seed st 3, P3, K1

Row 34: K3, Seed st 3, K3, Seed st 31, K3, Seed st 3, K3

Row 35: K1, P3, Seed st 3, P3, Seed st 19, P3, Seed st 7, P3, Seed st 3, P3, K1

Row 36: K3, Seed st 3, K3, Seed st 7, K5, Seed st 19, K3, Seed st 3, K3

Row 37: K1, P3, Seed st 3, P3, Seed st 17, P7, Seed st 5, P3, Seed st 3, P3, K1

Row 38: K3, Seed st 3, K3, Seed st 5, K9, Seed st 17, K3, Seed st 3, K3

Row 39: K1, P3, Seed st 3, P3, Seed st 15, P11, (Seed st 3, P3) 2x, K1

Row 40: Repeat row 38

Row 41: K1, P3, Seed st 3, P3, Seed st 15, P5, K1, P5, (Seed st 3, P3) 2x, K1

Row 42: K3, Seed st 3, K3, Seed st 5, K3, Seed st 3, K3, Seed st 7, K3, Seed st 7, K3, Seed st 3, K3

Row 43: K1, P3, Seed st 3, P3, Seed st 5, P5, Seed st 19, P3, Seed st 3, P3, K1

Row 44: K3, Seed st 3, K3, Seed st 19, K7, Seed st 5, K3, Seed st 3, K3

Row 45: K1, (P3, Seed st 3) 2x, P9, Seed st 17, P3, Seed st 3, P3, K1

Row 46: K3, Seed st 3, K3, Seed st 17, K11, (Seed st 3, K3) 2x

Row 47: Repeat row 45

Row 48: K3, Seed st 3, K3, Seed st 17, K5, P1, K5, (Seed st 3, K3) 2x

Row 49: K1, (P3, Seed st 3) 3x, P3, Seed st 17, P3, Seed st 3, P3, K1

Row 50: Repeat row 34

Row 51: Repeat row 33

Row 52: K3, Seed st 5, K3, Seed st 27, K3, Seed st 5, K3

Row 53: K1, P3, Seed st 5, P3, Seed st 25, P3, Seed st 5, P3, K1

Rows 54 to 76: Work Rows 24 to 2 *in reverse order*

Bind off in Seed st. Use Color A for Optional Edging.

OPTIONAL EDGING:

Start in a corner.

With RS facing you, pick up and knit one stitch.

*Pick up and K fbf. Turn.

K4. Turn.

Bind off 3 in knit, one stitch remains on right-hand needle.

Pick up and knit one stitch, and bind off previous stitch.*

Repeat from * around the edge of the washcloth. When you reach the beginning, finish on "Bind off 3 in knit" and weave your end into your initial stitch. Skip a stitch after each repeat for a flatter edge, or use every edge stitch and make the border extra floppy.

FINISHING:

Wet-block squares before knitting edging. Also, be aware that some dyes are left behind more than others, and washcloths are typically used in hot water, so you will want to rinse out as much residual dye as possible in the blocking process. Weave in your ends, fold the washcloths up with a cute handmade soap from a local artisan, tie with a ribbon, and make someone's day!

Ready to find
your next great read?

Let us help.

Visit prh.com/nextread

Penguin
Random
House